THE MUSE
IN A
TIME OF
MADNESS

THE MUSE
IN A
TIME OF
MADNESS

FRANCIS M. FLAVIN

BOOK ONE OF THE ALYESKA CHRONICLES

atmosphere press

To Mrs. Crawford, my fifth-grade teacher at Shenendehowa, who set this show on the road.

1570 Russia

Escape Route

from the

Sack of Novgorod

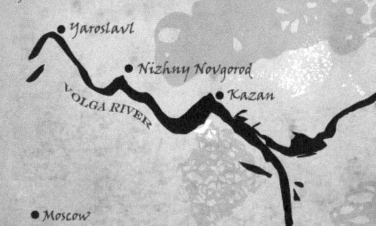

- Novgorod
- Yaroslavl
- Nizhny Novgorod
- Kazan
- VOLGA RIVER
- Moscow

IVAN THE TERRIBLE

TABLE OF CONTENTS

PART ONE
GROZNY

CHAPTER 1

Madness had a name, and death was his countenance. Dressed in black, with dog heads on their saddles, an inexorable wave of armed riders swept toward the sleeping city. Cloaked in darkness, they brought his message, and that message was terror.

But there was another messenger present that fateful night. Ephemeral in delivery and enigmatic in form, her message would reverberate through the ages.

Novgorod, Russia - January 2, 1570

Old souls, those who explore the boundaries of perceived reality and the shadow realm of possibilities, may find their muse. If their mind is receptive and their spirit pure, she will guide them — the shaman, the artist, the dreamer . . .

In the spirit land between slumber and awake, the sense of menace was palpable. The air was heavy with expectation; peril and promise were a heartbeat away. In the lake, the swans were clearly agitated as they swam in tight circles with their heads bobbing. They nervously watched a small grove of birch trees on the far shore. The birches were packed tightly on an island of high ground in an expanse of muskeg that extended a short distance back from the lake. Beyond the muskeg was a long, low ridge covered with magenta flowers — a vivid swath of color against the dark boreal forests that receded into the distance.

Movement at the edge of the birches sent the swans into a trumpeting retreat. The sound of their powerful wings beating the water rumbled down the lake as they struggled into flight. Two men and a woman silently emerged from the trees onto the shore. Dressed in tanned hides, they moved with the grace of forest people. The figures were dark complexioned like Tatars, but unlike Tatars, they were tall and slender. They lacked the aura of menace that usually attended Tatars — no matter how small the group or peaceful the setting.

The woman was nothing less than angelic. Her very countenance stirred a desire deep within him. He felt himself irresistibly drawn to her. She moved away from the men and cupped her hands to her mouth to call. At first, he could not hear her through the breeze that rustled through the overhead branches. He moved closer to the edge of the forest. She cupped her hands and called again. This time, he heard her, faintly at first —

"Petr."

Then louder — "Petr."

"PETR ALEKSEEVICH SAFRONOV. WAKE UP!"

Petr struggled to sit up — his mind reeling from lack of sleep and the effects of the fine French wine that had gone down all too smoothly only hours before. His mother used his full name when she wanted his complete attention — when he was in trouble. Only this time, it wasn't his mother. She was visiting in Lithuania with his father — a blessing, as he was about to discover.

"Matrona! What is it that compels you to turn my dreams into nightmares? I just got to sleep. Can't it wait until tomorrow?"

Even in the dim candlelight, the frightened look in his sister's eyes told him it could not.

"No, Petr. I'm afraid that you will not smile in your dreams for a long time. Ivan, the Holy Tsar of all the Russians, is approaching Novgorod with an army of Oprichniki. His mission here is undoubtedly neither peaceful nor holy."

"Grozny!" Peter growled this Russian epithet for the Tsar with bitter loathing and contempt. The literal translation of "dread" or "awesome" seemed particularly suited to the temperament of this Tsar with his predilection for violence and cruelty.

"I knew it would come to this, little sister. It's the damned Oprichniki. They want to control Novgorod like the rest of Russia. They continually feed the Tsar's paranoia with rumors and lies."

The Tsar was Ivan Vasilevich, "Ivan the Fourth" — or "Ivan the Terrible" as he was now known throughout Russia and the rest of Europe and Asia Minor. A title that was well deserved due to the ingenious and hideous methods of torture he used on his enemies.

"Hurry, Petr. Andrei Stepanov is waiting at the entryway. We need to leave Novgorod now."

Petr had never seen such fear and panic on his sister's face. "But I thought Andrei was on his way to Moscow with Dimitri and the trade delegation."

The Veche had selected several key Novgorodian artisans and merchants to open a dialog with the authorities in the capital, perhaps even the Tsar himself. It was hoped that with increased communication between the two cities, some of the suspicion and intrigue would dissipate, and the ever-increasing levels of taxation would be stemmed and eventually rolled back.

"He was, but some of their horses had wandered into the forest. Andrei and Dimitri went to retrieve them. Upon their return, they found the Tsar's men butchering their encampment."

Choking back sobs, she fought for control.

"Only the darkness and luck saved them . . . Oh, Petr . . ."

Petr took her in his arms and softly stroked her hair in a vain attempt to calm her.

Andrei, at the entryway, remained agitated as well. "I'm afraid we have little time for consolation and solace. The

Oprichniki have sacked every town and village between Klin and here."

This was a distance of over 260 versts.

"They will soon cordon off the entire city, and we will be sealed in to receive whatever punishment Grozny wishes to visit upon us. Lately he has taken to frying his subjects alive in a giant pan. I do not wish to participate in this activity, nor would I wish it upon my worst enemy."

"What about Dimitri?" Petr asked.

Her fiancé, Andrei's brother, had been one of the artisans selected for the delegation.

"Dimitri has gone on to Yaroslavl to secure a sanctuary for you and Matrona, as well as any other boyars we can save," Andrei replied. "To that end, I must be on my way. There are many at risk tonight. In order to prevent a warning, the Oprichniki are slaying anyone they encounter. I am that warning."

Andrei paused and looked directly into Petr's eyes. Like a good many Novgorod citizens, Andrei had a substantial amount of Tatar blood in his veins. With his swarthy complexion and fierce black eyes, few would challenge his ancestry or opinions. Saint Alexander Nevsky, the Prince of Novgorod, who was canonized by the Russian Orthodox Church in 1547, had submitted to the rule of Mongol overlords three centuries ago. While, to this day, it was considered a controversial act, Nevsky averted needless bloodshed and led the way to increased commerce with the Tatar Empire. Since that time, Novgorod accepted those of Tatar blood more willingly than most cities in Russia. Indeed, like Andrei, a goodly number of the citizens of Novgorod carried Tatar blood in their veins.

"I would leave now, my friend." Andrei counseled Petr.

"Only by taking seldom-used trails and byways was I able to avoid capture and execution. Death is on my heels, and I fear that I am too late to do much good. Meet us in the cathedral in Yaroslavl. Speak only to Father Ivanov!"

With that, he was out the door.

CHAPTER 2

"We must leave, Petr. NOW!" Matrona was clearly shaken, and her voice trembled in fear. "Please!" She sobbed.

Petr's first instinct was to resist his sister's plea.

"We must fight these beasts, Matrona! First we must spread the alarm. We can rally the people at Saint Sophia's. Let us go and toll the church bells there. These lackeys dressed in black with their dog's head saddles may rule the night like the curs they are, but we can make a stand in the morning."

"Brother, there is no time to organize a force to fight them."

"Surely God will protect us from these devils," he replied with more hope than conviction.

"No, Petr! God was not on the road to Novgorod — I doubt he is here now. We have no army. We have no weapons. We have no time. We must go!" Great sobs shook her tiny body as she tugged frantically on his nightshirt.

Pushing her gently away, Petr crossed himself. "Do not blaspheme, little sister. God has not yet abandoned us. It must have been divine guidance that inspired our father to prepare for this day. I thought he was foolish and weak. I see now that it was I who was stupid."

Petr's father, Alexsei, had feared a military campaign by the Tsar against Novgorod. He had prepared a family contingency plan in the event the Oprichniki attacked the city. Petr had argued that Catholic Poland and Lithuania would protect Novgorod in such an eventuality, a view shared by his brother, Nikolai, and most of the citizens of Novgorod. Alexsei, however, was convinced that Novgorod's ties to its allies were purely commercial. No Catholic blood would be shed for Orthodox souls. Novgorod and Pskov would be on their own.

Petr and Nikolai had halfheartedly joined in their father's contingency activities, more out of affection for the man than respect for his views. Now his planning and logistics would be tested.

"Father has planned for this raid, Matrona. Check the bridge often — when the Oprichniki devils arrive, they will undoubtedly come over the bridge."

The Safronov household was situated on a hill in the Sofiiskaya section of the city, named for its great cathedral, St. Sofia. The house was located just outside the citadel that enclosed the cathedral and the archbishop's palace within imposing stone walls. It stood above the commercial section of the city to the east. The commercial area was connected to the Sofiiskaya side by the Volkhov Bridge. The number of windows in the house was limited, and they were small to cut down on heat loss during the bitterly cold Russian winters. However, there were two windows that gave a view of the bridge: one in the living room and one in Petr's room.

Taking Matrona by the arm, Petr returned to his room, lit a candle, and emptied the contents of a large wooden trunk in the corner of the room onto his bed. In the trunk were jewelry, a large sum of rubles, and sufficient Tatar clothing to outfit the entire Safronov family. He tossed a bundle of clothing to Matrona.

"Here — wear enough of these for protection against the cold and take several changes for the road. The Oprichniki will be looking for boyars — not Tatars."

Petr separated the clothing intended for him from that of his father and brother, Nikolai. Nikolai was two years older than Petr, but substantially shorter and stouter. He was visiting Lithuania with their parents. As the elder brother Nikolai had taken up his father's occupation as a merchant and trader. His primary reason for the visit, however, was his ongoing courtship of a wealthy and beautiful Lithuanian heiress.

As Matrona went to her room to change, Petr placed half of the jewelry and coins into several pouches attached to a belt that he fastened around his waist. The remaining items were put back into the trunk. He wanted the Oprichniki to believe that the Safronovs had fled the premises in haste and were somewhere in the city. Perhaps they could buy some time if the Tsar's men believed that they were still in the city and due to return. Petr had no doubt that once the Oprichniki entered Novgorod, this house would be one of their first stops.

Petr quickly pulled on a Tatar caftan and pants. The pants were somewhat short owing to Petr's height, which at 5[] 10[] was taller than average for Russians in general and Tatars in particular. In any event, the length of the pants would be concealed under high fur-lined boots and a long fur coat.

Once he had dressed, Petr went to the living room and stoked the fire in the fireplace. After first extracting a number of jewels that had been sewn into the lining of the coats and the folds of the fur hats, Petr burned the bundle of clothing intended for Nicolai and his parents. The rest of the family would have no need of them in Vilna now or Novgorod ever again.

Petr then burned the family's correspondence and financial records as well. There was no sense in leaving any clues as to the identity and whereabouts of the family or its assets.

The Safronov family had a great deal of influence in Novgorod. Alexsei was a leading merchant whose trading influence extended from the Lower Ob River region northeast of the Ural Mountains to Paris in the West. A natural diplomat, he was equally at ease with Tatar chieftains and Polish princes. This ability led to a seat in the Veche and a great deal of travel throughout Europe on behalf of the city.

Petr's mother, Svetlana, had been educated in Paris and was one of the most renowned hostesses in Novgorod. Her personal charm and social acumen greatly complimented her husband's business and political interests. She was his shrewd-est advisor and most trusted confidant. After thirty years of marriage, they remained totally and passionately devoted to each other.

At the age of twenty-six, Petr had come into his own as an artist. His icons exhibited the spiritual fervor of his soul, the passion of his heart, and the artistic dexterity and finesse of his training. Petr was a leading figure in the Novgorod school of iconography, noted for the intensity of the religious figures depicted. The gaze of the subjects directly engaged that of the viewer, resulting in a strong emotional and spiritual impact.

In the Russian Orthodox religion, icons were not merely pictures; they were sacramental objects of great veneration and devotion. They were windows to the divine spirit. Petr's icons had been placed on viewing screens, or "iconostasis," in cathedrals and monasteries throughout Northwest Russia. His prestige as an artist added to his family's religious and secular influence — and further marked the Safronovs for Oprichniki oppression.

As he was burning the last of the family records, Matrona arrived in Tatar dress. Unfortunately, her features matched his own. With her blonde hair, blue eyes, and fair complexion, she looked more Swede than Tatar. Applying generous portions of fish oil, ashes, and lampblack, Petr transformed the pair of siblings into passable Tatars. Matrona had always been some-what vain concerning her appearance, but in her shock, she acquiesced to these indignities without complaint.

When the disguises were completed, Petr was satisfied that their appearance would fool a casual observer, especially if the reek of fish oil kept the onlooker far enough away to miss noting the Safronov eyes. At the moment, Matrona's eyes were as fixed and vacant as death. Petr embraced her gently for a moment. He could feel an emotional tide of panic and grief surging through him. He fought off the rising emotion — pushing it deep within him, beyond consciousness and feeling.

He collected himself with a brief mental supplication:

Oh Lord, protect us. Keep your faithful servants safe from harm and have mercy upon the citizens of Novgorod in this time of peril. In Christ's name, we ask it. Amen.

Then he remembered that Matrona knew nothing of the Safronov escape plans. Ultimately, they would have to travel to the east as the Tsar would undoubtedly have the western escape routes well patrolled.

Petr wished that he had spent more time learning about his father's commercial trading practices, especially in dealing with the Tatars, who had become substantially integrated into the Russian population due to their years of conquest and administration. The Tatars still controlled most of the land beyond Muscovy rule to the south and east, the regions to which they must flee. However, his father had planned for this eventuality.

"Matrona, should we become separated, in the right sleeve of each of our coats is sewn a letter of introduction and a list of Father's most loyal agents and friends, including Tatars. These contacts should be extremely helpful to us in finding safe houses while we are in the area of direct Muscovy rule and the Tatar areas beyond. Our first goal is to reach Yaroslavl and join up with Dimitri, Andrei, and any other Novgorod exiles who manage to escape. With the assistance of our father's contacts, we should be able to get there in several weeks. If, God willing, we escape the Tsar and his Oprichniki tonight!"

Petr went to the window — glass had not yet been introduced into Russia, so he had to throw open the shutters to observe the outside world. To his horror, he saw hundreds of torches swiftly approaching the bridge from the commercial section of the city. He ran to the fireplace and lit a torch of his own.

He grabbed Matrona by the shoulders.

"Be strong. There is little time to flee and less time for panic. Father has prepared a hiding place, and we must get to it without delay! But first we must release our horses so the Oprichniki will think that we have fled."

Pulling their fur hats down over their ears, they opened the door and stepped into the night. The hair in their noses froze instantly in the bitter cold. Their cheeks stung with the bite of the west wind as they descended the outdoor stairway and hurried to the stable. They quickly released the family's three remaining horses and shooed them into the darkness. As they returned to the house, they could see torchlight on the bridge.

Petr paused at the door to the ground-floor storeroom and took one last look at the city. "Gospodid Veliki Novgorod," Lord Novgorod the Great, as it was known to its citizens, slept, unaware that the zenith of its civilization would pass this night. Petr left the door ajar to add to the impression that they had recently fled.

Once inside, Petr grabbed a bag of biscuits off a shelf laden with food for the winter. Grabbing Matrona's hand, he proceeded to another row of shelves along the far wall. It took Petr several minutes to locate a large peg that was concealed beneath the middle shelf. He tugged on it, and the adjacent bookcase swung open to reveal steps leading down to an underground room. Petr nudged his sister down the stairs as he swung the bookcase closed behind them.

They descended a short set of steps into a confined storeroom. The ceiling was lower than Petr's height, and he had to stoop as they worked their way around the many bundles of furs and trade goods that were stacked throughout the room.

"I had no idea this room existed," Matrona commented, with some consternation that she had not been informed.

"Father had it constructed while we were in Pskov last summer. He used Lithuanian laborers that he could trust to keep its knowledge from local residents. He kept it from most of the family so that the secret would never inadvertently slip from our lips. He showed it to me on the eve of their departure to Vilnius."

Petr was glad that time did not permit more discourse on this subject. He was not particularly proud of the manner in which he had handled the interchange with his father. Unlike his older brother, Petr paid scant attention to matters of commerce and politics. When his father revealed the secret room, Petr laughed derisively and asked his father if he expected a Tatar horde to sweep through Novgorod.

"Don't you know that our Tsar put the run to the Tatars in Kazan eighteen years ago?" he asked facetiously.

"I know my history, son! Perhaps your art and music lessons have not provided much insight into our Tsar. Ivan is cruel and fearful — brilliant and mad; terrible combinations that will inevitably lead to disaster for himself and his subjects. The boyars here are a free and prosperous people. But not all who live here enjoy this freedom and prosperity. This is a republic of nobles only. Those on the outside of commerce and public affairs are all too willing to whisper accusations of treason in Ivan's ear."

"But our prosperity fills the Tsar's tax coffers more than any other region," Petr responded.

"Yes, but none of our land and wealth are in Ivan's Oprichnina. Our boyars do not hide their contempt for the Tsar, and a few openly court foreign alliances. Greed and sedition will bring the Tsar to our doorstep sooner or later — I suspect sooner. On this trip to Vilnius, I am transferring as many of our assets as possible out of the country."

"So why aren't Matrona and I accompanying you on this journey?"

His father explained that to transfer the family's assets out of the country, he needed secrecy. If the entire family left, it would alert Ivan's agents, and the family would be detained before it could reach the frontier.

"I require your brother's skill in trade and finance," he had stated. "You and Matrona must stay behind for a short while. If the Tsar arrives before our return, you must protect your sister. Flee if you can — hide if you cannot. I will send for you as soon as possible."

So, my only value to this family is as a decoy, Petr thought. His impotence in affairs of commerce and state was never more apparent. In these troubled times, artists and musicians had little influence on the affairs of state, particularly in Mother Russia. But protecting his sister was a sacred trust, and to this, he turned his full attention.

The secret storeroom was about twelve feet long by ten feet wide. When they reached the far end of the room, Petr handed the torch to his sister, and placing his shoulder to the left corner of the wall, he gave a mighty heave. The wall slowly swung open wide enough to admit their passage in a single file.

Matrona entered first with the torch. Once Petr was inside, he pushed the wall closed and thrust three large beams through wooden holders into deep recesses in the adjacent wall. Thus secured, it would take many hours for an axe to break through the wall if the hidden storeroom was discovered.

Matrona's torch revealed a small room containing five cots heaped high with fur robes. These would be invaluable as the temperature in the room was the same as the outside air. Although the cold lacked a bite due to the absence of wind, any prolonged stay would be miserable, if not lethal.

The sanctuary consisted of a rough-hewn lumber ceiling and walls with a dirt floor. Hanging from the walls were containers of dried meats and grains. In one corner, opposite the hinged wall, were the best of Petr's icons, wrapped in oilcloths to ward off the dampness of the subterranean room. Stacked in the other corner were a variety of weapons, including two harquebuses, many pouches of gunpowder, three pikes, and two swords, as well as a variety of knives and daggers. In the center of the room were barrels of pickled vegetables, salt pork, and water. Alexsei had diligently replaced the water from time to time to avoid stagnation.

Petr went to the pile of weapons, selected a menacing Tatar knife with a curved blade, and affixed it to his belt by its scabbard. As he did so, they heard the sounds of muffled shouts and the banging of chest lids and overturned furniture from the rooms above. Petr lit a candle and then ground out the torch on the earthen floor to ensure that no smoke would seep into the living quarters above. His father had checked to be sure that no light from this room would show through the walls. Petr glanced at Matrona. In the candlelight, her face was ashen, and she trembled uncontrollably. He went to her and held her tight.

Above, they could hear angry curses as their absence was discovered. The clamor of men looting and pillaging continued for many hours. Petr and Matrona could only bite their lips in frustration and rage as overhead, the Oprichniki ransacked the fruits of a lifetime of commercial and artistic endeavor.

◊

Lying wide awake for many hours, Petr reflected on the circumstances that led to the ongoing catastrophe at hand. Tsar Ivan IV, clearly mad after the death of his wife, had established a personal estate that was seized from the "boyars," the feudal aristocracy that largely governed local and regional affairs prior to the Tsar's consolidation of power. Ivan's new estate was known as the "Oprichnina," "the widow's mite," the portion of a man's estate that was given to his widow upon his death. In recognition of her vulnerability, the law prohibited anyone from taking the designated widow's share of an estate. It was a reflection of Ivan's paranoia that, like a widow, he felt defenseless against his enemies, both real and imagined.

Ivan's Oprichnina comprised about a third of the realm. The remainder of the realm was called "Zemshchina" or "the Earth." The Oprichniki, a legion of spies, bodyguards, and henchmen selected by the Tsar, administered the Oprichnina.

It was the Tsar's fear that the citizens of the Zemshchina could not be trusted. Therefore, it was his will that their holdings and belongings were to be plundered by Ivan and his minions.

The Oprichniki seized land and power by using their influence with the Tsar to dispossess those suspected of opposing his spiritual or political agenda. More than one cleric or nobleman who had offended a member of the Oprichniki had been trussed up and tossed into the Tsar's oversized pan to be publicly fried in oil for the satisfaction of the Tsar and the delight of the Muscovite mob.

Suspicious and fearful by nature, the Tsar had become increasingly withdrawn, sullen, and paranoid since the death of his wife, the widely beloved Anastasia. The rumors and allegations of intrigue were administered to him in large doses by his ambitious allies, who easily manipulated the Tsar. He reacted swiftly and ruthlessly to eliminate any perceived threat to his authority or slight of his personage.

Novgorod, in Northwestern Russia, was a prime candidate for such intrigue. The Tsar was suspicious of foreign influences on Novgorod and nearby Pskov to the west. Ivan feared that the two cities planned to break away from Russia and join the Polish-Lithuanian Commonwealth. Moscow was a brooding and closed city that mirrored the Tsar's own temperament. Novgorod, in contrast, was an oasis of enlightenment in backward Russia. It was an open city, where art and commerce flourished, and the town council or "Veche" determined public affairs.

In most of Russia, the power of Muscovy, exercised through the influence of the Oprichniki and the Tsar's reign of terror, had stifled the intellectual, commercial, and political growth of the country. The Tsar had extinguished the power of the Tatars over a broad area of the Russian heartland. Now, the Tsar's levels of taxation exceeded the tribute previously exacted by the Tatars. Even with its strong trade base and immense wealth, Novgorod struggled under the yoke of Ivan's excessive taxation.

While the Muscovy tax burden had succeeded in dampening the regional economy, the Oprichniki had little political influence in Novgorod, a situation the Tsar found intolerable, for which the Novgorodians were about to pay a terrible price.

CHAPTER 3

Petr awoke from a fitful sleep. The candle was just a stump, and he lit another before it went out. He judged that it had been at least four days since the Oprichniki had entered the city and four or five hours since they last heard any activity overhead. The room was well insulated by thick logs and the surrounding earth. The candle and their body heat provided sufficient warmth to keep the temperature slightly above freezing in their subterranean room.

He moved to Matrona's cot and found her awake.

"It is time to eat," he whispered.

She shook her head.

"I am not at all hungry, Petr. All this lying about and listening to our home being violated is not conducive to a good appetite. Nor, might I add, is the food. When can we leave? It has been quiet for hours. Surely it is safe by now. The barbarians have had more than enough time to cart off everything we own. Besides, we cannot stay in here forever."

Petr did not reply but merely squeezed her shoulder before ladling out two portions of pickled beets and salt pork into wooden bowls. He placed a hard biscuit from his sack into each bowl and handed one of them to his sister.

"Eat," he said gently. "We must keep up our strength for the journey ahead. It will be time to leave soon enough, but first we must be sure that the Oprichniki have left Novgorod. I have a great sense of foreboding that the worst is yet to come."

Matrona was perplexed.

"But how will we know when we can leave? There could

be twenty men with pikes standing by the bookcase when we open the door. There is no way of knowing, short of revealing our presence."

"Ah . . . I have yet another surprise for you, dear sister."

Petr was clearly pleased with himself for keeping his father's secrets so well.

Piece by piece, he quietly moved the pile of art treasures onto the vacant cots. Then, with the blade of his knife, he pried free several boards near the floor, revealing a tunnel cut into the earth and lined with timbers.

Petr lit a second candle and held it near the tunnel's entrance. The tunnel sloped down toward the river.

"Won't somebody find the entrance and break into this room?" Matrona inquired. "Those boards certainly won't keep anybody out."

"No — the entrance is quite cleverly concealed." He lit another candle and handed it to her. "Come, I'll show you."

Petr entered the tunnel on all fours, with his sister proceeding several feet behind him. The tunnel was well-braced with timbers. It was reasonably dry but bitter cold, as in near-Arctic Novgorod, the frost line ran deep. For Petr, it was a tight fit, and he frequently scraped his back and shoulders on the roof and walls as they proceeded down the gently sloping tunnel floor.

They had crawled for about five minutes when Petr came to a spot where the tunnel bent sharply upward and was blocked by a wedge of peat. He whispered to his sister to leave her candle lit in the tunnel so that they could use it on the way back. He then extinguished his candle and dislodged the loosely packed peat to reveal the tunnel entrance.

The tunnel entrance was concealed beneath the wide growth of two young fir trees that stood on a hill overlooking the Volkhov River. The lower branches of the trees were only inches from the ground and were concealed beneath the winter's snowpack. The snow had failed to penetrate the thick conifer branches, creating a natural cave under the limbs and between the trunks of the trees. Petr inched his way into this cave. He was careful not to bump the trees and dislodge the snow that was layered upon their branches. He moved carefully to one side, and taking her hand, he gently guided Matrona out of the tunnel.

They sat very still for a long time. Patience was the one trait that Petr had mastered as an artist that would serve him well in times of peril. He sat motionless as his mind slowly wrapped itself around the state of their surroundings.

The silence was of little solace to Matrona. She marveled at her brother's cool demeanor. At first, her heart was pounding so hard in her chest that she was sure it could be heard on the road that was only one hundred feet down the hill from their hideaway. But with time, it was apparent that they would not be discovered without a stroke of extremely bad luck. This realization allowed her to achieve some degree of peace within their snowy den.

With time, their ears became attuned to the outside world. The sounds from the city carried a long distance in the dense, cold air. Unfortunately, most of the sounds consisted of curses and screams that emanated from within the citadel of St. Sophia. The screams were of such intensity and duration that their blood ran cold, and Matrona began to tremble again.

Their physical state soon began to mirror their mental and emotional condition. The longer they sat, the more the cold seeped through their robes and into their bones. Finally, Petr inched forward onto his stomach and, with the tips of his fingers, slowly scraped a small opening in the snowpack beneath the lower branches. After ten minutes or so, he had cleared an opening of several inches in diameter and was able to observe the section of road that swung down to the Volkhov Bridge. The sun was low in the sky and nearly behind the tunnel entrance. Anyone looking in the direction of the hideaway would be blinded by the glare.

Petr heard the scuffling of feet, and a group of nine monks came into view as they hurried along at a near run. The monks were clearly nervous and continually looked over their shoulders to observe the road behind them. This was unfortunate, as the leading monk tripped over a rock frozen into the road, and four of the following monks tripped over their fallen brethren. Petr had to stifle a laugh lest he shake the trees and send a telltale plume of snow into the air.

Petr's mirth was short-lived as the air was suddenly filled with the rumble of hooves and the shouts of many approaching horsemen. The monks began to scatter in all directions. Two were headed directly toward the trees that hid Petr and Matrona. Petr tensed in fear, and his breath came in shallow gasps. There was too little time to maneuver into the mouth of the tunnel without shaking the trees in their haste. If the monks tried to hide in the trees, they were sure to reveal the tunnel. Their tracks in the otherwise unmarked snow would mark the monks' route of flight.

The monks were almost to the trees when Petr felt the ground shake. The legs and bellies of several horses suddenly blocked his view. One horse swung close enough to knock snow off the branches and onto the back of Petr's neck. He resisted the impulse to brush the frozen crystals from his bare skin.

Petr counted six riders in the group that had cut off the escape of the two monks. There were several other groups of horsemen that were herding monks back onto the roadway, where a dozen or so of their mounted companions shouted taunts and insults at the captured churchmen. The riders had the attire and accouterments of Oprichniki. They wore long black cloaks and rode black horses. Each carried a staff with a dog's head on one end and a broom on the other, symbolizing their bite of authority and zeal to sweep Russia clean of treachery.

Half of the riders dismounted, handing the reins of their

mounts to their companions. They proceeded to shove and kick the monks into kneeling positions in a tight circle on the street.

A squat Oprichnik with a bloated face and slit eyes sunken between layers of bulging fat grabbed a monk by the hood and jerked his head violently upward.

"Where's your tribute, scum? You know you are not allowed on the streets of the Tsar's Oprichnina without proper payment!"

He kicked the monk in the side and tossed him on the frozen ground.

"Well? I'm waiting for an answer. Do you have the payment or not?"

"Please, sir," pleaded the trembling monk. "We have paid all that we have. We are humble clerics without wealth or material goods."

"Nonsense!" responded his interrogator with a vicious kick to the side of the monk's head. "Didn't you hear our Tsar inform your archbishop that you are no longer pastors or teachers but wolves, despoilers, traitors, and mortifiers of the crown?"

"Make way!" shouted one of the riders from the periphery of the group. "The Tsar approaches!"

A large coterie of mounted Oprichniki approached from the citadel of St. Sophia. In the center of the first row of horsemen was the Tsar. Petr recognized him from a painting that hung in the Veche chambers. Like his Oprichniki, he was dressed in black and rode a black horse. Around his neck was a gold chain that bore an enormous jewel-encrusted gold cross. Attached to the Tsar's saddle was a large, iron dog's head. Its metal jaws snapped menacingly with the gait of the oncoming horse.

The Tsar's countenance was both severe and ominous. A dark, full beard hid most of his face. His mouth was set in a permanent scowl, and his dark eyes glared coldly from behind a prominent nose. The Tsar's dark complexion and solid frame revealed his Greek and Tatar ancestry.

The Tsar was descended from Khan Mamay of the Golden Horde on his mother's side and Dimitri Donskoy, the Khan's enemy, on his father's side. It was a common belief that this mixture of warring bloodlines accounted for the Tsar's distrust of everyone he encountered.

As he rode, the Tsar's eyes darted from side to side. He alone, among all his Oprichniki, took notice of the two trees standing in the otherwise open field as a potential threat. The Tsar turned toward Petr, raised up in his saddle, and pointed to the trees. The sight of the Tsar sent a chill deep within Petr. He sensed both keen intelligence and great madness. This feeling was quickly replaced by alarm as two riders separated from the Tsar's entourage and galloped toward Petr and Matrona's hiding place.

The horses were slowed by the steepness of the hill, which was slippery from the compaction of snow by the horses of the Oprichniki that had captured the escaping monks. As the riders struggled up the hill, Petr carefully backed deeper into the tunnel while signaling Matrona for silence.

The riders circled the trees several times and began probing the tree branches with their pikes. Their thrusts caused the trees to drop some of their snow load. Using the falling snow for cover, Petr and Matrona quickly backed further into the tunnel. They could hear the deadly tips of the pikes plunging into the bare earth at the center of the recess where, only moments before, they had lain in hiding.

After several more thrusts of their pikes, one of the riders called out that there was nobody hiding in the trees, and they slowly made their way down the hill to the main group.

Petr found that the excitement of near-impalement had warmed him a good deal. He cautiously slipped back into the tight little lair under the trees. The hole that he had cleared for observation was a good deal larger due to the Oprichniki search efforts. This afforded him a much greater field of vision. The conifer branches still provided adequate cover, and he doubted that anyone would look their way after the recent search.

As Petr watched, the Tsar slowly rode up to the monks, who remained clustered in a tight knot on the frozen road.

"Who is senior here?" he asked.

A gaunt, balding monk murmured an unintelligible response.

"Rise, man — You may speak to your sovereign," the Tsar commanded in a calm and almost gentle voice.

The elderly monk rose on trembling legs, his head bowed in silent supplication.

"So, I am told that you have no recompense for your theft of the air and sunlight of my realm. Is that correct?"

"Yes, sire — that is correct," the old man stated in a small, tremulous voice.

"I find that quite odd, given the wealth of stolen riches you have hidden from me."

"Bring the sleighs," he commanded, pointing back toward St. Sophia. A rider quickly detached himself from the group and rode back into the citadel. The old monk began to sit.

"Did I command you to sit?" the Tsar asked calmly. The old monk shook his head. "We shall want to question you in greater detail in several minutes. Please be patient — as your Tsar is patient."

After several minutes, six overladen freight sleighs were pulled laboriously out of the citadel by teams of four horses each. As the sleighs appeared in Petr's field of vision, he gasped; the many treasures of St. Sophia were heaped onto the sleighs.

St. Sophia, a majestic successor to its original namesake in Kyiv, was one of the finest cathedrals in the world. A grand pair of embossed bronze doors from the twelfth century had opened into the magnificent interior of majestic cruciform piers, three semicircular apses, and a choir gallery. The central dome contained a head and shoulders representation of

Christ Pantocrator. The iconography included wonderful figures of the prophets, evangelists, and other religious figures. Petr had created several of the icons, a sign of his rising stature as an artist.

To Petr's great dismay, the cherished art of St. Sophia lay jumbled and despoiled in the approaching sleighs. The first two sleighs contained the bronze doors, the next two the broken remains of the iconography. The fifth sleigh held heaps of gold plates, goblets, utensils, and religious paraphernalia. At the bottom of this sleigh, sacred vestments lay in soiled mounds beneath the piles of booty. The last sleigh held a variety of equipment and utensils that Petr deduced were implements to service the Tsar's army of Oprichniki.

As the sleighs approached the Tsar's entourage, many monks, including the old one standing before the Tsar, began sobbing in despair at the desecration before them.

"Silence!" the Tsar commanded. He held out his hand and halted the train of sleighs just short of his men and the monks. He motioned for the old monk to come forward.

"Tie him with his face to the sleigh and see if the sight of the doors of St. Sophia will open his brain." Two Oprichniki came forward with ropes and tied the monk to freight hooks on the side of the sleigh.

"Now then," the Tsar continued, "tell me where you are hiding more treasure from your Tsar." His voice was calm but heavy with menace.

"I know not, sire," the monk replied — his whole body trembling with fear.

Ivan frowned. "It appears your fidelity to Archbishop Pimen exceeds your loyalty to the Tsar." He directed his attention to the nearest Oprichniki. "Apparently, this monk needs a little encouragement to loosen his tongue."

One of the Oprichniki went to the last sleigh and returned with an armload of implements, which he dumped on the ground. Ivan dismounted, kicked at the pile, and picked up an object that Petr, at first, thought was a broom handle or stave. Petr, and the knot of monks, gasped as the Tsar shook the object and numerous leather straps fell free. It was a flogging whip.

The Tsar handed the whip to a broad-shouldered man who stood head and shoulders above the rest of the Oprichniki.

"Assist this poor monk in remembering where his true loyalties lie. I know that you will not spare any effort on behalf of your Tsar."

At the first stroke, the monk whimpered. At the fifth stroke, his tunic darkened and he screamed. At the tenth stroke, the tunic disintegrated and blood splattered the side of the sleigh. At this point, the Tsar raised his hand to halt the flogging.

"There now . . . That should clear your memory," he stated calmly. "Names . . . I need names. You have been in the church a long time. You must know many names . . . Those with wealth . . . Those who conspire against me; evil men. Give them up to your Tsar. I am in a forgiving mood this day. I just need a few names, and we can all be on our way."

The monk shook his head and said nothing. Petr admired the spirit and fortitude of the old man. He suspected that many of his own friends would have condemned all of their colleagues upon the first lash. Petr had never been particularly religious and generally considered monks to be both devious and pathetic. This monk was neither.

The Tsar shook his head in disappointment. He pointed to the heap of tools and equipment. "Unfortunately, we must find other means to open the minds of these monks. See what you can do to assist your Tsar."

With obvious relish, several Oprichniki began selecting a variety of torture implements from the pile. As their fate became apparent, the monks began moaning and sobbing.

"Must the air of my realm be fouled with the sounds of whimpering vermin?"

Three of the Tsar's men began to subject the monks to

"pravezh," or cudgeling. One monk screamed and was immediately clubbed senseless by a burly Oprichnik.

Petr had never felt such rage and powerlessness. His body was tightly coiled and ready to spring into action, yet he was unarmed and, even if armed, could do nothing against so many adversaries. His father had provided him with extensive instruction in the use of sword, harquebus, and bow in the hopes that Petr would participate in the family's dangerous commercial enterprises in the east. Under the existing circumstances, that training was as useless today as it had been in his iconography studio in Novgorod.

Petr always doubted that he could kill. Today he realized that he could — wanted it — craved it with an uncontrollable longing, an overpowering lust for blood and vengeance. He wanted to grab the Tsar — to squeeze his throat between his hands until Ivan's face turned purple, and his eyes bulged from their sockets. Only Matrona clutching frantically at his legs prevented him from running at the Oprichniki like a wild bear, blinded by madness and rage. Instead he wept in great sobs that wracked his body and threatened to bring the remainder of the snow load down upon them.

The Tsar suddenly held up his hand and halted the mayhem. Petr took a deep breath. *Perhaps it is over*, he thought. The depth of this depravity must sicken even a madman.

"Names ..." said the Tsar. "I need names."

The names came. Slowly at first:

"Andrei Kurbskii ... Grigor Volynsky."

Then in a torrent:

"Kirilko Onichkov" . . . "Grisha Tryznov" . . . "Pervoi Dmitriev" ..."Ondrie Aliabev" ..."Dmitrei Eremeev" ... "Ivan Ushakov" ... "Aleksei Kotoshikhin" ... "Afanasei Lukin" ... The monks murmured on ... A mantra of names that continued even after the Tsar turned his back on them and called to his men.

"Now that we have loosened their tongues, it is time to

build a fire and enjoy a little warmth and conviviality. Round up a few citizens so that they can enjoy our company. Make sure the boyars are well represented at our gathering as befits their princely station. I am sure that with a little warmth and encouragement, these good monks will be happy to entertain us all."

Two large groups of Oprichniki separated from the main body of men. One group rode back into the citadel of St. Sophia; the other crossed the bridge into the eastern section of Novgorod. Smaller groups of men broke into nearby dwellings and expropriated the firewood and furniture that remained after the first wave of ransacking by the Tsar's men. These were piled into a large bier that would be ignited for the bonfire.

Six Oprichniki began to lift a huge pan out of the last sleigh. The diameter of the pan was as wide as Petr was tall, and the men struggled with its weight. They were barely able to lift it off the sleigh, and after several failed attempts to carry it to the fire, they resorted to sliding it along the frozen street like a giant metal sled.

Petr felt an almost overwhelming sense of foreboding. He doubted the Tsar was planning a celebration that anyone but Ivan would appreciate. Whatever was coming, he did not want Matrona to be a witness to it. Her emotional stability was already hanging by a slender thread. He tapped her shoulder and motioned for her to return to their hidden room. She nodded and quickly scurried into the tunnel.

CHAPTER 4

Over the course of the next hour, a crowd of over two hundred citizens was herded into a circle around the bonfire, which had been built to a height that exceeded the tallest man in attendance. Using their pikes, the Oprichniki hollowed out a depression at the center of the inferno. Large buckets of lard were shoveled into the pan, which was then pushed into the center of the inferno. At length, the lard in the pan began to sizzle and smoke. At this point, the Tsar emerged from a knot of Oprichniki to address the crowd.

At first, many in the crowd did not recognize the Tsar. Those that did immediately dropped to one knee; those that did not were clubbed onto the frozen ground by the Oprichniki who were circling the crowd like so many wolves.

"What has become of Great Novgorod?" he began. "How great is your reputation of commerce and wealth. Yet, here is your Tsar — cold and exhausted from his long journey to meet his loyal subjects! And what have you brought him? Do I see one fur? One blanket? One robe? Nothing! Is this my reward for the yoke of sovereignty — the pain of service?"

An old man attempted to reply, "But, sire — these men have taken everything..." He was quickly clubbed into unconsciousness by two Oprichniki.

The Tsar continued, "Excuses! Is this all that you can bring me? Lies and Excuses?"

"I have gifts, sire!"

Petr recognized the voice of Pavel Vorotntsov, a trading rival of his father. Vorotntsov was notorious for his ill treatment of the Komi and Samoyed peoples in his trading operations. His avarice and unscrupulous dealings with these aboriginal tribes made it difficult, and at times extremely dangerous, for other Novgorod traders to do business in the territories to the North and East of Russia.

As Vorotntsov stepped out of the crowd, Petr was not surprised to see that he was garbed as an Oprichniki in a monk's black robe with a dog's head pendant around his neck. *The dog's head suits you,* Petr thought. *Perhaps it is one of your rapacious relatives.*

In his hands, Vorotntsov had two ropes. The other ends of the robes were around the necks of two of the boyars that the monks had identified under torture.

"Sire, I have brought you two traitors — Ivan Ushakov and Grigor Volynsky!"

Peter gasped. Both men had been in the Safronov home many times. They were well-known leaders of the Veche who advocated closer ties with King Sigismund Augustus of Lithuania. Petr offered a prayer of thanks that his father, a political ally of both men, was now safely out of the Tsar's clutches.

The Tsar smiled and clapped Vorotntsov on the back. "It is good to have one loyal citizen in this den of subversion. Let us see what kind of entertainment we can cook up for our two wealthy and treasonous hosts."

"Mikita — the pan!" he commanded.

A stocky Oprichnik with a porcine face and matching piggish eyes grabbed the rope around Ivan Ushakov's neck and yanked the boyar violently to the frozen earth. Another Oprichniki, thin and with a weaselly face, came forward. He pinned Ushakov's neck to the ground by stepping on the rope that encircled his neck.

A third Oprichniki, whom Petr recognized as a salt merchant, approached with two knives. He handed one to the Oprichnik named Mikita, and both men proceeded to recklessly slash at Ushakov, removing his clothing and a good deal of flesh in the process. Ushakov cried out in horror and pain as the blades bit into his flesh. By the time he was disrobed in this fashion, Ushakov was awash in blood and hoarse from the terrible screams that had rent his throat and lungs.

The Tsar smiled and called for a goblet of mead. He nodded at Mikita to continue.

Ushakov was jerked roughly to his feet by the rope that remained around his neck. He was then dragged forward to the base of the bonfire. Sensing his fate, his bladder and bowels simultaneously released as he howled incoherently.

Petr crossed himself. He wanted to avert his eyes, but was unable to divert them from the impending horror.

Ushakov was doused with a bucket of cold water to wash away the waste clinging to his legs. Four burly Oprichniki grasped him by his wrists and ankles. Swinging him back and forth, they counted out loud. On the count of three, Ushakov was tossed in a high arc toward the pan of searing grease. He began screaming at the top of the arc.

Mercifully for Petr, the wailing of the crowd drowned out all but the highest-pitched shrieks of the frying man. Even so, these anguished screams caused Petr's skin to crawl. The blood rushed from his head, leaving him gasping and disoriented. Throughout the crowd, men, women, and children were fainting. Those who remained conscious were sobbing and vomiting in horror. Petr could not release himself from the vision of Ushakov, his body parboiled red, attempting to flail his way out of the pan, only to be poked back into the oil by pikes wielded by laughing Oprichniki. Even at a distance, the sickly-sweet stench of frying flesh hung in the cold air. Petr retched uncontrollably beneath the sheltering bushes.

For what could only be minutes but seemed like hours, the doomed man writhed in agony. Eventually, with his body scorched and crusted, he rolled onto his back and expired with his arms stretched out in unanswered supplication.

The Tsar nodded to Mikita, and the corpse of what was

once Ushakov was snagged from the pan with a rope and grappling hook. The body hissed and steamed as it was dragged through the snow beyond the fire.

Ivan gestured to Volynsky, who stood leashed like a dog, trembling before his master.

"Fetch me my subject!" Ivan pointed to the corpse of Ushakov. Volynsky did not move. The Tsar walked up to him and gently shook him. Volynsky's eyes came into focus, and he shrunk back from Ivan. "Bring me my subject," Ivan repeated — almost tenderly.

Volynsky stumbled forward and began to drag Ushakov's remains toward the Tsar by one foot.

"That is no way to treat the Tsar's subject!" thundered Ivan. "Pick him up!"

Volynsky cradled the crusted corpse in his arms and, staggering under the weight, carried it to the glowering Tsar. Ivan took some time to inspect Ushakov's body. His face softened noticeably as he quietly addressed Volynsky.

"See how he reaches out in entreaty to his Tsar. If only he had confessed and sought my mercy sooner. Is there anything you would like to say to your Tsar now?"

Volynsky dropped Ushakov's corpse and threw himself at the feet of the Tsar's feet.

"Forgive me my treason, sire," he begged. "Spare me from the horrors of the pan!" Ivan smiled at Volynsky. Patting the man's head, the Tsar gently pulled him to his feet.

"Your Tsar is merciful," Ivan announced to the crowd. "Despite his subversion, I shall spare this man from the pan." Smiling, he began to gently remove the clothing from the trembling man. At length, Volynsky stood naked and shivering in the icy breeze.

Ivan handed the rope that still encircled Volynsky's neck to an Oprichnik and walked over to Mikita. The Tsar and Mikita talked quietly for some time. Then both men laughed, and Mikita gestured to a group of ten Oprichniki to join them.

After a short discussion punctuated by laughter and guffaws, eight Oprichniki approached Volynsky, and two went to the bonfire.

Volynsky was quickly wrestled to the ground. He was spread-eagle on his back with two Oprichniki holding each arm and leg. When he was completely subdued, the two Oprichniki waiting at the bonfire drew two huge iron tongs from the bed of coals. The crowd gasped as they observed the pincer ends glowing white-hot. The pincers hissed as they were struck by the falling snowflakes from a passing squall.

Petr did not want to see what was coming next. Yet, he felt compelled to watch, for whether on earth, in heaven, or in hell, he knew that someday he must bear witness to this terrible brutality.

Volynsky's loud and rhythmic moans sounded almost like a chant as the Oprichniki approached with their sizzling pincers. Soon Volynsky's moans turned to keening and then to shrieks as the searing pincers were repeatedly thrust into his chest and his ribs torn viciously from his body. Mercifully, Volynsky passed out upon the extraction of the second of his ribs. This did not deter the Oprichniki from their ghastly task. They grunted and swore as they labored upon the shredded remnants of their still-living victim.

The crowd stood in stunned silence, their minds shocked into a catatonic state by the gruesome exhibitions that they were forced to witness. Many had wet themselves, while others drooled and rocked rhythmically as if the ground were undulating beneath their feet.

At length, the Tsar spoke, "Who will claim the remains of this traitor?"

No one spoke. If Volynsky had relatives in the crowd, they were too fearful to identify themselves. The Tsar glared at the throng. His face became purple with rage as he paced up and down in front of his silent subjects.

"This is not an old man. He must have relatives — a wife,

children, cousins, and nephews? Bring them forward! Now!"

A low murmur swept through the crowd, but no one spoke, and none came forward.

The Tsar turned to Mikita and gestured to the terrified citizens.

"Very well — since nobody has come forward, I will assume that they are all relatives!"

He paused and looked over the crowd. "And all treasonous!"

The man named Mikita rushed forward and clubbed an elderly monk with his cudgel. As if upon cue, the Oprichniki fell upon the citizens with pike and cudgel, wantonly beating and skewering men, women, and children alike. Those who were not immediately set upon by the Oprichniki fled in every direction.

Petr, both fearful of discovery and ashamed of his helplessness, withdrew into the tunnel, pulling branches and snow in behind him to conceal the entrance. For a long time, he lay sobbing in the entryway, and then gradually, he backed down the tunnel, letting the soothing darkness spill into the hideous images burning in his mind.

CHAPTER 5

Matrona came awake, choking. She wanted to cry out from the bloody horror of the nightmare that assaulted her subconscious. Her survival instincts choked back her screams before they could clear her throat. She lay trembling under the fur robes for several minutes before the visions of bruised and tortured flesh that had plagued her sleep dissipated in the dank air of the cellar hideaway. She could have used some comfort from Petr, who slept fitfully a few feet away in the darkness. She dared not disturb him, however, as he had precious little sleep since he returned from the tunnel two days ago.

Despite her frequent inquiries, Petr refused to talk about what he had observed after she had descended into their subterranean den. She surmised that whatever he saw, it had been even more horrific than what she had observed of the Oprichniki's cruelty toward the monks. Twice, she had to spring to his bed to stifle the screams that wracked his sleep. She feared he would be heard by the Oprichniki who were intermittently present in the main house above.

Matrona longed to be in her own cluttered room at the top of the house. The Safronov home was constructed and maintained in accordance with the *Domostroi*, the universally acknowledged guide to good household management of the era. Their home was self-sufficient, with gardens, orchards, barns, stables, and storage facilities. An outdoor stairway bypassed the ground-floor storage rooms and led to a foyer on the second floor.

The Safronov household furnishings were sumptuous,

consisting largely of tables, benches, and chests. Chairs were quite rare in Russia at this time and generally reserved for the master of the house when present. However, due to the Safronovs' wealth and Alexei's devotion to Svetlana, their house boasted two chairs that sat side by side in the sitting room, a physical testament to the bond between the master and mistress of the home.

The Safronov home was lavishly decorated with taffetas, brocades, and velvets. The wooden floors were covered with oriental carpets and exquisite throw rugs. Most of this by now was on the way to Moscow, the booty of some thieving Oprichniki. Tears welled as Matrona remembered the family's shrine, known as the "beautiful corner," which contained a lovely array of candles that illuminated Petr's icons. As visitors genuflected at the Safronov shrine, they often caught their breath as if glimpsing a part of heaven.

While the Safronovs generally followed the *Domostroi* in matters of household management, they varied from its precepts in regard to family relationships. Marriage alliances were vital to the propagation and prosperity of the lineage group or "rod." Young girls were generally contracted off in arranged marriages to foster commercial or political relationships.

At sixteen years of age, Matrona was older than most of her unmarried contemporaries. Alexsei had the absolute right to marry Matrona to anyone he chose. However, he waited until he was sure that there was an emotional attraction between Matrona and Dimitri before approaching his commercial ally, Filipov Stepanov, to arrange their marriage.

The fact that Alexsei knew anything at all about his daughter's feelings or thoughts would be unique in Muscovite society, where the *Domostroi* was strictly observed. The *Domostroi* required the seclusion of elite women to prevent social attachments that might undermine the family's ability to arrange a politically or socially advantageous marriage alliance. Under its tenets, separate household spheres were established and maintained for men and women. Men and women ate and lived apart. Women left the home only to attend church or, on rare occasions, to visit other women.

Like many successful boyars in Novgorod, Alexsei was both too kind and too shrewd to abide by the more draconian of the *Domostroi*'s strictures. He was passionately in love with Svetlana and valued her social and intellectual contribution to his career. Unlike most of the elite of the day, he did not consider his wife to be a mental and moral inferior. He ensured that his daughter received an education sufficient to mirror her mother's attributes.

While Matrona did receive an education, her training and tutoring were conducted separately from that of her brothers. And although she wasn't secluded from the male members of the family, the divergent roles and responsibilities of men and women precluded any sustained close personal interactions at work or play. Consequently, she was ill-prepared for her present situation, where she shared the same small space with her brother.

Indeed, Matrona had almost burst from holding her bladder for the entire first day that they were underground. Only the excruciating pain from this ordeal enabled her to use the chamber pot in Petr's presence — even though that presence was buried under every robe she could find in their subterranean den. She would never forgive him for not immediately telling her about the tunnel leading from their lair. His penance was to ascend the tunnel every time that nature called to her, which was frequent in the dank hideaway. She also insisted that he nightly empty the chamber pot into the hole in the corner of the room that had been prepared for this eventuality.

Her thoughts turned to Dimitri. They were to be wed at Easter time. She had been somewhat apprehensive about this union. To be sure, she was attracted to him. In many respects, he reminded her of Petr. Dimitri had the same easy laugh and sophisticated style as her brother. He was an accomplished musician. On many a winter evening, Dimitri had enchanted both their families with his mastery of the harpsichord.

Dimitri was handsome, elegant, and very European, in contrast with his brother, Andrei, who appeared to have captured most of their family's Tatar lineage. Andrei was solid, rugged, and fierce. Dimitri was being groomed by his father for negotiation and diplomacy in the family's commercial and political endeavors. Andrei was responsible for expanding their trading empire into the barbarous lands beyond the eastern frontier.

Matrona was attracted to the refined manner of Dimitri, but in Andrei's presence, she found herself stirred in a way that was, at once, both exhilarating and unsettling. As, day by day, the danger grew and her physical and mental resilience flagged, it was Andrei that she longed to see descending the tunnel. She knew her feelings were wrong, but her frequent prayers were unable to summon Dimitri into her thoughts or expel Andrei from her dreams.

Petr rolled over on his side, and his breathing became less labored. He slipped into a deep sleep. Matrona pulled her woolen sleeping cap down over her ears, pulled the robes up under her chin, and closed her eyes to sleep some more. Sleep was a blessed escape from their wretched existence.

Suddenly, there was a loud thump on the outdoor stairway leading to the living quarters above. In an instant, Petr and Matrona were standing. Matrona clutched the sleeping robes to her breast, and Petr brandished a dagger that he kept within easy reach.

There were several more thumps, and a woman cried out in terror. Her scream was cut off with a hollow thud, and two men guffawed loudly as if greatly amused by her fear and pain. Matrona felt her skin crawl, and she shrank back into her bedding.

"Petr!"

But Petr was already in the tunnel heading for the surface.

CHAPTER 6

Petr stopped briefly to collect himself. He stilled his racing heart and gasping breath, before he poked his head out of the tunnel. He had no plan as to what he would do once he was above ground. He only knew that there was a woman in peril from at least two men. For too long, he had played the silent observer. He prayed that there were no more than two adversaries and that the element of surprise would be in his favor. As Petr poked his head out of the tunnel entrance, he was relieved to see that the moon and stars were obscured by clouds, and the night was pitch black.

Petr was lightly armed, as the tunnel was too tight to permit the passage of a heavy weapon. In case it was necessary to bind one or both of the Oprichniki, he carried a dagger and a strong leather thong. Regardless of the danger or consequences, Petr was ready to act. His impotence in the face of Ivan's cruelty had consumed his conscience in an inferno of shame. He would not allow himself to hide in cowardice a second time.

Sensing that time was of the essence if he were to save the woman, Petr raced through the orchard and then slid along the side of the stable. He could hear the sound of horses nervously stomping around within. He carefully moved to the end of the stable. This enabled him to observe the main entrance to the house. The door stood open and was backlit by torchlight from within the foyer. A short, stout Oprichnik came to the door and glanced up and down the street. Petr doubted that he was on guard. More than likely, he was looking for more of his comrades to join in their sordid assault. As soon as the Oprichniki went back into the house, Petr ran to the bottom of the stairs.

He cautiously ascended the stairs, keeping his shoulder as close to the wall as possible without touching it. He was careful to step close to the stair support beams to eliminate any noise from a loose board. The steps were covered in snow. Petr knew that snow that was frozen to a very low temperature would squeak and squeal when it was compressed by a footstep. To minimize this noise, he slowly and carefully transferred his weight from one foot to the other.

As Petr moved quietly and deliberately up the steps, he could hear his heart pounding within his chest. All of the night sounds seemed greatly magnified. He could hear shouts and laughter from the streets far beyond the cathedral. A wolf howled by the river near the bridge. He was surprised to hear a wolf so close to the city and wondered what drew them out of the wilderness — was it starvation or opportunity?

Petr's climb seemed endless, but at last, he was at the top of the stairs. There was a good deal of turmoil from within the house. He could hear the woman groaning and the sounds of bodies hitting against the wall. After a particularly loud thud, a man groaned and then cursed loudly.

"You little whore! You're as slippery as an eel. But if you won't take it one way, I'll sure as hell give it to you another!"

The other man guffawed raucously. Petr could hear him chortling as the man's footsteps approached the open door. "It looks like you have too much to handle there by yourself, Liron! I'll look for reinforcements again. I'd help you out, but I've poked more than my share already today."

Still laughing, the man stepped out of the doorway. His eyes widened and then bulged as Petr thrust the dagger through the man's jugular and trachea in one swift stroke. The cursing and groaning that emanated from within the house drowned out the Oprichnik's gurgling death rattle outside.

Petr carefully lowered the quivering body to the snow-laden landing. As he stepped away from the body, the woman inside began a forlorn wailing that spoke of unspeakable pain and humiliation.

Petr sprang into the foyer, forgetting his dagger that remained protruding from the neck of the dead Oprichnik on the landing. At first, he could not locate either the victim or her attacker. The woman began sobbing loudly, and Petr detected her and her assailant in the corner that had been, at one time, the family's shrine.

A tall and burly Oprichnik had pinned a young woman by jamming her head into the corner of the room. He was attempting to sodomize the maiden, but she continued to squirm in resistance. The man struck the girl in the side of her head with one hand while he pulled her hair with his other. His lust-flooded senses failed to detect Petr's approach until the leather thong encircled his neck and bit sharply into his flesh. Struggling mightily, Petr was able to pull the larger man up a sufficient amount for the girl to twist out from under him.

The Oprichnik outweighed Petr by at least forty pounds, but this was of little advantage in the face of the fury with which Petr clung to the makeshift garrote. Petr thrust his knee into the rapist's back, and with this leverage, he was able to withstand the violent writhing of the choking Oprichniki. Petr's adrenaline and hatred blocked the pain of the leather thong biting into his hand. Petr continued to cling to the garrote long after the Oprichnik's death throes signaled that he had succumbed to strangulation. Petr's face, contorted in hatred, was almost as purple as that of the dead man.

After several minutes had passed, the young girl tugged on Petr's sleeve; she struggled to talk through her swollen lips.

"He is dead, Master. He cannot hurt us now."

Petr slowly released the garrote and, with it, his hold on his emotions. He shook and sobbed uncontrollably as he pulled his thighs to his chest and buried his head between his knees. The girl said nothing but sat beside him, pulling the tattered remains of her torn clothing together.

After several minutes, the girl tugged on his arm again.

"Do not mourn him. He deserved to die. If we do not leave soon, we will join him."

Petr slowly pulled himself together and rose, wiping his tears away with his sleeve. "I do not grieve for him. I grieve for the loss of the better part of my soul. I fear I shall never regain it."

The girl looked at the open door and shrugged. "An unblemished soul is of little use in Novgorod. It is best to be free of it in these times!"

Petr looked at her for the first time. She was slender, fair-haired, and tall for a Russian girl, almost as tall as Petr. He judged her to be a year or two older than Matrona, seventeen or eighteen years old, perhaps. He could tell little of her countenance as her face was a mass of bruises, and her left eye had already swollen shut. She fixed him with the gaze of the undamaged eye, which was icy blue and fierce.

"We must dispose of these bodies; then we must escape!"

Petr was amazed at the girl's composure. The rape had not been consummated, but she had still been brutally violated.

"What is your name, girl? Do you have a family nearby?"

The young woman looked away before answering.

"My name is Anna, and I have no family. I am a servant ... Rather, I was a servant in the Ushakov household. There is no Ushakov household now, and no Ushakovs either."

"Well, Anna — avert your eyes because I have need of this swine's garments."

Instead of turning away, she went directly to the corpse and began disrobing it. "There is precious little innocence left to protect. Better that we do what we must and be on our way."

Petr helped her remove the clothing. With its chalky white

body, purple head, and obscenely swollen member, the corpse was a grotesque monument to man's lust.

Petr handed the garments to the young woman. "Hold onto these while I drag the other body indoors."

The corpse of the Oprichnik at the top of the stairs was heavy. It took several minutes for Petr to drag it through the foyer into the family room. Anna scowled at the body. "Do you want his clothing as well?"

Petr shook his head. "No. There is too much blood on them, and we have no means to wash it out."

Anna handed the bundle of clothing to Petr. She then reached down and pulled Petr's dagger out of the corpse's neck. "I have need of this."

She strode to the body of the strangled Oprichnik and sliced off his erect manhood — hurling it into the corner. "Perhaps the next Oprichnik will think twice before trying to rape another woman!"

Petr was surprised but not stunned. He had seen so much cruelty in the last several days that the mere mutilation of a corpse did not shock him.

"Come," he said. "We must be out of Novgorod by daybreak."

Petr led Anna down the stairs and in through the storeroom to the secret hideaway under the house. When they entered the lair, Matrona gave a little cry and rushed forward to hug him. Petr could not help but notice that both their hideout and his sister smelled like moldy cabbage that had been left in the cellar too long.

As Matrona stepped away from Petr's embrace, she noticed Anna standing quietly outside the zone of light cast by the one candle that burned in the room. She took the girl by the hand and led her into the light. Matrona gasped when she saw the girl's bruised face and torn clothing.

"You poor thing," she whispered as tears welled in her eyes. "You poor, poor thing." She reached out and gently stroked the girl's hair.

The fierceness that had supported Anna through her ordeal departed in a tiny tremble that rippled from her lower lip into a tidal wave of sobbing convulsions that shook her whole body. She clung to Matrona, salving her wounded spirit with the kindness and understanding that only another woman could provide in the wake of such horror.

Petr silently slipped away from the two women and made his way to the stable. He was relieved to find four horses — all sturdy and apparently fit for a long winter journey. Three of the horses were mares and appeared quite docile. He saddled two mares, one each for Matrona and Anna. He saddled the stallion for himself and haltered the third mare for a spare. He would rather have a coach, or even a sleigh, so that they could carry more goods in greater comfort. But with these mounts, they would have the advantage of speed. With death lurking in every shadow, speed was a better ally than comfort.

On the way back to the house, Petr filled one of the buckets from the stable with snow. When he returned to the hideaway, the young women were sitting on Matrona's bed, engaged in a quiet dialog. Each of their spirits seemed elevated by the other's presence.

It is good that their morale is improved, Petr thought, *for the coming journey will test their bodies and their will.*

Petr handed the bucket of snow to Matrona. "It looks like you will not become a Tatar after all, sister. Wash off what is left of your dark complexion, for you are about to become my slave — albeit a stolen slave."

"I would rather be a Tatar," Matrona snapped.

"It is not so bad being a slave," Anna volunteered wryly. "I have been a slave for five years now. Except for getting fondled on occasion by my master's dull-witted son, it was quite bearable."

Neither Matrona nor Petr were surprised. Many of the servants in Novgorod, as in Moscow, were serfs bound to the household and land. There was a common Russian bond between serf owners and their subjects that was due in part to the shared cultural background of serfs and masters. The serf system in Russia served as a welfare system for families or individuals with no other means of support. When they fell on hard times, people sold themselves or their offspring into serfdom to survive.

Petr took two ropes off the pegs on the wall.

"Well, we are all slaves to circumstances now," he explained, gently knotting a rope around each of the women's necks. He handed a sack of supplies to each of them. "Now it is time to bid farewell to Lord Novgorod the Great," he said sadly.

"I fear that the greatness of our civilization is vanishing quickly. Stamped out under the Tsar's ruthless heel — or cast to the four winds."

"And to which wind are we cast, Master?"

"To the East, Anna," he replied. "And we best be on our way."

CHAPTER 7

At first, the detachment of Oprichniki at the bridge over the river Volkhov did not notice the three riders descending from the city. They were too busy enjoying the merriment of their latest endeavor. The river was unfrozen in this section due to the increased speed of the current near the bridge. The Tsar's men had put this anomaly to good use. The open stretch of water contained hundreds of corpses. The number was about to increase by two. A mother and her toddler had been found hiding in an outbuilding of a boyar's estate. They had been tied together and cast into the river from the bridge.

The mother's will was strong, and she struggled to the surface over and over again. Two guards stood by in small boats. They would let her struggle on the surface for a while with her child. They would feign interest in her pleas of mercy for her son. Laughing, they would then paddle over and push her under the water with their pikes.

By the time the riders approached the bridge, the mother and child had finally ceased their futile fight against madness and death. Ice fog from the open water hung over the bridge and obscured the riders' features.

The lead rider, a male, rode a black horse in typical Oprichniki fashion. He carried the signature broom mounted on a staff as well as a dog's head on the saddle. He was dressed in a black cloak resembling a monk's habit. If not for the ice fog, the Oprichniki might have noticed that the rider's cloak was several sizes too big for him.

As the leader of the Oprichniki detachment approached

the horseman, the rider guffawed and pointed to the bank where a dozen severed heads of monks were mounted on stakes in the ground. "I see that not all of the intellectuals I sent down to you made it into the river. It's a shame, as they were all complaining about being thirsty after we so graciously made them toasty warm!"

The Oprichniki laughed, but the two trembling women who were secured by ropes around their necks diverted most of his attention. He pointed to the woman nearest him, who quaked under his gaze. "This one is a real prize, but it looks like you ruined the other one."

"I'm afraid you're right. That's the reason I'm on the road so early. Our Tsar wants these two back in Moscow for some public education that he has planned there. He probably wouldn't care that I had to knock this one around a bit. But why take chances? It's best to be on the road early."

The detachment commander shook his head in agreement. "That's probably wise," he said. He studied the male rider for a long moment. "I don't recognize you. I know just about every Muscovite here, but you aren't familiar."

"That's because I'm not from Moscow. I'm from here in Novgorod. I have been spying for the Oprichnina for months. Another reason I hate to leave now. I want to be here when Ivan divvies up the boyar estates. I'm afraid I'll lose my fair share taking this pair back to Moscow. I've been banking on two estates that adjoin my own. Maybe the Tsar's wise to me?"

The Oprichniki laughed. "You'll be alright if you hurry. The Tsar has a lot of thinning out to do before he is ready to establish the new order here. We should be entertained for another week or two before the fun is over."

The rider clucked to his horse and moved out onto the bridge, tugging on the ropes that were securing the two women. "Well, off we go then. Save some fun for me."

When the riders reached the far end of the bridge, they were enveloped in ice fog. The Oprichniki could not observe the male rider hang his head in shame or the women shuddering as the horses shied from a wolf dragging a severed arm across the roadway. By the time a light breeze dissipated the fog, the riders were gone.

◊

The night was clear, and the starlight reflecting off the snow provided sufficient illumination for the safe passage of the three riders. The horses generated tiny clouds of ice fog as their warm breath hit the frigid air. Petr's stallion rebelled at the slow pace, and he had to work to keep him under control.

But it wasn't his mount that concerned Petr. He was most worried about his sister. As day broke, Matrona was already slumped forward, barely able to stay in the saddle. Anna was concerned as well and offered her whispered encouragement.

Anna was indefatigable. She stood more than her share of watches during the day while Matrona and Petr tried to sleep. Fortunately, there was no lack of shelter for the travelers or their horses. By ransacking every village between Moscow and Novgorod, Ivan had unintentionally provided them with many abandoned dwellings.

As each day broke, they carefully selected those buildings far from the road and close to the forest to preclude discovery and provide a quick avenue of escape and concealment. One man had tried to sneak back into his house, but one sight of Petr's Oprichniki attire sent him fleeing in panic.

On the fourth day, Anna pushed her mount forward to catch up to Petr. "We must find a sleigh for Matrona soon, Master. She is near total exhaustion, and if she falls, she may be gravely injured. We will be without assistance of any kind for many days."

"Thank you for your concern, Anna," he replied. "We will search the next village for a sleigh. I am afraid that anything of value has been carted off to Moscow by now."

Anna nodded and began to rein her horse to the rear.

Petr reached out and gently tugged on her sleeve. "There is no need to call me 'Master,' Anna. I do not own you — have no desire to own you. I am in your debt for your devotion to my sister. Without your assistance, I doubt we would have made it this far."

She glared at him defiantly. "No, Master Petr, it is I who am in your debt. You saved me from ruination, and I have treated you quite badly. I am truly sorry." She paused for a moment — softening. "It's hard for me to be near any man ... After ... After all that happened ..." she stammered. "Even you."

Petr wanted to reach out to her — hold her. He restrained himself. "Perhaps time will heal your wounds, Anna — even the ones that you carry inside," he said gently.

"I will pray for this," she said.

They proceeded in silence for half a league. At length, they neared another village. Petr thought it might be Mologa. He had traveled there quite often with his father, who maintained several warehouses of furs in the community.

Something was not quite right. Petr's stallion could sense it, and he snorted in dismay as Petr urged him on. As he approached a grove of firs, Petr could make out several shapes that were out of place. He motioned to Matrona and Anna to stay put, and pulling his sword, he rode forward cautiously.

As he entered the tree line, he felt a great sense of foreboding. It was not just the gloom of the dark trees that blotted out the starlight. The mood was darker and deeper than that. A small, forlorn rural road ran north from the main road. Petr could sense that he was once again in the presence of a great evil.

He found the bodies next to a small clearing. They were propped up on pikes with the frozen gore that had once been their bowels piled at their feet. Their tongues had been severed, and their lifeless eyes that were lifted heavenward registered shock rather than supplication. There were four in all. The last one was Dimitri.

CHAPTER 8

Andrei

They spotted Andrei from the crest of a small hill about ten versts from Yaroslavl. Petr had the women remain where they were and rode out to meet him. The gravity of the situation demanded privacy, and Petr was somewhat apprehensive of Andrei's response to the news. With the discovery of Dimitri's body, Matrona had become a mental and physical wreck. If Andrei became unhinged, it would only aggravate his sister's condition.

Andrei received the grim news stoically at first. Only a tiny tremor that coursed across his face from his lower lip to his left eyelid betrayed the shocking news that assaulted him. For several minutes, he remained silent and rigid in his saddle. There were no tears, but his eyes gradually hardened into black ice. Tiny sparks ignited in the pupils of his eyes and soon grew into a conflagration that consumed his entire countenance. He drew his sword, and with a terrible roar, he galloped past the startled women and disappeared over the hill behind them.

◊

It was early morning when Andrei arrived at the site of the slaughter. The bodies were not difficult to locate. A dozen or more ravens could be heard croaking and screaming in the forest as they fought over the most scavenger-delectable parts of the ten corpses hanging just off the roadway. By the time Andrei arrived on the scene, the eyes, eyelids, and lips of the massacre victims had already been consumed by the ravens. The jays were content to devour the severed tongues and bowels on the ground, where they were free from the harassment of the ravens. The bodies resembled macabre scarecrows from a wormwood-induced nightmare.

Petr's small party had not had the time or resources to provide a proper burial for so many bodies. Petr and Anna had done the best they could to bury Dimitri. Matrona had been too grief-stricken to participate. Pushing the limits of time and safety, they had put Dimitri to rest in a shallow depression and covered him with loose logs and large branches from road-clearing debris. That would have to do until the Church could recover the bodies and re-enter them in consecrated ground. Andrei knew that the forest animals would harvest most of the bodies, including Dimitri's, before any retrieval by the Church could be undertaken. Nevertheless, he appreciated the efforts of Petr and Anna, who had risked detection by any pursuing Oprichniki in order to honor and respect his brother.

Andrei made no effort to locate his brother's grave. A veteran of many battles and skirmishes, he was accustomed to riding away from death, even the death of friends and loved ones. His eulogy to his brother would be written in vengeance and blood rather than liturgical dogma.

Pushing his grief aside, Andrei searched the area near the corpses for any sign of the victims' assailants. Heavy hoarfrost covered most of the gore near the bodies. Footprints and hoofprints were almost totally obliterated, but under some of the taller fir trees, the boughs had blocked the fall of ice crystals, and a few tracks were visible. It took him some time to sort them out. He had to be sure that the tracks he followed were those of the assailants and not those of the victims.

Under a tall fir tree near the bodies, Andrei found what he was looking for: the track from a horse with a defective horseshoe. A deep indentation in the side of the print indicated a casting error, a minor defect for the horse that could prove fatal for the rider. Andrei knew that if he could follow this print north on this rural road, he would be able to locate at least one of the assailants. If the horseman had company, woe to them who wore black.

Walking back to his mount, Andrei noticed an odd-looking object beneath the hoarfrost. He gently brushed off the frost and discovered a ceramic dog's head encased in leather. An unfortunate Oprichniki had lost his insignia and identified his participation in the slaughter. It must have been snagged in the bushes and torn off the saddle. Now Andrei had two of the assailants identified. He wanted nine more.

Andrei rode slowly northward. After following the defective horseshoe track for several versts, he was certain that he was on the trail of the attackers. The victims had been going in the opposite direction, innocent third parties who had undoubtedly suffered the same fate as the Novgorod trade delegation.

It was not long before Andrei's supposition was born out. As he approached a sharp curve in the road, he could hear the raucous squawks of ravens on the far side of the turn. As he rounded the turn, he spotted three bodies swinging from a tree near the bridge over a small stream.

At another time, it would have been an idyllic setting. Vapors rising from open water turned into ice fog as they rose to form a sun dog, a rainbow shard of ice crystals in the clear blue sky. The horror below was nothing less than hell frozen over. Andrei did not reflect on the biblical juxtaposition of beauty above and carnage below. He concentrated on whatever information the scene presented. Vengeance is a focused endeavor.

There were three bodies, two females and a male. They appeared to be a small family: a husband, wife, and teenage daughter. In the extreme cold, they were frozen in abject horror and degradation. The male had been castrated and disemboweled. His trousers dangled obscenely at his ankles. The wife's throat had been slit. The blood flowing down her dress had frozen into a crimson gore, reduced here and there by the pecking ravens.

The daughter hung stark naked. She had been violated with knives and sticks in ways heretofore unimaginable to Andrei. He had seen many facets of death, but what was before him was too shocking to observe, let alone contemplate; he had to look away.

The victims' plain dress revealed that they were serfs. The Tsar's quarrel was with the nobles and boyars. The gratuitous slaughter of innocent serfs demonstrated the depraved state of the Oprichniki. This level of debauchery further strengthened Andrei's resolve for vengeance, now not only for his brother but for all who suffered from the degeneracy of the Oprichniki. But to exact revenge required that he catch the Oprichniki assailants, so he rode on, leaving the dead for the scavengers and the Church. He looked back once. The grisly scene served as a macabre reminder of the madness of the Tsar and the wickedness of his henchmen.

After the bridge, the roadway took a sharp turn to the west and broke out of the forest into an area of small fields and woodlots. A humble wattle-and-daub hut of sticks and mud with a thatched roof was close to the right-hand side of the road. The door had been kicked in, and blood stains on the threshold marked the beginning of the end for the peasants who had been dwelling there. There were no trees nearby, so they were strung up where Andre had found them. In a pen behind the hut, the carcasses of a cow and several sheep were scattered in frozen disarray. An abundance of feathers indicated that many chickens had gone under the knife as well. Apparently, the bloodlust of the Oprichniki had no limits. Andrei intended for the stolen chickens to be their last meal. But he had no time for contemplation of the evil circumstances or visualization of retribution. Again, he rode on, leaving the physical horror behind. The mental scar would remain.

The sun was almost at its zenith in the southern sky. The warmth it created was so minimal that most people could not discern its effect. But Andrei was a man of the vast, forlorn lands that lay east of Muscovy's influence. He noticed that his nose hairs no longer tingled with ice. The hoarfrost on his saddle blanket was gone, as were the shards of frost around his horse's mouth and nostrils.

In contrast to the crystal-blue sky, the landscape was barren and bleak. Wherever the wind had scoured away the snow and frost, stubble from the previous year's crop stuck through the underlying ice sheet. It was a scene as dismal as the lives of the serfs who tended the fields for the sustenance of their families and the profit of their master. Peasant serfs could be sold, but they could not be sold away from the land to which they were attached. In all respects, they belonged to the land.

As he pushed northward, Andrei had a fleeting image of a trip he and Dimitri had made to the steppe, the ancestral homeland of their Tartar kin. He pushed the thought aside. There was no time for that. Grief and remembrance could come later. Urging his horse on, he sensed the presence of Oprichniki. The opportunity for revenge was near.

As he journeyed onward, Andre encountered three more peasant huts that had been ransacked, their inhabitants butchered. Chillingly, he only discovered the bodies of men, boys, and older women. There were no slain girls or young women in any of the huts. As with the first hut, the large animals had been slaughtered, but here, even dead chickens littered the landscape. Unlike the human victims, the animals had not been mutilated.

Approaching a low-lying ridge, Andrei observed smoke drifting up at the base of the hill. Arriving at the site of the smoke, he discovered a fourth hut that had been set afire. Snow on the roof of the hut had prevented a complete burn. He could see charred human remains in the ash and rubble. Again, animal remains lay scattered about the adjoining pen. He did not pause to investigate further.

Andrei, the veteran of several military campaigns, dismounted at the military crest so that he would not be skylined on the ridge top. He tied his horse behind a copse of alder where it could not be seen from the road. He climbed the remainder of the hill on foot. Due to the possibility that Oprichniki were observing the road from a location beyond the hill, he avoided any movement that would show his presence. There were few shrubs at the top of the hill to hide him, but as he neared the crest, he saw the thatched roof of a shed, or small hut, off to the right side of the road. He moved to place the roofline of the building between him and any observer on the far side of the hill.

The building turned out to be a small, windowless shed generally used to store field implements and seeds. Its state of disrepair indicated that it had not been used in some time. The door was broken, and here and there, wood had been scavenged for use elsewhere. This proved fortuitous for Andrei, as the openings provided him an opportunity to observe the road ahead without revealing his presence.

The view from the top of the hill provided Andrei with a panoramic view of feudal Russia — and hell. The road circled a two-story, boyar manor house, and even at the distance of several versts, its elegance and opulence stood out. The stone columns on its veranda gleamed in the afternoon sun. Stables and various outbuildings stood to the back of the manor. Beyond the outbuildings was an extensive orchard, and beyond that was the peasant village surrounding a stone church. Beyond the village, the fields of the serfs stretched to the horizon.

Under normal circumstances, this winter scene would

have been peaceful, but a score of houses was ablaze, marking the active presence of Oprichniki. The church, too, was on fire. The smoke from the many fires merged into a wide plume, illuminated by the crimson rays of the setting sun, casting a hellish glow on the scene below.

There was nothing Andrei could do to halt the distant debauchery. There were no trees or shrubs to provide concealment for a daytime approach to the village and manor. He knew that an army of one could only be effective in the dark of night. Stealth and surprise were not available in daylight. He would bide his time. Choking back loathing and fury, he took out a small whetting stone from his pocket and began sharpening his knife and arrowheads. Pushing all thoughts aside, he focused on his implements of war and retribution.

CHAPTER 9

An Army of One

Dusk can be a magical or terrifying time, depending upon what one envisions in the subdued light and descending darkness. The world is wrapped in shadow, hiding detail and obscuring movement. It is a time for lovers. It is a time for assassins.

Graveyards are particularly foreboding at dusk, especially for those with a superstitious mind or a guilty conscience. The cemetery next to the little church had two sections, one with humble grave markers for the serfs and an area of crypts and monuments for the nobles and clergy. Andrei was concealed behind a large monument in the latter.

The adjoining church had been gutted by a fire within that had consumed pews, draperies, rugs, and the wooden infrastructure. The walls being stone remained, a hollow testament to the spirit and piety of this rural community.

Outside the church, the intermingled bodies of a score of clergy and townspeople were strewn about the premises. There were no Oprichniki bodies. The carnage was the result of a mass execution, not a battle. One reason for the slaughter was contained in a large wagon in the churchyard. It was overflowing with plunder taken from the church. The gold, precious stones, and jewels purchased with tithings from the miserably poor serfs now belonged to the coffers of the mad Tsar and his henchmen.

A black horse without the accouterments of the Oprichniki was tied to the wagon. A tall, angular man was quietly sifting through the booty. In the flickering light of the church,

Andrei was able to identify him as a member of the clergy. The gold embroidery on the vestments indicated that this was a high-ranking bishop from Moscow. This was not entirely unexpected. Church officials were not above engaging in sinister intrigue to catch the Tsar's ear and expand their own standing and influence. So what if a few monks had to be martyred? It would only improve their standing in heaven.

A lusty roar and loud female sheiks from the manor house split the night air. The bishop looked up briefly but went right back to sifting through the wagon's riches. Andrei wondered why the cleric hadn't joined the Oprichniki in the manor house. Perhaps he was only present to sanctify the slaughter. The Muscovy clergy had convinced Ivan that since he was God's emissary on earth, he had all of the God-given powers to torment and execute those who defied the Holy Realm of Rus.

The bishop looked to the manor house after another roar from the rampaging Oprichniki. Andre used this opportunity to move quickly to a gravestone less than twenty paces from the cleric. His Tartar bow was under his cape, where it was protected from the extreme cold. He withdrew it and tested its draw. It remained supple and strong. It appeared short and unimpressive, but its recurve would supply ample power. Andrei's training would provide accuracy.

Andrei was growing impatient. His attack required darkness, and the quarter moon would be rising soon. It did not take much moonlight to illuminate the snowy landscape. At last, the bishop moved to the side of the wagon facing Andrei. He took off the cross hanging from his neck and threw it in the wagon. He then withdrew a much larger cross from the pile of plunder. Andrei realized that the bishop did not avoid the carnal reverie out of any moral standard; he merely wanted the best loot for himself.

Totally absorbed in the beauty of the jewel-encrusted gold cross, the bishop never heard the twang of bowstring or the soft rush of displaced air. Darkness descended at the tip of a speeding arrowhead that pierced his brain stem and dropped him silently to the frozen ground.

Andrei moved quickly to shove the body of the bishop under the wagon before any telltale blood could pool in the snow. The horse, scenting blood, became agitated. Andrei moved quickly to calm him. His grandfather was full Tatar and had trained Andrei in the ways of nomads and the steppe. He knew horses.

The horse was a fine steed: tall, muscular, and sinuous. It would be fleet, and Andrei would need a fast mount to reach his horse, which was tethered on the far side of the hill. He was confident that once he was on his own mount, no Oprichniki could catch him. He checked the horse's shoes. The defect he had been tracking was on the right rear shoe. So, the bishop had been present at the slaughter of his brother. That explained why the delegation from Novgorod had not put up a fight. Being merchants and tradesmen, they had obviously been complacent in the presence of clergy.

It was likely that the villagers had been also similarly surprised. Most had their hands bound, and all but a few adjacent to the church were gagged. The bodies lay in small groups of two to four individuals. Andrei suspected that the Oprichniki had used the bishop to gain entry to each house. They had then quickly overwhelmed the inhabitants before they could sound an alarm. Even though Dimitri had been a devout Orthodox Catholic, Andrei now had no remorse for killing a member of the clergy.

Andrei threw all but one of the bags attached to the horse under the wagon. He quickly filled the remaining bag with as much gold and jewel-encrusted treasure as it would hold. The Novgorodian refugees would need all the wealth they could muster to escape from the tyranny of Muscovy.

As he finished securing the bag to the horse, he noted a slight lightening of the eastern skyline. He must hurry. As he moved through the bodies of the slain serfs and clerics, he noticed a cudgel that had been crudely converted to a battle axe by lashing a pointed iron head to its shaft. He picked it up. He instantly appreciated its heft and balance. Covered in peasant blood, this simple weapon would soon be washed in the blood of the village's assailants.

Andrei moved quickly and stealthily through the orchard and slid into the shadows behind the stables. Through gaps in the stable walls, he ascertained that there were nine horses that bore the dog's head and the broom insignia of the Oprichniki. One horse was missing the dog's head, further proof that he was confronting his brother's murderers.

In a corral adjacent to the stable, there were more than a dozen horses from the manor. One Oprichnik was on guard at the corral gate near the stable entrance. Andrei had a good view of the stable and the kitchen-side entry to the manor house.

Secure in the belief that the manor and village had been completely subdued, the heavyset Oprichnik was not very vigilant. He sat dejectedly on the corral rails and swilled wine from a looted ornate decanter. As he was seated, he had no view of the corral behind him. In a drunken stupor, he mumbled to himself, disconsolate that he could not participate in the ongoing debauchery.

The ongoing laughter and screams from the manor masked Andrei's approach to the corral. Treading lightly and softly stroking the horses as he slid by, Andrei quickly crossed the corral. The Oprichnik saw no stars and felt no pain as the crude battle axe crushed the back of his skull.

Andrei propped the body up against a hay mound at the back of the stable. He placed the decanter in his hand. To a casual observer, the Oprichnik appeared to be asleep. Andrei selected a perch in the loft of the stable from which to observe the manor and plan his next move. The loft was barely above Andrei's head, and its height would present no obstacle to quickly abandoning the stable if the need arose. The growing illumination from the approaching moonrise was a disconcerting but unavoidable obstacle to his deadly activities.

Andrei focused most of his attention on the kitchen of the manor house. As was usually the case in rural Russia, the kitchen was external to the main building. It presented him with the opportunity to sneak closer to Dimitri's assailants.

Over the next half hour, Andrei observed three individual Oprichniki exit the kitchen door to relieve themselves. Two of them staggered past the chimney, but the third, apparently more drunk than the others, urinated out the door. A fourth reveler came out onto the raised veranda at the front of the manor. He was so intoxicated that he had to hold on to a stone column to keep from falling over the edge. Andrei surmised from the man's level of drunkenness that the observed behavior would continue well into the night.

As Andrei watched, the moon slowly crept above the eastern horizon. Reflecting off the snow cover, it provided ample illumination to observe the entire village. However, there was one factor that worked in Andrei's favor. As the moon was still low on the horizon, it created long shadows on the lee side of most of the structures. Andrei noted that the veranda was well-illuminated but that the kitchen chimney shaded an area large enough to conceal him.

Andrei was ready to chance a dash to the back of the chimney when the kitchen door was thrust open, and a half-naked young woman was flung into the snow. Landing face first, she tried to rise, but a burly Oprichnik emerged from the doorway and stepped on her back, pinning her to the frozen ground.

"Look, Sergei," he bellowed. "I have a present for you! Where the hell are you? You can't join the festivities, so I'm bringing the party to you."

The Oprichnik roughly pulled the woman to her feet. She could not have been more than seventeen or eighteen years old. Even in her distressed state, she was beautiful. Her flaxen hair that fell well below her shoulders shimmered in the moon-light. Andrei ignored her nakedness and focused on her coun-tenance, which was marked by beauty, strength, and defiance. Her chin was up, and her eyes glared at her captor with con-tempt and hatred.

"Wake up, Sergei. You're supposed to be on guard, not sleeping off all that wine I saw you take." He laughed and dragged the struggling woman toward the stable.

Andrei moved to the edge of the loft and lay on his stom-ach in order to keep a low profile. Once situated, he grasped his battle axe and fully extended his arm. In this way, when the weapon was deployed, the arc and sweep would compen-sate for the lack of muscle purchase due to his supine position.

The Oprichnik continued in his one-sided conversation. "This is a feisty one, Sergei. Unlike the others, she refuses to submit. More fun that way, I say. I had to sodomize her, so she is still fresh for you."

As he dragged the woman into the stable, Andrei could see deep scratch marks on the Oprichnik's face. She had indeed put up a good fight. Too bad the men were not so valiant.

The Oprichnik spotted his colleague's body. "Ah, there you are, you drunken sot! Well, at least you didn't break the decanter. Our bishop will want that one for sure."

A slight flicker in the moonbeam coming through a crack in the stable wall caused him to look up. It only provided a momentary cognition of his doom as the axe head caved in his nose and eye sockets, rendering him instantly unconscious. Andrei jumped down to deliver the coup de grace.

The girl stood transfixed in bewilderment. Andrei took her head in his hands and looked directly into her eyes.

"I am a friend. Do you understand?"

She slowly nodded her head.

"I intend to kill them all."

She nodded again. "Yes," she whispered, "kill them."

"I might not succeed, so you must hide." He wrapped her

in one of the horse blankets that were strewn about the stable and directed her into the loft. "You are a strong girl. Hide here until you collect yourself, and then hide in one of the ransacked houses. They may torch this stable in the morning, but they probably won't go back through the village. Don't go to Novgorod; it has been sacked, and the people largely exterminated."

After the girl was securely hidden in the loft, Andrei dragged the body to the back of the stable and covered it with hay. The Oprichnik's cloak and hat were large enough that they could be used as a disguise. On close examination, his swarthy Tartar countenance would quickly reveal the ruse, but his makeshift disguise could buy him a few seconds of surprise, and that may be all that he needed.

Counting the bishop, there had been eleven raiders. There were eight left. A daunting number for sure, but Andrei had stealth, surprise, and sobriety on his side. He fetched his bow from the other side of the corral. He could not rely on the work of his battle axe in close quarters for much longer. Once he had his bow in hand, he quickly crossed the yard between the stable and the manor's kitchen annex. He slipped into the shadows behind the chimney and waited.

He did not have to wait long. Within minutes, a drunken Oprichnik staggered past and was felled with a violent stroke of the battle axe. Andrei counted his blessings that the Oprichnik had not come out of the manor while he was crossing the yard. A half-hour later, another Oprichnik joined his slain comrade in the bloody shadow of the chimney.

Andrei knew that he was on borrowed time. Even in their advanced state of inebriation, the Oprichniki were bound to notice that four of their group were missing.

As if on cue, a fat Oprichnik lurched out of the door. "Grigor! Aleksei! Where the hell are you guys? Sergei, you're supposed to be on watch! Vitaly!" He paused and leaned forward, listening. "I saw you leaving with that yearling, Vitaly.

The best one by far. Time to share, comrade."

Andrei stepped partially out of the shadows with his back to the loud Oprichnik. He grunted softly and pretended to be urinating.

"Ah, Grigor. There you are."

When he was within ten paces, Andrei turned, drew, and sent an arrow on the way, all in one motion. The Oprichnik's eyes widened as the arrow pierced his throat. With his jugular and larynx severed, he could only gurgle in surprise. Oblivious to the man's death throes, Andrei dragged him into the shadows. The flowing blood formed a black stain in the moonlight.

There were now five Oprichniki raiders left in the manor. Andrei knew that in order to prevail against these odds, he would need to act quickly and take chances. Bold action or retreat were his only choices. He didn't feel like running away. Vengeance must be meted out, not only for Dimitri but for all the innocents slaughtered for plunder, politics, and pleasure.

To eliminate the remaining Oprichniki, Andrei would need cover and diversion. Unfortunately, cover was in short supply. Most of the buildings were too far from the manor house to allow him to use his bow to great effect. He settled on a lone spruce tree that was a little over twenty paces from the veranda. It would not totally conceal him, so he would need to create something to distract his adversaries.

Stealth was becoming increasingly difficult. As the moon rose toward its zenith, the shadows that provided concealment were ever shortening. As the temperature dipped to sixty degrees below freezing, every footfall, no matter how soft or carefully placed, resulted in a loud crunch that was amplified in the heavy air.

Moving quickly, Andrei left his bow and quiver behind the tree and sprinted to the kitchen entryway. He placed his ear near the wooden door, careful not to touch it to avoid frostbite. He heard nothing inside and quickly entered, his battle axe at the ready. The kitchen was well stocked and orderly, as one would expect in a prosperous manor. The large flat iron stove was warm to the touch. In normal times, some of the inhabitants would have slept on the stove for warmth. Perhaps the Oprichniki had surprised the inhabitants there.

Andrei was pleased to find a bed of hot coals banked within the stove. He found several seasoned sticks in the tinder box next to the stove. He inserted these into the coals. As he waited for them to ignite, he searched the kitchen for something flammable. He found a large crock of cooking oil on a shelf near the inside door of the manor. As he took the crock down, he could hear moans and laughter from inside the manor.

Andrei set his battle axe outside the kitchen door and proceeded to drench the inside and outside of the kitchen door with half the oil. He took a deep breath, and with his bow, the crock of oil, and the firebrands, he walked briskly to the stable. He was unobserved, as there were few windows in the manor due to the extreme cold and length of the winters. What few were there were shuttered against the cold.

Andrei looked for the young woman he had rescued. He called softly to her, but there was no answer. He regretted that he had not asked her name. He quickly searched the loft, but apparently, she had left the stable. Once he was convinced that she was safe, he opened the rear door of the stable and untied all of the horses. He then opened the corral gate as well.

Now it was time to create a glimpse of hell for the fiends remaining in the manor house. Andrei drenched the hay and straw in cooking oil and set them on fire. He followed the terrified horses out the stable entrance and sprinted to the kitchen door. He was alarmed to find that his firebrands went out as he was running. He blew desperately on the remaining embers at the end of the sticks and finally produced enough flame to ignite the oil on the door.

Grabbing his battle axe, Andrei sprinted to the spruce tree. A wild scene encircled the manor house. Horses fled every which way, and the twin infernos from the stable and kitchen brightly illuminated the surroundings. He nocked an arrow and waited, and waited . . . The drunken debauchery continued unabated for several minutes. Andrei became concerned that the fires would burn out before any Oprichniki noticed the manor was on fire.

Finally, an Oprichnik staggered out onto the veranda to relieve himself. Andrei did not fire. The man froze as if paralyzed and then let out a bellow. "Fire! Fire everywhere!"

The remaining Oprichniki lurched onto the veranda. One was armed with a harquebus; others carried only flagons of drink. Shocked, drunk, and bewildered, they huddled together in a tight group. Blinded by the raging fires, they peered vainly into the darkness.

"Sergei?" one called plaintively into the night.

Swiftly, three arrows were on the way. Three Oprichniki were suddenly writhing in pain on the stone floor of the veranda. Two were struck in the chest, and the third in the stomach. All doomed, two quickly and one slowly and painfully. Andrei was not concerned with the murderer's agony. He turned his attention to the two remaining Oprichniki. The one with the harquebus frantically fired a shot in Andrei's general direction. The only result of his effort was his own temporary blindness from the weapon's flaming discharge and the thick black smoke from exploding black powder. He never saw the flight of the arrow that pierced his breast and found his heart.

Avoiding the light from the doorway, the remaining Oprichnik ran to the far side of the veranda and leaped into the darkness. Grabbing his bow and battle axe, Andrei left the cover of the spruce and cautiously ascended the steps onto the veranda. He expected that the unarmed remaining Oprichnik was fleeing to the safety of the distant forest. He was surprised to hear loud moans from the far side of the veranda.

Fearing a ruse, Andrei went back down the steps and circled the manor house to approach from the dark side. He did not want to be illuminated by the fire or the light from the open entrance. The fire at the kitchen door had largely burned out by the time he passed it. Again, his timing had been fortuitous. If the fire had gone out sooner, he could have been attacked from two angles, an untenable situation at best.

As he approached from the dark side of the house, he noted that the moans, although still present, had become shallow and muted. The Oprichnik, spotting his approach, tried to crawl away but gave a loud shriek as soon as he moved. Andrei surmised that he had broken both legs in the fall. His feeble moaning indicated he was in shock. The extreme cold would end the Oprichnik's misery soon enough. Andrei had done enough killing; the drive for vengeance slowly dissipated as he circled the man and ascended the veranda.

All the Oprichniki on the veranda were dead, even the one with the stomach wound. The combination of shock and cold was a quick killer. The blood of the slain was a frozen gore that shone black in the moonlight. Andrei took a deep breath, nocked an arrow, and entered the manor. Inside, it was no longer a princely manor; it was a charnel house.

Two men, one older and one younger, hung lifeless from the railing. Each was strung by a rope around their neck that was tied off at the railing. A bench lay on its side near each corpse. The Oprichniki had obviously wanted their victims to observe the violation of the women of the household. The men had helplessly clung to life, supported on tiptoe by the small benches. Eventually, their strength had waned, and gravity had had its grisly way.

Andrei judged the older man to be the boyar and patriarch of the household. His hair was gray, he was well-fed, and he had a round face that had probably been jovial in life. Before he was hung, his ribs had been broken, and he was castrated. The final degradation was the shearing of his beard. The boyars were entrusted with maintaining tradition. Religious order required that all males wear beards, and the shearing of the beard was apostasy and humiliating.

The younger man, probably the boyar's son, was similarly humiliated but did not have enough of a beard to be shorn. He looked to be in his early teens, barely old enough to hold a sword, let alone fend off a band of murderers.

Andrei turned his attention to the women in the room. There were five in all. The oldest woman, presumably the boyar's wife, lay in a pool of blood. Her throat had been slit, but she appeared otherwise unmolested. The four younger women were not as fortunate, if fortune had any meaning in such savagery. All had been stripped naked. All had multiple bruises on their throats, breasts, buttocks, and thighs. The purple, swollen faces of two of the women indicated that they had been strangled. Blood flowed from every orifice of each body. Although he was steeped in war, Andrei had to look away.

A weak and shallow sigh brought his attention back to the situation at hand. The youngest victim, a girl who appeared to be a pre-teen, did not have the pallor of death. He set down his weapons and kneeled to listen for a heartbeat or detect a wisp of breath on his cheek. It was a mistake.

"Stand up with your arms spread and turn around!"

With his peripheral vision, Andrei glanced at his weapons.

"Don't even think about it. Even with this ridiculous weapon, I can blow a hole in you at this distance."

So, he has a harquebus, Andrei concluded. There may be a modicum of hope. It took the better part of a second for a harquebus to discharge. Time to dive for his battle axe.

He slowly turned to face his adversary.

The Oprichnik stood in the doorway ten paces away. He was tall and angular, with a full black beard streaked with gray. A hawk nose and high forehead framed cold black eyes that glared intensely at Andrei.

"How many are you?" His harquebus twitched menacingly.

"Just me." Andrei had surmised that whatever he said

would not be believed, so he may as well tell the truth.

"You butchered many of the Tsar's men here tonight. You and your comrades wherever they are."

"Your Oprichniki were worse than animals. I merely killed them. They deserved worse."

"The Tsar reigns under divine authority. Whatever occurs is God's will."

"I think this madness belongs to men alone. The Metropolitan blesses it for his own evil ambition."

"What does a half-breed Tartar know about Orthodoxy?" The Oprichnik laughed. "No matter, the Tsar would love to fry you up in his big pan. I doubt your arrogance would last long in the skillet."

Andrei said nothing. His eyes focused on the harquebus.

"My men will be here shortly to take charge of this estate for the Oprichnina. I rode ahead to make sure there was something left to annex. I don't share in the appetites of my comrades. I would, however, like to hold you for their entertainment, but you are too clever."

Andrei tensed; it was now or never.

As he sprang for his battle axe, the harquebus dipped and, with a roar, discharged harmlessly into the floor. The Oprichnik took one lurching step forward and fell face-first through the black powder smoke.

Collecting himself, Andre stared in amazement as the young woman from the stable stepped through the smoke, holding a blood-drenched dagger.

"Thank you," he said softly.

"The least I could do," she replied.

"You have saved me and avenged my family," she continued. "Or as much vengeance as one can provide in the face of such wanton depravity."

"Was all your family here?"

"Yes, that is my father and older brother there." She gestured toward the stairway. "My mother," she said as she motioned toward the older woman. "And my sister." Her voice broke, and she sobbed quietly as she gently stroked the hair of the young girl who now had the alabaster sheen of death. Collecting herself, she stood, her legs trembling. "The others are valued servants, as close as family."

Adrenaline gone, Andre sagged physically and emotionally as the full weight of the tragedy descended on him.

"Do you wish to spend some time alone with your family?"

"No. I cannot find grief. Only emptiness. And hatred."

"Do you have any remaining family?"

"Only an uncle, aunt, and several cousins in Novgorod. They probably met a similar fate."

"No husband?" Many young women were married as young as thirteen.

She shook her head sadly, a hard glint in her eyes. "No. I was betrothed."

"It is well that he was not here then."

"Oh, he was here," she said bitterly.

Andrei followed as she strode through the entryway. At the edge of the veranda, she stood over the Oprichnik with the broken legs and spit on him. "My fiancé!"

"Samara," the broken Oprichnik called plaintively.

"Rot in hell with the rest of your Oprichniki comrades, Vadim! You are a treacherous bastard and deserve a worse death than you are getting!"

She turned and strode back into the manor.

Andrei followed. "Well, now I know your name, Samara; mine is Andrei."

She nodded and tried to smile, but couldn't.

"We best leave, Samara. The rest of the band following the Oprichnik you killed are on the way. I don't know how many or how far away they are, but I think we have an hour at most, maybe just minutes."

"Let me change, Andrei. I don't mind the peasant garb, but I do mind the biting little things that are in them. I'll be quick." She headed for the stairs but turned around at the top. "Prepare to set fire to this place. I don't want the Oprichniki to have the manor or the bodies. We can't take my family. The fire will have to consecrate their deaths."

While Samara changed clothes, Andrei moved all the bodies together, side by side, and covered them with carpets. He then drenched the wood paneling, tapestries, and the carpets, covering the bodies with lamp oil. The manor house was stone, but the fire would consume all inside.

As he finished, Samara came down the stairs. She was dressed in wool and fur outerwear, well suited for a winter ride on horseback. She saw that the bodies were not visible and nodded to him in appreciation. She waved two small sacks at Andrei. "They didn't find all of our gold and jewels!"

Despite the circumstances, Andrei could not help but notice that she was beautiful, the loveliest woman he had ever seen. He stood transfixed for a moment, then sprang into action. He handed her a lit candle, noting that it was beeswax, a sign of wealth.

"Start with the tapestries. I'll put more lamp oil on the stairs so that the fire will find its way to the second floor."

By the time he was finished, the fire was already halfway across the floor. He picked up his weapons and headed for the door. He knew they would be illuminated by the fire and wanted to get to the shadows as soon as possible. Samara followed, pausing only long enough to pick up a crossbow and bolts that had belonged to a dead Oprichnik.

"Don't look back," Andrei counseled as they descended the veranda steps.

Andrei gave the large spruce a loving pat, cut off one of its boughs, and tucked the bough in his cloak. They made their way through the orchard to the church. Andrei untied the bishop's horse.

"We'll have to ride double until we get to my horse on the far side of that hill."

"That won't be necessary." Samara put her fingers to her mouth and gave a shrill whistle. A tall, dark charcoal stallion emerged out of the darkness to nuzzle her insistently. It was all saddled and ready to travel. A smaller bay mare stood several paces away in the darkness. Samara brought her forward and tied her to the stallion. The mare was burdened with several large sacks.

"I left the stable, but I didn't leave alone. I was prepared to flee, but I didn't. I had to see it through with you."

Andrei smiled. "You may be a princess, Samara, but you are a warrior princess."

"Well, I may be a warrior princess, but I have had enough of the Oprichniki for a lifetime. I don't want to run into them on the road. I know a back way to get to your horse. By the way," she continued, "I would like you a lot better if you got rid of your regalia."

Andrei had totally forgotten his Oprichniki disguise. He quickly shed the hated cloak.

Andrei looked wistfully at the treasure wagon. "These will never make it back to the church, or any church for that matter. However, it seems much reduced from when I last saw it."

"I told you I was busy while you were slaying Oprichniki. The mare has quite the treasure on her back. Enough to help your fleeing Novgorodians and perhaps a bit of a dowry for me. There are also some items of liturgical value, if we can ever find an honest member of the clergy."

"Let's be off then, Samara. You lead."

"Lead where?"

"First to my horse, then to Yaroslavl."

"I'll lead you to your horse, Andrei, and to the road to Yaroslavl. Then we will see," she said equivocally. "If we make it that far."

CHAPTER 10

The Forlorn Forest

Samara led them north, parallel to the long hill on which Andrei had tied his horse. The extreme cold precluded a swift flight. Lathering the horses under these conditions could prove fatal to beast and rider. After several versts, the long hill grew in elevation and curved west toward their route of travel. It terminated in a sharp ridge just east of the roadway.

As they swung east toward the ridge, they observed the light of at least a dozen torches descending the hill toward the manor.

"Well, we are outnumbered," Andrei remarked wryly.

"But we have a head start, and their horses are tired," she replied. "Perhaps they won't follow us."

"They will," he countered. "They will assume we took some of the plunder and try to recapture it. This road is lightly traveled. Our tracks will stand out."

He dismounted and took out the spruce bough. "Take the horses up the hill at least one hundred paces, and I will join you. First I have to buy us some time."

As Samara continued up the hill, Andrei swept their tracks away with the bough. He hoped that hoarfrost would form quickly, further obscuring their progress, but the air seemed to be warming. He looked up and saw that low clouds were moving in. A mixed blessing at best. The moon would soon be obscured, aiding their surreptitious flight. If it snowed, it would be easy to follow them unless there was wind or an accumulation quick enough to fill their tracks before discovery. In any event, he had no control over the weather and set to sweeping their trail, something he could do to increase the odds of escape.

Samara rode up the ridge and stopped on a narrow bench of ground that would allow the horses to rest on level ground. There were several wind-stunted spruce trees that would shield her presence from the eyes of any searching Oprichniki.

This was the first time since the arrival of the Oprichniki that she was free from action that required her full attention. The horrors of the night quickly flowed into the vacant spaces. She buried her head in her horse's mane and let the anger, pain, and loss flow out of her. Great sobs wracked her body as her great grief took its course. As Andrei approached, she pulled herself together. She realized that she could easily fall into a great despair that would define the rest of her life. She resolved not to let that happen. Defiance slowly replaced her grief. Her revenge would be her survival. She was Samara Anastasia Kucherov. She would amount to something, for herself and her family.

Andrei finally arrived and mounted the bishop's horse. He either didn't notice, or ignored, her distraught state.

"Lead on," was all he said.

The trail they followed was well suited for stealthy passage. It was a hidden game trail that Samara and her brother had found and utilized many times. As an animal trail, it took the easiest physical route from cover to cover. Samara's horse knew the way without being led. Depending on elevation and drainage, they passed through groves of spruce, pine, or birch. Particularly damp areas had stands of willows. They might be tracked, but they would not be sighted.

When they reached the top of the ridge, the hill turned back south toward where Andrei had left his horse. The game trail continued on into the forest, but they were forced to abandon the trail to reach his horse. Unfortunately, much of this area had been cleared to provide grazing for horses and cattle. The elevation provided relief from summer's heat and insects. It provided little concealment for their furtive journey. The moon was periodically obscured by clouds, which aided their concealment. They were careful not to skyline themselves during one of the periodic breaks in the clouds.

They stuck to the military crest on the eastern side of the hill. Every so often, one or the other would poke their head over the crest of the hill to look for Oprichniki. At last, they reached the shack where Andrei had first observed the manor house and village. Samara did not wish to look upon the manor in its ravaged state. She remained outside as Andrei entered to observe from inside the structure.

When he exited, his face revealed his concern.

"Well, they are on to us. At least a dozen torches are moving up the road that we used to escape the manor. There are probably several other riders with no torches. It is a formidable force."

"Not good news," she responded glumly, fatigue beginning to show in her demeanor.

"Not all bad. All of the torches are on the roadway and none to either side. If any of the Oprichniki had military experience, they would have put flankers on either side of the road to look for our tracks and prevent any type of surprise attack. There is a good chance they will ride by our trail and have to come back once they discover their error. With any luck, most are drunk."

"They can't all be drunk all the time," she responded wearily.

"Yes, but there are also no torches coming on this road, so we have a good head start. I just don't know how long we can stay on this road. With the sacking of Novgorod, the countryside seems to be crawling with Oprichniki."

"I know a way around this road," she replied thoughtfully, seeming to gather new energy for the challenge ahead. "There is a peasant hut a short way down this road. It marks the end of our estate. Behind the hut, there is a major trail through the woods cut by deer and other animals. The serfs in that house are good people. They won't report us."

"Unfortunately, Samara, they were the first of your estate to be slaughtered. The Oprichniki spared no innocents. Even the animals were killed."

She said nothing, just sagged in her saddle. Her renewed energy was dissipating with the continuing bad news.

Andrei's horse was where he left it. It was clearly happy to see him but was too well-trained to nicker. As he approached, the horse put his nose in Andrei's face, sharing air as happy horses are wont to do. As Andrei patted him, the horse draped its head and neck over his shoulder.

Ah, a horse hugger, Samara thought. *I could really use a hug myself right now.*

Her father had been a hugger, a great, lovable man who delighted in all of his children. A vision of her father struggling to stay on the little bench, his face bulging purple, intruded on her thoughts. She pushed it back, concentrating instead on her companion. *No hugger here. He would probably rather step in front of an arrow or harquebus for me than give me a hug.* At the moment, she envied the horse.

"Happy horse," Samara observed.

"Yes, we are comrades of many years."

"What's his name?"

"He doesn't have a name."

As someone who loved horses, she was surprised. "No name?"

"He's a horse; he knows who he is without me telling him. What about your horse?"

"Smokey," she said, patting him on his neck.

"I can see that."

"I named him when I was thirteen and he was a colt. He was lighter in color when he was young. Will he have a problem with my stallion?"

"No, my horse is used to being with many horses. There won't be a problem unless your mare comes into season. Then there would be a problem. He is a horse, not a philosopher. We should be off," he said, mounting his horse and taking the reins to the bishop's horse for the short trip to the serf dwelling ahead.

They went in silence. Images of horror and pain pushed into their consciousnesses as they grew too fatigued to push back. Snow began to fall, the flakes sharp against their faces as they rode. Andrei knew it would be a hard and stinging journey if they had to ride into a stiff wind.

The southeastern sky was lightening as they approached the partially burned serf hut. The coming dawn was dulled by the thick cloud cover. It would have been a dismal scene in the best of times; now, in the worst of times, it was oppressive.

Samara remembered the happy serf family who lived there. She stopped to visit them many times in her exuberant teenage riding expeditions. "Where is the family?"

"Hanging from a tree on the other side of the bridge."

"We should attend to them."

"No, the ravens and jays have attended to them already. You have seen enough horror for one night. We will notify the Church in due course. They will put what remains in consecrated ground." He turned off the road toward the hut. "Besides, we have precious little time."

Her spirits sagging, she did not argue.

They found some rough fodder near the animal pen and allowed the horses to feed. Samara's horses had been fed at the manor stable and were too skittish of the slain livestock to eat. Andrei's horse, having not eaten in many hours, was more enthusiastic.

Samara dismounted. "I should check inside for some food that may have survived the fire."

"I got a small sack of food while you were upstairs changing," Andrei responded. "It is not much, and we could use more. Also, we have no pot or utensils other than my knife."

Samara knew that even in good times, the serfs would have only humble fare. However, she was able to locate a small sack of buckwheat and another with turnips. Neither had sustained fire damage. She also found a large cooking pot and two wooden spoons. The spoons were singed but still usable.

She was on her way out the door when, on a hunch, she went back in and looked inside the oven. There, in all its glory, was a perfectly baked golden-brown loaf of bread. She fell to her knees and burst into uncontrollable sobbing at this homely display of domestic order.

Suddenly, she was lifted to her feet by and enveloped in strong and sympathetic arms.

So, I am a horse, she thought. *Nothing is more important to Tatars than their horse.* She nuzzled in for a moment.

Then it was over.

"The bread is a good omen," was all he said.

They remounted and, with Samara in the lead, headed into the forest beyond the hut. She turned in the saddle. "I will go in the wrong direction at first, in case they find our trail before the snow fills it in."

Andrei nodded in approval. *How much like a fox she is: strong, beautiful, and cunning.*

His thoughts were interrupted by a new sound, just a sigh in the distant pines at first. The sigh strengthened into a moan in the nearby spruce, and then the trees bent under the onslaught of the onrushing wind.

The snowfall increased with the wind. The snow was hard and sharp as it was driven into the side of their faces. They headed northeast at first. After several versts, Samara turned southeast. The wind was now directly in their faces. The wind found gaps in their clothing, chilling them to the bone. The snow was a frozen rasp gnawing at their exposed skin.

Andrei knew they could not survive the blizzard conditions for very long. He rode up beside Samara. She was covered in crusted snow, as was Smokey. "We must find shelter soon or take a chance and stop to make a lean-to out of pine and spruce bows."

She brushed the snow off her clothes and pointed to the left. "There is an abandoned cabin in a clearing off to the side. It is not on our route, but not very far off our trail. A little over a verst if I remember correctly."

"That sounds good, Samara. Lead on."

After a short distance, she stopped and turned in the saddle, yelling, "It looks so different in the winter. I could swear it is right here."

He could tell she was apprehensive and rode up beside her.

"I'm confident you are right. Let's split up so we can see more. Move to the right, and I will move to the left. We must be sure to keep each other in sight so we don't lose contact."

They slowly moved forward, gray shadows in the forest gloom and driven snow. At length, he heard a familiar shrill whistle and headed toward Samara. He found her in a very small clearing, relief radiating from her face. The dilapidated cabin was covered in snow and nearly invisible.

"Good eyes, Samara. I probably would have missed it."

She now had an air of confidence around her that Andrei had not seen since she killed the Oprichnik and saved him at the manor. The storm, for all its ferocity, was acting as a buffer between the horrors of the previous night and a new life that must be embraced and mastered.

They tied the horses on the lee side of the cabin. The entryway to the cabin was drifted in with snow, so they had to dig out the doorway. Inside, the cabin was gloomy but dry and largely intact. The only light came from openings in the cabin walls where the log chinking had weathered off. There was snow in small amounts here and there on the floor where small openings in the walls and roof thatch were open to the elements.

The cabin had no stove or oven, but there was a stone

hearth. There was fresh snow and an old bird's nest in the hearth. The storm had done them a favor by clearing the chimney so that there would be sufficient draw to maintain a fire. There was cut wood near the hearth, but it was too large to start a fire.

As Andrei cleared the hearth of snow and debris, Samara fetched dead limbs and twigs from under the nearby pines. The broad boughs of the trees protected the lower branches from snow, and she soon had an armload of kindling. Once they had an ample supply of wood of all sizes, Andrei removed a small char cloth and fine tow from his sack. With deft handling of flint and steel, he soon had enough flame to light a small ball of tinder. Within minutes, he had a blazing fire in the hearth.

As soon as possible, Andrei substituted aspen and birch hardwood for the initial pine and spruce kindling. The hardwood produced much less smoke, particularly the pieces from the cabin, which were dry and well-seasoned. Even so, he hoped there were no Oprichniki close enough to observe the light smoke.

As soon as he was warm, Andrei announced that he would cover their back trail to be sure they were not being followed. He would leave his horse with Samara, as stealth was of primary importance, and a man on a horse was easy to spot.

"If I am not back by dark, take the horses and head for Yaroslavl as soon as the wind lets up," he instructed.

Samara did not want to be left by herself, let alone run off into the stormy night alone. She had come to rely on his steady presence. He didn't look like a guardian angel, but he certainly felt like one.

"Won't the wind and snow scour and cover our tracks?"

"Most of them, but the trees will block some of the effects of the weather, and a determined tracker will be able to discover our trail."

"Wait," she said, slipping out the door.

She returned shortly with a white cloak and fur hat of ermine.

"Take these. I grabbed them on impulse at the manor. They were my father's winter hunting clothing. He was heavier than you, so they should easily fit over your outerwear."

"Thank you," he said, somewhat awkwardly. Her presence was disconcerting. He had a fleeting impulse to pull her to him — hold her. He pushed it aside and slipped on the cloak and hat. "These will help me blend in with the snow and birches. It may be very important."

Samara reached out and touched his sleeve. He caught the concern in her eyes, and with that, he was out the door. He quickly disappeared into a passing flurry.

CHAPTER 11

Birches and Blood

The wind was brisk and biting. It froze the hairs in Andrei's nostrils and caused his eyes to water. He was nonetheless thankful for its presence. It gnawed away at their trail and quickly dissipated the icy cloud created by his breath. Absent the wind, even in the flat light of late afternoon, his breath would be a dead giveaway of his presence in the forest.

He stayed well off their trail, operating more by memory and feel than any observation of tracks or broken branches. He took advantage of every edge of elevation that the terrain afforded. Staying off the ridge tops, he went slowly from grove to grove and tree to tree. He never took more than two steps at a time before stopping to survey the surrounding forest.

A small black swath moving in the branches gave the Oprichnik away. In a land dominated by winter, black was a stupid choice of color. It would be this one's demise. The rider came out of a stand of fir trees on a small knoll. There was a large spruce within a few feet of Andrei. When the rider rode through another small stand of trees, Andrei slowly moved behind it.

Andrei let the rider come closer. The closer the range, the surer the shot. He wasn't worried that the rider would see him, as his attention was riveted to Andrei's and Samara's trail. Andrei was mostly worried about a possible second Oprichnik. Safety would dictate that one rider would follow the trail, and one or more others would watch the flanks.

A side-on shot presented a small target area. A frontal or rear shot was more certain. Andrei let the rider pass, then sent an arrow on its way. His shot was true, striking the man in his torso and piercing his lungs. The man fell to the ground and lay moaning on the trail, a widening pool of blood staining the pristine snow. Andrei considered putting the man out of his misery, but thought better of it. Something wasn't right — he could feel it.

Some slight movement in the periphery of his left eye alarmed him. He turned slowly to get a better view. As he did so, he realized that he should have stepped behind the tree. The thought had not cleared his mind when a loud twang was followed by an impact in his left shoulder that spun him half-way around. The shock and pain would have taken a lesser man to his knees, but Andrei stayed upright — focused. He stepped behind the tree for cover.

Through the branches of the tree, Andrei saw a large Oprichniki struggling to reload his crossbow. He was obviously panicky as he dropped the crossbow bolt several times in an attempt to quickly reload his weapon. Wincing in pain, Andrei grasped his bow and, with great difficulty, managed to straighten his left arm. With his right arm, he pulled to full draw, stepped out from behind the tree, and let fly. The shot took the Oprichnik in the stomach. He took two steps toward Andrei and collapsed into a writhing heap.

Andrei dared not approach the dying man. He did not have enough strength left to draw his bow, and if he got close enough to use his knife or battle axe, he would risk a close-in attack from the dying Oprichnik. Besides, he was already feeling light-headed. He glanced at his left shoulder. Blood was already seeping through the ermine cloak; it was becoming a frozen mass of gore.

To Andrei's good fortune, the first Oprichnik's horse had not strayed from the body. It was skittish but allowed him to mount. Light was fast fading, and he hoped he could reach the cabin before Samara left. He would need her help. He would need her grit.

◊

Samara anxiously paced back and forth across the dirt floor of the hut. She frequently put her ear to the crack in the door, hoping to hear Andrei's footfalls in the snow. It was close to nightfall, and she knew she should go. She was packed and ready, but she remained. She had become very attached to this Tartar with the stony countenance and piercing eyes. Despite her family tragedy, it brought joy to her heart to see his eyes soften and his bearing relax whenever she came near. His demeanor, while not what anyone would call nurturing, had become protective in a guarded but gentle way. He was not given to touching her, but she wished he would. She needed his strength and craved his embrace.

Samara kept herself busy by melting snow for drinking and cooking water for when Andrei returned. But at length, the daylight through the door cracks completely disappeared. It was night, and she must go. With a sinking feeling, she set her belongings near the door. She first had to prepare the horses for travel. But she thought of Andrei, alone and cold in the darkness. She added some sizeable logs to the fire. If Andrei returned after she left, at least he would be warm.

As she prepared to unbar the door, she heard a muffled thump on the other side. Her heart raced with hope and alarm. She put her ear to the door and listened. Nothing. She drew her dagger. She would not go down without a fight. Again, she pressed her ear against the crack in the door.

"Samara, I have returned."

Andrei's voice was very weak, and her joy was suddenly replaced with apprehension. She unbarred the door, and he stumbled in, almost falling over the doorstep. The ermine cloak she had given him was covered in frozen gore. He had obviously been bleeding for quite some time.

Samara felt faint. Useless. She knew she had to act, so she gritted her teeth and got on with it, half carrying him to one of the crude stools near the fireplace.

"I don't know what to do," she said plaintively.

"I do, but you must help me, or I will die," he said, his voice barely above a whisper.

"First bar the door. Then put the iron poker into the fire and let it heat up until it glows red."

She did as bidden and then returned to remove his garments to reveal the shoulder wound that was still steadily seeping blood. The crossbow bolt had passed through his shoulder and exited without doing damage to vital organs or bone, but the bleeding persisted.

"We must cauterize the wound, or I will bleed to death, or it will fester and I will die of fever. I can do the wound in front, where the bolt entered, but you must do the back."

"I have heard of this, but I have never seen it done. I don't know how. I can't!"

"You must. There is no one else. You are strong, Samara. Watch me, it is simple."

She took a deep breath. Steadied herself. "I will try, Andrei. What if I fail?"

"You won't," he said firmly.

He reached down and picked up a piece of wood from the stack of kindling near the stool. He placed it into his mouth and bit down on it. He pointed to the poker, the end of which was glowing menacingly in the red-hot coals.

She handed him the poker. He paused a second. She could see his jaw tighten as he bit down hard on the wood. He quickly plunged the glowing end of the poker into the wound. His flesh sizzled and steamed as he rotated it to completely sear the wound. Dropping the poker, he groaned loudly and fainted.

Samara kicked the poker away from his legs so that he

wouldn't be further burned. The smell of burnt flesh was nauseating, and she felt her knees buckle. She fought the urge to collapse. Now she knew what to do. He needed her. She needed him. She put the poker back into the coals.

As the poker reheated, Samara placed one of her robes on the bed so that the straw would not stick to his wound. It took all of her strength, but she managed to drag Andrei to the bed and roll him onto his stomach. By this time, the poker's end was glowing red once more. She returned to him, straddled his body, took a deep breath, and thrust the poker into the exit wound. His body writhed in pain, but her weight kept him down. Ignoring his groans and the stench of seared flesh, she thoroughly cauterized the wound. Finished, she cast the poker into the fire and collapsed into a sobbing heap next to him.

◊

The fire had burned down, suffusing the room in a soft glow from the dying embers. She realized that she must have slept, but she had no idea for how long. The bed, though sturdy, was shaking. She turned to look at Andrei. To her alarm, he was shaking violently, his teeth chattering, and his eyes were open and wild. She quickly fetched fur robes from her belongings and covered him with them. He continued to shiver uncontrollably. The loss of blood, shock, pain, and fatigue were taking a toll.

As the shaking continued, Samara knew what she must do. The forces at hand were stark and elemental. There was no room for pretense or modesty. She removed all of her clothing, wiggled under the robes, and pulled him to her. Gradually the shakes and tremors subsided.

As morning approached, he woke to the presence of the lithe young woman beside him. He touched her shoulder, and in the darkness, her hand found his. She pulled him toward her. His fatigue and pain were replaced by desire. He wanted what all men needed — craved. He surrendered to it, embraced the soft and supple splendor. It was awkward. It was rushed. It was magical and perfect.

◊

Andrei woke to the smell of woodsmoke and the scent of steaming food, something familiar.

"Porridge?" he asked softly. Porridge was a favorite food in medieval Russia.

"Yes, I grabbed it on impulse when we left."

"I did not expect porridge here," he said, delighted with the surprise.

"It is my wedding porridge. Very special. It seemed some-how . . . appropriate," she stammered, blushing profusely.

"I agree," he said, smiling.

She was his woman now, and he was her man. They did not need a priest or Iman to sanctify the union. It had been sanctified in struggle and blood.

As they ate, she sat on the stool facing him. He sat on the bed, surrounded by the dark stains of his ordeal. They spoke little. The age difference had been bridged, and the cultural barrier between them had been breached, but they were cautious, unsure of themselves. At length, she reached over and touched him gently on his knee. Their eyes met, and he smiled broadly. Everything would be fine. It would just take time.

Perhaps the long journey ahead won't be so hard after all, he thought.

◊

It was mid-morning before they were ready to leave. Several helpings of porridge had restored his spirit, if not his vigor. Andrei was anxious to leave. The sooner they reached Yaroslavl and the collective protection of his comrades, the better. He unbarred the door and opened it just a crack so that he could observe their surroundings while still remaining largely protected behind its wooden mass.

All looked tranquil and safe, but he remained cautious. At this northern latitude, the sun still remained low on the horizon, casting giant shadows from the surrounding trees. A dozen enemies could hide in those shadows without being spotted. Visibility was poor, and due to his injury, he had not had the strength to cover his own trail. He could plainly see his bloody course in the bright morning sun.

Andrei and Samara could not huddle in the illusory safety of the small cabin any longer. They had to leave. There was no telling how many Oprichniki were on their trail. If discovered, they could be burned up in the cabin with little or no chance of escape, let alone survival.

Before Andrei opened the door, Samara handed him the large cooking pot that she had filled with most of their remaining food.

"We will need this for the trail. We have an extra horse now, so it shouldn't be a problem, should it?"

He shook his head in agreement and opened the door.

Andrei was temporarily blinded as he left the dark interior of the cabin and entered the brilliant sunlight that reflected off the pristine snow. He looked away from the piercing light. As he did, he noticed that his horse was agitated and looking to his right. Sensing danger, he spun in that direction. Too late. He heard the awful and now familiar twang of the crossbow and the hiss of the bolt as it sped toward him. He moved just a little, but it was enough. This time, there was no impact or pain, only a dull clank. The bolt had deflected off the cooking pot.

Not more than ten paces away, an Oprichnik stepped out from behind a large spruce. "Die, you Tatar bastard!"

His assailant had reloaded his crossbow and was raising it to fire when Andrei's battle axe hit him square in the chest, staggering him and knocking the crossbow to the ground. He reached for it, but he was slow. The long, cold night had taken a toll on his reflexes. He had one hand on the crossbow when Andrei slit his throat with one swift swipe of his knife.

"Someday, Oprichnik. Someday. But not now."

Andrei quickly scanned the forest but could detect no other threat. Still, he feared that more Oprichniki were close by. They would be investigating what happened to their comrades. He and Samara had to leave and quickly. He rushed into the cabin to help her collect their things.

Upon entering the cabin, he was distressed to find her trembling on a stool, holding her left leg. Blood ran between her fingers.

"It is nothing. Just my leg. It went straight through."

He gasped. Staggered. Righted himself. He realized, to his horror, that the crossbow bolt intended for him had deflected off the cooking pot and struck Samara. It had severed the large artery in her leg. There was no hope. None. He wanted to scream but controlled himself. He gathered her into his arms and laid her gently onto the bed, cradling her head in his lap. The color was already draining from her face.

She looked up at him. "I'm dying, aren't I?"

"Yes," he gasped, "it should have been me."

"Then I, too, would have died, Andrei. Either way."

He swayed slowly back and forth, not knowing what to do.

"You saved me, Andre." Her voice was now not much more than a whisper.

"Not enough, Samara. Not enough."

"Yes, Andrei. In the last two days, I have gained my freedom, found my strength, and discovered my one true love. Enough for any lifetime."

She closed her eyes for a moment and gathered herself — "Now it is time to join my family." She reached up and touched him on the cheek. "Remember me, Andrei."

"I will never forget you, Samara."

She smiled. Her hand slipped away.

◊

Time passed unnoticed. Still, he sat in the darkness with Samara's head in his lap. From time to time, he gently stroked her hair. He did not weep. Tatars are not given to tears. Yet a deep ache tore at his heart. There was a growing darkness in his soul where he kept his guilt for surviving while those he loved died. He did not latch the door. He hoped the Oprichniki would come. He had always buried his sorrows in a lust for vengeance. But not this time. He realized that he could kill a hundred of them and it would not alleviate the pain that tore at every fiber of his being.

PART TWO

VOLGA RIVER
PASSAGE

CHAPTER 12

Father Ivanov

The five figures huddled together in the nave of the cathedral did not look out of the ordinary. From a distance, it appeared that the Russian Orthodox monk was attempting to convert four heathen Tatars who hung with rapt attention on his every word. Yaroslavl, founded in 1024 and the oldest city on the Volga, had been a religious center of Orthodoxy since the eleventh and twelfth centuries. The city had been sacked by the Tatars in 1238. Since that date, a significant number of Tatars had been converted to Christianity on this very spot. However, despite history and appearances, there was far more plotting than proselytizing involved in this particular conversation.

Father Timoshka Ivanov was an imposing figure whose very presence commanded respect. His height of slightly over six feet was tall for Russians of the era. His heavily muscled frame was more befitting a carpenter or laborer than a monk. His blue eyes blazed with an intensity that bordered on incandescence.

Petr's father had told him numerous stories about Ivanov's courage in missionary work in the lower reaches of the Ob River — stories which Petr had been disinclined to believe. Now, awed by the size and intensity of the monk, Petr found himself wishing that he could use the man as a model for Christ in one of his icons. Crossing himself, he quickly dismissed this blasphemy from his mind and focused on their present predicament.

"We appreciate your hospitality and protection, Father, but it grows increasingly apparent that we cannot remain here much longer. It is just a matter of time before we are recognized by one of the Oprichniki."

The monk considered Petr's statement a moment before replying. He realized that the trickle of refugees from Novgorod would soon become a flood. Yaroslavl was only a little over two hundred versts northeast of Moscow, and the Tsar's local henchmen, augmented by Oprichniki from Moscow, would soon be among them, seeking to identify any boyar or other prominent citizen fortunate enough to escape the initial slaughter in Novgorod.

"You are essentially correct, Petr. I believe you would be safe enough here for a few months, but it would be time better served by putting distance between your party and the Muscovites."

Yaroslavl was on the main cart road connecting Moscow to Arkhangelsk. While it might be possible to conceal Petr's party for the next several months of winter, with the increased trade and traffic of summer, their discovery would be inevitable.

Father Timoshka said, "As I see it, you have two choices — neither easy. You can try to reach Poland by going south and circling around Moscow to the west. You would risk the Oprichniki in every community you encounter — or you could head east beyond the Urals into Siberia. I believe the latter is your best option."

Matrona gasped. "Siberia! How can that forsaken place be the best choice?"

Petr and Anna vigorously nodded their heads in agreement. "Siberia," Tatar for "the sleeping land," was a word that sent a chill through even the most stoic of Russians who were accustomed to the harsh Russian winters. This was a forbidding territory of endless mosquito-infested swamps in summer and bone-chilling winds sweeping unimpeded across taiga and tundra in winter. Even Petr, who had some knowledge of his father's trading activities in western Siberia, was aghast at the prospect of venturing into this trackless wilderness.

He said, "Surely there is a better option. What about Khylnov and the Vyatka River valley? That is an old Novgorodian trading zone. We should find allies there."

The 850-mile-long Vyatka River was a prime gateway to the Central Urals for the Novgorodian fur traders. Khylnov had been founded on the banks of the Vyatka as a principal trading center in 1181.

"That will not work, my son," said Ivanov, shaking his head. "Khylnov is certainly full of Oprichniki. A lot has changed there since it passed from Novgorodian control."

Khylnov had owed its main allegiance to Novgorod until plundered by the Tatars in 1391 and 1477. It had been annexed by Moscow in 1489.

Petr remained unconvinced of the priest's recommended itinerary. "Father, I can see why you feel that we would be safer in Siberia, but we have no guide to take us there. And how would we travel in such a harsh land once we arrived? From what I have heard from my father's trading agents, our horses will be useless in the Siberian lowlands in the summer."

"Petr, even in Kazan, you will not be beyond the reach of the Tsar. You must go further. The Church has been sending missionaries over the Urals for decades. I know there are monks in Kazan who have traveled through the Urals into Siberia on many occasions. In good weather, we can reach Kazan in several weeks."

Petr looked at Andrei. "What do you think, Andrei? Stay here? Circle back to the north and west, or go east?"

Andrei said nothing at first. He had said little to his companions since the night they had fled Novgorod. By nature, he was not prone to casual conversation. His grief for his slain brother and Samara had driven him further into silent introspection.

When Andrei had returned to Yaroslavl, he had brought with him the body of a young woman. He himself had been more dead than alive. He had spoken little of his absence from the Novgorodian refugees. He had told no one about his ordeal or his relationship with Samara. All remained bottled up in his heart and soul. Only the bonds of duty to his brother's fiancé restrained him from returning to Novgorod to exact a greater measure of revenge.

It was this duty that compelled him to speak now. "I'm afraid I must agree with Father Ivanov. To go west is suicide. I have many relatives along the Volga to the east, and my father often mentioned that we had other relatives on the other side of the Urals in Chingi-Tura. Perhaps my cousin in Nizhni Novgorod can be of assistance in directing us through the mountains. At any rate, it seems logical to continue down the Volga to Nizhni Novgorod and then on to Kazan. I feel confident that we can hide among my Tatar relatives there long enough to make some long-range plans. In my view, the sooner we leave Yaroslavl, the better."

Petr did not like the direction this conversation was taking. Clearly agitated, he repeatedly clasped and unclasped his hands behind his back. He barely maintained the posture of deference and reverence customary in the presence of the clergy. He was an artist, a man of civilization and culture. He was no hunter or trader, and the thought of the Urals — the "Ural'skiy Khrebet" — and the Siberian wilderness filled him with dread.

He said, "Siberia! I can't believe we are considering this. From what you are saying, we are headed for the Upper Ob River Basin. A region that remains largely unexplored. As much as he loves travel and adventure, even Father never ventured into that dreary land. He leaves that up to his agents — his most expendable agents, I might add. I don't know how we would get there, let alone what we would do once we arrived — if we ever did arrive! I know we can't return to Novgorod, but surely there is a better homeland for us than this."

Matrona appeared on the verge of collapse. In Novgorod, she had lived a privileged and protected life. The journey to Yaroslavl had taken its toll on her health and spirit. Never robust before, she was now gaunt, her eyes sunken, and her skin virtually transparent. Only the constant presence of Anna by her side had enabled Matrona to continue on their arduous journey.

She said, "I'm not sure I can go on much longer. Even Kazan seems impossible. It doesn't seem to matter — it's all so hopeless."

Father Ivanov placed his hands on her shoulders and looked directly into her eyes. "You have too much life ahead of you to give up now. What you need is rest, Matrona — and faith. Then you can make it through the Urals and beyond. To hardships? Yes — but also to freedom — freedom from the Muscovites, freedom from the conventions of class and privilege. With the grace of God, you will have the freedom of a new beginning."

Petr remained confused and troubled. "But Father, we do not know the way. Who will be our guide?"

His answer astonished them all. "Remember, Petr, our true faith comes from the East. The rising sun signifies the coming of Christ. Trust in the Lord, Petr — and his humble servants. God willing, through me, he will be your guide."

Barely an hour had passed when Father Ivanov received a knock on his door. When he opened it, he was surprised to see Andrei. Tatars were generally reluctant to visit within Orthodox religious quarters.

"Andrei, what brings you out so late in the evening?"

"Sorry to bother you, Father, but this is important." He laid a large bulging sack on the priest's table.

"It is not a bother, Andrei." Ivanov chuckled. "I've been up studying maps. I'm trying to get as knowledgeable about our travels ahead as I may have led everyone earlier to believe I am. You strike me as a man who knows the difference between bluster and reality."

Ivanov hefted the bag curiously. "What have we here?"

Andrei opened the bag and spread the trove of gold and jewels out onto the table. The contents sparkled and gleamed in the candlelight. "Most of this is Oprichniki loot, taken from the people in and around Novgorod. Some is from the family of the young woman that I brought here."

"This is quite some treasure, Andrei. You risked your life to get it; by rights, it is yours."

"It is blood booty, Father. I want nothing to do with it. I have several more sacks that I will give you to provide for our journey to the East."

"That is very generous of you, Andrei."

"I have only one demand, Father. The woman's name is Samara. I desire that she be buried in consecrated ground. I know that would be the wish of her family. Her headstone should read thusly." He handed the priest a paper:

SAMARA
A WARRIOR
SHE EARNED HER FREEDOM

"I will see to it, Andrei; there are still several graves that were dug in the autumn for dignitaries that might pass in the winter. I will see that she is interred in one of them and that the headstone is cut as directed."

Andre left and returned shortly with several more sacks of valuables. The priest was more somber than excited. "I will give ten percent of this to the church here. They will be most pleased. The rest we will use to finance our escape."

"Very good, Father. I could not ask, or hope, for more."

"Andre, you said this is blood booty. But we will sanctify it through our own struggles and righteousness." He touched Andrei on the shoulder. "I can see that you are deeply troubled. Whatever you have done has been forced upon you. I know you are not of our faith. That is but a trifling matter to me. Dogma is for fools and schemers. In this world, there are good men and bad. You are a good man, and all good men walk with God."

"Thank you, Father."

"I will pray for you, Andrei. God bless and comfort you."

◊

As he returned to his quarters from Father Ivanov's cell, Andrei was surprised to encounter Anna in the passageway.

"Anna, it is very late. You should not be out and about alone."

"I am fine, Andrei. We need to talk. We can go to the chapel; that way, nobody can make up stories about us."

Once they entered the nave, she sat down cross-legged on the floor and motioned for Andrei to do the same. She paused a moment, gathering herself.

"Something is deeply troubling you, Andrei. Something more than your brother's death. Others don't see it; well, maybe Father Ivanov. I saw a look of concern on his face."

"It is difficult," he stammered. Her directness was disconcerting. It reminded him a bit of Samara.

"I know, Andrei. I have my own demons, but you must talk to someone, or it will consume your spirit — your life. I will keep your confidence. I will not even tell Petr."

He stumbled for words at first, but then they came in a flood. Long into the night, the anguish spilled out of him in a flood, all of it: the blood, lust, hate, fear, love, and remorse. With a long sigh, he was at last drained of his inner torment.

She said nothing, only gave him a light touch now and

then to show her attention and caring.

When he returned to his quarters, he slept soundly for the first time in many nights.

CHAPTER 13

Nizhni Novgorod on the Volga

The stone monastery stood two hundred feet above the river ice on the northern bank of the Volga. It was the first sign that Petr's party had finally reached Nizhni Novgorod, a city built by the Grand Prince Vasilii and peopled by those he exiled from Novgorod in an earlier, though significantly less bloody, purge. Its gray face barely visible against the leaden winter sky, Nizhni Novgorod did not present a cheery picture. It was, however, a welcome sight to Petr, who was as tired and cold as he had ever been. For the past two days, he had been wishing he had trained as a snow sculptor rather than an icon painter. At least then he would have built up some tolerance to the cold.

The group of dispossessed Novgorodians was strung out over several miles. Their numbers had swollen to over a hundred in Yaroslavl. Because Nikolai Safronov was a leading boyar, they looked to Petr for leadership, that, due to his station, he was obliged to provide — regardless of his experience or desire. Petr, in turn, sought advice from Father Ivanov and strength from the indefatigable Andrei Stepanov. Andrei had been unbowed by the fierce winter storms that had ravaged them as they proceeded southeast along the Mother Volga.

Petr did not know how the horses, let alone the frail Matrona, had managed to survive the journey. He was deeply worried about his sister's mental and physical condition. She ate little and spoke less. She had a gaunt and forsaken demeanor that chilled Petr's spirits more deeply than the numbing cold air or the freezing river ice.

Ever since they had departed Yaroslavl, Petr and Anna had tried to engage Matrona in conversation. He hoped that the shock of exile, if not her grief, would lessen with the miles. Opportunities for discourse were frequent due to the numerous times the group holed up to sit out the worst of the storms. His efforts to draw Matrona out of her despondency were in vain. Though she no longer cried, her speech had evaporated with her tears.

In her silence, Matrona was the perfect companion for Andrei, who had spoken little in the best of times. Since learning of his brother's death, he scarcely spoke at all. Stepanov must have felt Petr's gaze on his back. He turned and pointed to the monastery.

"If I spend another night in one of those, I'll turn into a monk myself — as strange as that one!" He gestured toward Father Ivanov, who was riding out ahead to hail the gate-keeper.

In the various monasteries in which they had sought shelter, Petr had been surprised that the wild-eyed monk had gained access for himself, let alone the crowd of refugees that followed him. With his sunken eyes blazing from his gaunt and haggard face, the priest appeared more like a demon than a holy man.

Yet, in spite of the elements, Father Ivanov maintained a religious discipline that provided sustenance for the soul and a sense of normalcy for the psyche of his forlorn flock of exiles. In the face of the fiercest gale, he gathered the group for Mass. Petr could still picture the priest with his hair whipping in the wind, his eyes so alight with religious fervor that the simple chalice in his raised hands might well have been the Holy Grail.

Petr's reverie was interrupted as Andrei moved to take the reins of Matrona's horse. "I have relatives here in the city. If you have no objections, I will take Matrona with me while you attend to the rest of our party. It will be several hours before the last of them straggle in."

"That is fine with me, Andrei," Petr responded wearily. "We could probably all use a warm hearth and a soft bed."

Petr hoped that the presence of women and children would elevate Matrona's spirits a bit. Besides, she would be safer with a Tatar family than at the monastery. Fearing the political influence and organizational power of the church, Tsar Ivan had shown no reluctance to hang, burn, or even fry the clergy right along with the rest of the enemies that his demented mind conjured up. However, the Tatars in this region had already been brutally subdued and forced into Christian conversion. The Tsar took little interest in their affairs once they had been bent to his will.

Petr rode up close to Stepanov and lowered his voice so as not to be heard above the wind. The Tsar's agents were everywhere — it must be assumed that the group of refugees contained more than one spy. "Meet me at the monastery tomorrow at sundown, Andrei. We need to plan the rest of our journey, and we dare not tarry here more than a day or two. I will need most of the day tomorrow to contact my father's agents."

Situated at the juncture of the Volga and its main right bank tributary, the Oka, Nizhni Novgorod was a hub for the Russian fur trade and a center for the Safronov trading empire. Tsar Ivan's huge standing army had virtually bankrupted the country. The costs fell particularly hard on landowners, who taxed their peasants and serfs to their knees in most regions, and to their graves in some provinces. The Safronov wealth, however, was based upon trade rather than land, and Alexsei had wisely, and widely, dispersed his assets from the Urals to Western Europe. While the Tsar's Oprichniki enforcers had undoubtedly seized all Safronov property in Novgorod, most of the family's wealth remained intact — at least for the time being.

Nizhni Novgorod marked the boundary between European and Asian influence. Since the time of the recently sainted Alexander Nevsky's rule in the mid-thirteenth century, the merchants of Novgorod had maintained strong trading ties with the Tatars throughout the region surrounding this cosmopolitan city. Among these people, Alexei Safronov had several agents and friends located in Nizhni Novgorod – resources that Petr must tap for funding and counsel. What Petr could use most right now, however, was a little encouragement. Except for the Mother Volga, the lands to the east were terra incognita to most Russians, Petr most definitely included.

CHAPTER 14

The fire in the hearth had been banked for the night. The two men huddled as close to its embers as safety allowed; they spoke in hushed tones in deference to the four families that slept within the simple one-room dwelling. In the presence of the women and children, Andrei had said nothing about the events that had transpired in Novgorod. He had not wished to interrupt the attention lavished upon Matrona, although, unfortunately, it had not lifted her spirits in any visible respect.

After the families had fallen asleep, Andrei related the events surrounding the death of Dimitri and the flight from Novgorod to his oldest surviving cousin, Ogotai. Ogotai was one of the few relatives who had visited the Stepanov family in Novgorod. He received the news of Dimitri's death in silence — any grief his face may have shown was obscured in darkness.

It was several minutes after Andrei had completed his story before Ogotai spoke. "I'm truly sorry to hear of Dimitri's death, Andrei. He had a most promising future. I fear that Novgorod has suffered the same fate as poor Dimitri."

Andrei gripped Ogotai's shoulder tightly. The shadows could not conceal his malice and resolve. "I shall avenge his death, Ogotai. I shall exact a blood toll so terrible that all the Oprichniki brooms in Russian cannot sweep it away!"

Ogotai grasped his cousin's wrist with one hand, and with the other hand, he pulled Andrei's head close so that he could look him squarely in the eye. "The Tsar is a madman, Andrei.

One cannot revenge madness. You can only survive. Revenge is for the rich and powerful. For us, it is folly — deadly folly. We Volga Tatars know much of death and hopelessness. Too much! Do not add to our legacy of misery. Escape with your friends while you still can."

In his heart, Andrei knew that Ogotai was right, but hatred had carried him this far, and without it, he had no bearing to guide him. He slumped forward despondently.

"To flee is cowardice, Ogotai. How can I live with myself if I run from this? Is not revenge a duty? I cannot avenge my brother by running from his murderers!"

Ogotai quickly replied, "Your brother was a peaceful man, Andrei. To share his fate only magnifies the tragedy. Avenge him by surviving and prospering. Revenge is your personal affair. It ignores your brother's life and aspirations. It won't bring him back. It will just lead to retribution against the rest of your family — here and elsewhere. Besides, you have other duties that transcend your personal honor. Have you forgotten that young woman over there?" He gestured toward Matrona.

Andrei shrugged. "You are right, cousin, but tell me, Ogotai — how far must we run? How far to the east can we go before we are swallowed up by wilderness? I hardly think that Dimitri intended to have Matrona chewing hides and eating dogs!"

Ogotai did not respond. He recognized that his cousin felt guilty about Dimitri's death and was deeply ashamed that he had survived while his brother was butchered. Consequently, Ogotai remained silent while his cousin mastered his emotions and collected his thoughts.

After several minutes of silence, Andrei continued. "Of all of my relatives, you are the most traveled, Ogotai. Unfortunately, it appears that I may soon surpass you in this respect. What lies beyond the Urals? That crazy priest Ivanov is convinced that only in Siberia will we be beyond the reach of the Tsar. My friend Petr has come to believe him."

Gazing into the ember, Ogotai considered Andrei's questions for several minutes before replying.

"I'm afraid your friend Petr is right. Since our last revolt was crushed in 1556, Ivan has paid little attention to us Tatars. As long as we maintain the trappings of the Russian Church, we are practically invisible. We are merely 'Starokreshchennye' — forced Christians! But your friends will be noticed. Just today, I saw two men flaunting their dog's heads and brooms to demonstrate their devotion to the Tsar. I doubt there are enough Oprichniki here to cause you grief, but by now, the word of your arrival is on its way west. Tsar Ivan is always in need of fresh blood — particularly Novgorodian blood, from what I hear."

Ogotai sighed and continued, "It will be no better in Kazan. There are more Oprichniki there than here. They have not finished picking over our bones from the last failed revolt. You must make for Chingi-Tura on the eastern slope of the Urals. It is still in Tatar control, but your friends, as enemies of the Tsar, should be welcome there."

"Can you give us directions?" Andrei asked.

Ogotai clapped him on the back. "Yes, cousin. I learned them from a friend who was one of the few to go there. The directions are straightforward, but the journey is difficult to contemplate, let alone complete. You must follow the rivers, but I fear that the spring breakup will render them impassable before you can reach your destination this year."

Ogotai then proceeded to outline the river itinerary that the refugees must follow in order to reach Chingi-Tura. From Nizhni Novgorod, they would proceed eastward on the Mother Volga into a region of mixed forest where a broad plain lay on the river's left bank and the northern portion of the Volga upland rose steeply from the right bank. The party would re-provision at the Tatar city of Kazan, which was conquered by Ivan in 1552.

From Kazan, the refugees would need to proceed down the

Volga as it swung southward and was entered by its main tributary, the twelve-hundred-mile-long Kama River, whose headwaters lay in the low outlying ridges of the central Urals. They
would then proceed first northeast and then north along the
Kama until they reached the Chusovaya River, which would
lead them into the heart of the Urals. It would be an epic journey, as the Urals were extremely broad in this region.

In the Urals, the party would encounter a swampy taiga
of pine, birch, and larch, which would be difficult to navigate
and arduous to traverse. Here, they would have to somehow
locate the Serebryanka River and ascend that river to its headwaters. From there, they would trek east to the Tagil River and
descend it to the Tobol River. Then they would need to proceed up the Tobol to the Tura River and Chingi-Tura. If they
missed the Serebryanka River, there was an alternate route
down the Iset River.

Ogotai finished his description of the journey. He put his
hand on Andrei's shoulder.

"You must reveal these directions to no one. If you are
captured, you will know what to do. If any of the others are
taken, I fear they would give up the plans under torture."

Andrei was despondent. "Even if we are able to find these
rivers and know which one is which, I doubt our party has
the strength to make it to Chingi-Tura. If you and I were to
attempt such an undertaking by ourselves, it would tax us to
the limit. I don't know how a party of refugees, many in as
bad or worse shape than Matrona, could ever complete such
a journey."

Ogotai responded quickly. "Yes, cousin, it will be a most
strenuous journey, and many will die — perhaps even Matrona.
A few fur traders and missionaries from this region have been
to Chingi-Tura and returned, so it is not impossible. Besides,
to remain here is certain death. I don't see any other choice
for you."

"Can you guide us, Ogotai?" Andrei asked. "I have no faith

in that crazy priest. Although I must admit that he sustains the spirits of the others. Still, I would feel much better with you in charge, cousin. You, after all, know the way."

Ogotai shook his head sadly. "I'm afraid not, Andrei. I must remain here with our families. Look around. I am the only adult male in this household. When our last revolt was crushed, there were few surviving males left to provide for the people. We have four families in this one house, yet we are better off than most."

Ogotai lifted his tunic and pointed to a nasty scar that ran from his sternum diagonally to his left hip. It was clearly visible even in the faint light cast by the embers in the hearth. "My wounds are healed, cousin. It will take many generations to heal our people."

Though no emotions marked his face, Andrei's voice betrayed his despondency. "I still don't see how we can get through the Urals without a guide. We could flounder around for months without finding the proper route to Chingi-Tura. If we are just one drainage off from our route, we could end up hopelessly lost in the heart of Siberia. Dealing with fellow Tatars in Chingi-Tura is one thing — throwing ourselves to the mercy of Voguls, Ostyaks, or Komi is something else again!"

Ogotai shook his head at the strange dilemma faced by his cousin — be captured by the Oprichniki or venture into the heathen lands of the non-Russian Eastern peoples, or the "Inorodtsy" as they were known to the Muscovites.

"Well, Andrei, unlike Ivan, I doubt the Inorodtsy have a frying pan big enough to fry the likes of you!"

Andrei was not amused. "By the time the ice, snow, floods, and mosquitoes are done with us, I doubt whatever is left will present much of a challenge to whichever of the Inorodtsy we blunder into."

Ogotai chuckled. "Perhaps you have given up on that crazy priest a bit too quickly, cousin."

"What do you mean?" Andrei asked. "Do you know something about him that I don't?"

"I only know what you have told me, which isn't much," Ogotai replied. "But I do know a few things about the Russian Church thanks to our late friend Archbishop Gurii of Kazan."

Andrei was surprised that his cousin would acknowledge any understanding of the Russian Church, which was an anathema to most Muslim Tatars. "I did not know that you had converted to Christianity, cousin!"

"Oh, I thought everyone in Russia knew that we Volga Tatars flocked to the Church once Ivan demonstrated the true spirit of the Christian faith!" Ogotai replied sarcastically.

He continued in a more serious tone, "But perhaps a brief explanation is in order. You see, not all Tatars have enjoyed the freedom that has been afforded those fortunate enough to reside in Novgorod. You have had the legacy of Alexander Nevsky to dampen the excesses of religious zealots of whatever ilk. We on the Volga have not been so fortunate."

"That's true — Nevsky was canonized as a saint a little over twenty years ago — even so, not everyone agreed with his policies of coexistence between Christians and Tatars," Andrei responded. "But how does this fit into our present situation?"

Ogotai shrugged. "Only indirectly. I'm sorry, cousin. I suppose this branch of the family has always been a bit envious of your situation in Novgorod. But that is all past history. Now it is you that must be somewhat envious — at least we have a place to call home!"

"I understand your sentiments," Andrei replied. "But please continue."

Ogotai threw several logs on the fire and then continued. "After the Tsar defeated us at Kazan in 1552, he believed that our subjugation would not be complete until we were converted to the Russian Church. To this end, he appointed Archbishop Gurii to convert us. Flushed with his new victory, Ivan must have felt magnanimous at first because he gave Gurii special powers, the 'jus asyli.' These powers were given to protect non-Christians who ran afoul of Russian civil authorities."

He continued, "Well, knowing what you do about the Oprichniki, you know the ultimate fate of the jus asyli, but at first, Archbishop Gurii did what he could. My older brother — your cousin, Cyril — was a spokesman for our community here. I accompanied him on many of his trips to Kazan to petition Archbishop Gurii on behalf of a townsman."

"Gurii was a just man, but we Tatars are devout — and stubborn. There were few conversions, and eventually he could hear the Tsar's big frying pan sizzling back in Moscow. He began to forcibly convert Tatars in this region, which resulted in the revolt of 1556."

Andrei was growing impatient — "But, cousin, I still don't understand what this has to do with our crossing the Urals."

Ogotai smiled. "You are not leaving tonight, Andrei. A little of our history will not be much of a burden to carry into your new land. But I will come to the point."

"In addition to Tatar and various animist supplicants appearing before Archbishop Gurii, there were many missionary monks reporting on their journeys to so-called 'heathen' lands. I personally talked to two monks who claimed to have traversed the Urals to Chingi-Tura."

Andrei was perplexed by this explanation. "That is interesting information, but how do we know if these missionaries are still around, and if so, why would they want to guide us over the Urals? I would imagine they fear Ivan's hot pan more now than ever!"

Ogotai clapped Andrei on the back. "That, cousin, is where your crazy priest comes in. One thing I have noticed about the Russian Church is that they write down everything. There is undoubtedly a detailed written description of every missionary expedition over the Urals. While I'm sure the degree of hardship will be exaggerated to emphasize the religious fervor of the missionaries involved, the directions should be accurate enough. There must be more than one route; it is best to know as many as possible."

"And you think that Father Ivanov can get access to this information," Andrei responded.

"I do not know. That depends upon his contacts in Kazan and his powers of persuasion. At any rate, it is best that he be approached through your friend Petr. It is best that we let the Christians handle this."

Andrei nodded his head in agreement. "I am supposed to meet Petr at sundown tomorrow. I will discuss these matters with him then. I am very grateful for your advice, Ogotai. I still find our situation bleak, but I have some hope now."

Ogotai patted his cousin's shoulder. "A little food, a warm place to sleep for a night or two, and some dubious advice is little aid and small comfort, I'm afraid. I wish I could go with you, but . . ." Ogotai's voice trailed off, and the cousins stared silently into the glowing embers for many minutes before bidding each other good night.

CHAPTER 15

Matrona was exhausted yet could not sleep. Two of the many babies in the household were fussing, and the grandmother of the extended family was snoring loudly in the far corner of the room. While she hated the trail and the winter hardships she had endured, Matrona would gladly trade this human racket for the sound of the wind and pelting snow, even if it meant giving up the warmth for a night.

The house smelled strongly of sweat, mildew, and cooking odors. Her stomach turned as the odors reminded her of the meal she had gagged down several hours before.

"It smells even worse than it tasted," she muttered to herself.

Matrona crinkled her nose and pulled her robes up over her nose to block the smell.

I wonder where Anna is staying tonight? she thought. *My brother probably has her set up in a boyar's home while I languish in this hovel!*

Petr had advised her that it was safer to stay in the Tatar quarters, where the Oprichniki were less likely to be looking for them. She suspected this was just a ploy for Petr to get some time alone with Anna.

Matrona squirmed in her sleeping robes as she considered Petr's obvious infatuation with Anna. She had not noticed it while she was sickly and weak during the first several days of the journey. But now that she was regaining her strength, it was painfully obvious. The more she thought about this relationship, the more upsetting it became. The death of Dimitri had pushed all thoughts of male companionship aside; even her fantasies about Andrei had vanished. Her only solace was her brother, and Petr's attentions were elsewhere.

It is unseemly for someone of Petr's station to dote on a slave girl. He hardly pays any attention to me. It appears I have lost everything. First my home, then my fiancé, and now the affection of my brother!

Matrona heard one of the women moaning softly in the darkness.

"Good night!" Matrona snapped loudly as she turned over on her side and pulled the covers over her head.

◊

It was well past sundown, which came early in winter this far north. Yet, Petr was not drowsy despite his fatigue from the many days of hard and frigid travel. It was as if his eyes had frozen open and his brain was too heavy to drift into sleep. He sat on a cushioned bench, stoking the fire in a large clay stove, a "pech'," which was located on an expansive earthen area of the floor. This stove was a new invention and provided sufficient heat for a large household to remain comfortably warm for most of the winter. The stove was flat on top, and on extremely cold nights, the master and mistress and several of their children would sleep on it.

Except for the crackling of the fire and the creaking of the building as it contracted in the extreme cold of the night, the house was still. By the time Petr had located Leon'yev Belov, his father's trading partner, and returned to the monastery, Father Ivanov had already attended to the quartering of most of the refugees. Only Anna and a small boyar family needed a place to stay. Petr took them back to the Belov residence with him. Belov's family had journeyed to Moscow to visit his wife's grandparents, and he offered to provide lodging for as many of Petr's entourage as his dwelling could accommodate.

Belov was a very wealthy merchant, and the small party that accompanied Petr easily fit in the spacious home. The boyar and Petr roomed with Belov in the master's quarters, while the boyar's wife and daughters stayed in the mistress's section. Despite Petr's objections, Anna had insisted on staying in the servant's quarters at the top of the house.

Petr had argued that since Anna's master was dead, she was no longer a slave, especially when she was under his care and protection. She had responded that she was dressed like a slave, spoke like a slave, and had no more wealth than a slave. Secretly, Anna feared that to act otherwise was bound to bring approbation and dishonor upon Petr. While many a nobleman, married or unmarried, would climb under the blankets with a servant in secret, it would be scandalous to flaunt their association in public.

The evening meal had been taken quietly and without ceremony. Due to their host's relationship with Petr's father, Belov wanted to organize a banquet in honor of Petr and his companions. But Petr prevailed on him to provide simpler fare and ceremony in light of their exhausted condition. Soup and bread, accompanied by aqua vitae, or Russe wine, were quickly consumed. After a brief prayer session in front of Belov's beautiful iconostasis, the travelers, except for Petr, were quickly off to bed.

Over several cups of mead, Petr and Belov lingered to discuss which of the Safronov assets Petr would need for their journey to the East. Petr remained quite vague as to their ultimate destination. Although his father had absolute faith in Belov's integrity, Petr knew from direct observation that the Tsar's ingenious torture techniques could loosen the lips of any man. Without actually naming a destination, Petr left the impression that they were headed for Perm. Belov had bought into it.

"Sounds like you are headed to Perm? That's Stroganov territory, and from what I hear, old Anika Stroganov has repudiated his family roots in Novgorod and thrown in with the Muscovites, even joined the Tsar's Oprichnina."

Petr remained noncommittal. "Well, the weather will have more to do with our final destination than any plans we make this far up the Volga."

"If you do go north, be cautious," the old man continued. "From what I hear, Stroganov's sons, Yakov, Semeon, and Grigorii, are as hungry for power and wealth as the old man. If they see you as a threat, you'll be trussed up by their hired Cossacks and sent back to Moscow to entertain Ivan."

With that happy thought, Belov bid Petr good night and retired to the master's quarters. Petr remained to reflect on the suffering and horror they had so far endured and to fret about the hardships yet to come.

Petr threw another log on the fire and watched the steam curl up from the cracks in the wood as the frost melted and boiled away. His mind drifted with the smoke and steam, and he lost track of time. It may have been hours or merely minutes when he heard the stairs creak behind him. He turned and caught his breath as his heart skipped a beat. It was Anna — but not as he was accustomed to seeing her.

Except for her rescue, when he was distracted by fear, combat, and shame, he had only observed Anna in her layered outdoor apparel. On the trail, her face was covered. This was due to the bitter cold and, no doubt, in some measure, the facial trauma resulting from the attack in Novgorod. Often, only her eyes were exposed to view. To be sure, her eyes were beautiful, though disconcerting in their intensity and directness. Petr had found it impossible to meet her gaze for more than a moment.

Petr knew that Anna was fair from the occasional lock of hair that would fall from beneath her fur hat. Like all Russians in winter, she presented the image of a formless lump of wool and fur; at a few paces, they were barely discernible from one another or any accompanying men. When the refugees found shelter on their journey, the women would disappear into their separate lodgings in the evening and reappear in the morning in the same shapeless forms as the previous day. Whatever metamorphosis might have occurred during the night remained a mystery.

Despite his lack of familiarity with Anna's physical appearance, Petr was thoroughly captivated by the young woman. Unlike his sister, who seemed to become a greater burden with each passing verst, Anna was a source of energy and caring. She tirelessly ministered to the waning strength and flagging spirits of the Novgorodian refugees. If a young mother were beside herself due to the relentless wailing of a disconsolate child, Anna would tend the child until the mother's nerves were mended. Anna treated a host of bumps, abrasions, sores, and frostbite that plagued the winter travelers. She chastised the belligerent and encouraged the disheartened and seemingly never lost her own energy or good spirits.

Petr would try to ride beside Anna as often as he could manage, but she would usually shoo him away to his other duties. He wasn't sure Anna liked him very much. She still called him "Master" even though she knew he found this distasteful. Although he had managed to save her from ravishment, he supposed she saw him as weak. Indeed, he had only overcome the Oprichniki with the element of surprise and had not taken any action in the face of the atrocities that had been observed while leaving Novgorod. He certainly did not project the strength of Andrei, and with several hundred versts of travel under his belt, he no longer looked the gentleman. No, there was not much there to attract a young woman; no wonder she shooed him away.

But now here she was — her golden hair cascading to her shoulders. She moved with an easy elegance, the simple blue gown pressing gently against her body. Petr stood transfixed by the subtle revelation of generous breasts and a lithe and graceful frame.

Petr was unprepared for the appearance of this nubile apparition in the night. He held his tongue for fear that he would stammer and betray his physical arousal and mental disarray. Noticing him sitting near the stove on the far side of the room, Anna stopped at the foot of the stairs.

"Forgive me, Master. I did not intend to intrude on your privacy. I could not sleep and thought that I might tend the stove so as to warm the house for the morning."

Petr took a deep breath and collected himself. "No, no. Think nothing of it. Your company is welcome — most welcome!"

He winced and then recoiled with the thought that she could read his reaction, maybe even his mind — which was going places that would require a trip to Father Ivanov. *My God, man*, he thought, *pull yourself together before she thinks you a pervert and a fool.*

"Forgive my lack of manners, Anna. My mind is fogged by fatigue, yet I cannot sleep. Perhaps it is something we ate — or didn't eat." He started to stand up, remembered his condition — and rapidly sat back down.

That's it, he thought. *She now knows me to be a total idiot.*

Seeing his discomfort, she moved to the woodpile and retrieved some fuel for the fire. As she fed the logs to the fire, Petr had an opportunity to study her face, heretofore hidden by hoods and scarves. In profile, her hair formed a virtual halo in the soft firelight. Her face was luminous, seemingly too lovely to touch — like soiling sunlight. Her lips were full and ripe, and the eyes that had always seemed so icy were as soft and alluring as blue topaz.

Petr's artistic endeavors had brought him into contact with many women, and he had known a few intimately. Seduction was a cherished game of those Novgorodians with wealth and title. There was no love in it — only sport. Noblewomen were used to having their way, and several had had their way with Petr. Not that he minded. He was as much a slave to his lust as any other young man. Even the priests seemed unimpressed by his intermittent and modest dalliances as they doled out his penance of prayer and reflection at confession.

But those women, housebound and parched by the dry and intense heat of their winter stoves, bore little resemblance to the fetching maiden before him. Their faces had been painted in garish red and white colors to hide the ravaged complexions. Softened by fire and candlelight, Anna's residual bruises from the attack in Novgorod were all but invisible. Her skin was as pure as Italian marble. Despite the cruel attack in Novgorod and the bitter cold that had besieged them for many leagues, she retained an unsurpassed beauty that was breathtaking to behold.

After she had fed the last log into the stove, Anna stood, still facing the fire. She was not yet ready to confront this man, not on this night when her need was high and her resolve low. Her right hand clenched and unclenched, betraying her inner conflict. She could feel Petr's eyes on her — wanted his eyes, his hands — his lips. She turned and smiled, her lips slightly parted — her eyes betraying a desire that her mind struggled in vain to contain.

Petr's heart melted in a flood of emotion unlike any that he had ever known. He moved to the edge of the bench. "Please sit here awhile, Anna. You must be exhausted. I know I am."

He paused for a second. "No, what I mean is that I would like you to sit by me. I would very much like your company."

"Very well, Master," she said as she settled onto the bench, trying to look and sound more dutiful than interested.

They sat staring ahead in silence for several minutes. He wanted to reach out to touch her but knew that the tiny ripples of that touch would return as a tidal wave of desire that would sweep him away. Sensing his tumult, she turned to him with a smile so disarming that his tension quickly melted in its warmth.

"What should we talk about, Master?" she inquired. "I have had a narrow and uninteresting life, so I'm afraid you will have to carry this conversation."

"Well, your life is interesting to me, Anna, so why don't we start with your parents? I can see that you are not from the usual Russian stock."

She nodded. "Is this a bad thing, Master?"

"No, it is a very good thing — you are very fair and, dare I say — slender." He looked into her eyes so that she would not misconstrue his admiration as baser feelings.

She said, "My mother was from Kexholm on Lake Ladoga. My father was a trader who worked for Master Ushakov, transporting furs to the West. I favor my mother, who was taller and fairer than my father."

"What happened to your parents?" he inquired.

"My mother was taken by a fever when I was eight. For the next four years, I was my father's companion and help-mate. That is why I know how to read and write, ride a horse, and steer a boat. We were inseparable . . ." Her voice trailed off.

"I'm sorry, Anna," Petr said softly. "I should not have opened old wounds."

"No, it is good to talk about them," she replied. "I need to keep them alive in my memory, and there have been so few people to talk to — only you, really."

She took a deep breath and continued. "My father died in a boating accident. We hit a sweeper in the river, and I went overboard. I got caught in the branches, and he jumped in to save me. He managed to free me from the snag, but he him-self was swept under the tree and drowned. I was picked up by a nearby boat and brought to Master Ushakov, who took me in. I was his servant until the day that the Tsar executed the entire family. I was out on an errand, or I would have perished with them. The Oprichniki killed everything, even the dogs."

She was quiet awhile. Then, smiling, she turned to Petr. "And what of you, my Master who rescues slave girls from evil Oprichniki?"

"And cowers in his cave in the face of evil and flees the enemy under the cover of darkness," Petr responded ruefully.

She rose and knelt before him; taking his face in her hands, she looked him directly in the eyes. "Do not think yourself a coward, Master. You are a kind and gentle man with great inner strength and courage that we all rely on. Your intelligence will not allow you to perish foolishly — rely on it, as we do."

Without breaking eye contact, Petr gently took her hands and pressed them to his lips. He leaned forward until their lips almost touched.

His voice quavering with emotion, he said softly, "You know, dear Anna, I am falling in love with you."

Her eyes welled with tears, and she lowered her head. "Yes. Yes, Master, I know this. But you must never act on it — never!"

And then she was gone — a silent apparition disappearing into the night, not even a footfall to echo in the darkness.

CHAPTER 16

Kazan on the Volga, 1570

Matrona shuddered as another icy blast hit the sleigh. She pulled her hand from her mitten and dabbed at the ice crystals that had formed on her eyelids. She, like the other refugees from Novgorod, was exhausted from two days of travel with no sleep and very few breaks. To avoid detection by the Tsar's henchmen, they had been forced to make a long detour around Sviyazhsk, the Tsar's fortress on an island at the mouth of the Sviyaga River. It was about twenty versts upriver from Kazan.

The fortress was the engineering marvel of its time. In 1551, it had been cut from the forests of central Russia and floated over a thousand miles to its island site. It had been assembled in less than a month for the siege of Kazan. Now, it was the region's administrative and trade center — and filled with Oprichniki.

Matrona cared little about engineering feats or history; her only thoughts were of a hot meal and a warm, clean place to sleep. It seemed like hours since they had left the Volga and headed inland. Petr had come by to tell her that they were only a few versts from Kazan. She thought that this storied city was situated along the river. However, all that remained in this area was the ruin of the old Tatar headquarters that Ivan had destroyed in 1552 when he defeated the Tatars and sacked the city.

Petr explained that the Volga and Kazanka rivers flooded this plain every spring; consequently, the city sat inland on several hills above the plain. She wished that her assumption had been correct. The wind had been at their back for most of the day. Now that they were headed inland, they were quartering into the wind, and it was brutal.

Matrona pulled the fur robes up to her chin, seeking to block as much of the slashing wind as possible. She tugged the robes away from three small children who had burrowed completely under them. Since Yaroslavl, she had had the sleigh to herself until this abominable wind had come up. Anna had brought the children to her because the sides of the sleigh were high enough to block most of the wind.

Matrona was not happy with this turn of events. There were several other sleighs in the party that were better equipped than hers to handle children. Besides, she had barely enough blankets and robes to keep her warm, let alone several squirming brats. She thought of protesting, but Petr had arrived on the scene, and she had known that he would take Anna's side. He was clearly smitten with this slave girl, and there was no sense in starting an argument she couldn't win.

Matrona pulled her scarf up and her hat down and burrowed as deeply into the sleigh as she could. No matter what she did, the wind found a seam to work through. Just when she thought she could endure the cold no longer, Andrei hailed her from the side of the sleigh. Wincing, she thrust her face into the wind to see what he wanted.

Lord knows how long he's been there, she thought. A picture of stoicism, he sat on his horse as if it were a warm summer day. He pointed to a magnificent architectural structure in the distance. It was the Kazan Kremlin, which had been constructed from 1556 to 1562, after Ivan had captured the city in 1552. The Kremlin was enclosed by high stone walls that were white with characteristic loopholes and thirteen towers.

In the Kremlin was the "Taynitskay," or "Secret Tower," which contained an underground secret passage to drinking water. The Kremlin also contained the Annunciation

Cathedral, which had replaced the former Kremlin Mosque. The "Spasskaya," or "Savior Tower," stood at the opposite end of the Kremlin. In the storm, this tower nearly blended in with the gray clouds.

Andrei was unmoved by the magnificent architecture. "Kazan," he said.

Ever the conversationalist! She glared at him. *If I must have a constant companion, I wish he would have something to say. It doesn't even have to be interesting. Just something!*

"I don't see a thing, Andrei," she said, blinking as the wind and snow assailed her eyes. "Are you sure you are not imagining it?" She could not miss the looming city walls and knew full well that he was certain, but she wanted to pull some conversation out of him. Besides, he was all she had for company since her brother was so taken with Anna.

If he knew that she was baiting him, he didn't show it. His face betrayed no emotion. "Yes, it is. Look there." He pointed. "There are the walls of Kazan. Below them will be Staraia Tatarskaia Sloboda, the Old Tatar Quarter. Petr will probably want to stay there tonight. I will go and see if that is his plan."

Matrona hoped that it was not. She did not appreciate being quartered in a Tatar hovel in Nizhni Novgorod while Petr had secured lavish lodging for Anna and himself. Andrei had barely spoken to her, preferring to converse late into the evening with his cousin. Everyone had assumed that she would enjoy the company of the Tatar women and their squalling horde of undisciplined children. She had feigned exhaustion and went straight to bed.

However, Matrona was glad to see that since they left Nizhni Novgorod, Petr had spent a good deal more time with her and significantly less time with Anna. She guessed that he felt guilty about abandoning her and was trying to make it up to her. Consequently, she was unpleasantly surprised when Petr rode back to her sleigh to announce that they would indeed be staying in the Old Tatar Quarter.

"For God's sake, Petr," she responded angrily. "Doesn't Father have any friends in Kazan? I thought he had friends and associates in every city west of the Urals?"

"Don't blaspheme, Matrona!" he chided. "Yes, Father has a contact here, and I intend to visit him tonight. But it isn't safe inside the walls. The Tsar certainly has many agents in Kazan, but I doubt there will be any Oprichniki outside the walls where the heathen Tatars are forced to live. Most of the Muscovites still consider the Tatars 'Gog' and 'Magog,' devils incarnate and agents of Satan, and as cruel as the wind. Tatars are not allowed inside the City walls unless they convert to Christianity."

She replied, "From what I've heard, there is a lot of truth to that. Tamerlane certainly had a reputation for sacking Russian cities and erecting towers of human skulls to mark the occasion."

Petr rolled his eyes. "You forget that the Tatars ruled Novgorod for a generation, during which there were no atrocities. In fact, some of our finer citizens, like your protector, Andrei, are a result of that peaceful occupation. The Tatars were much kinder and abler administrators than the Tsar's Muscovite scum. And, in fact, the residents of Kazan are mostly Volga Bulgars. We in the West fail to discern the distinctions between the peoples of the East."

Petr went on to explain that the Golden Horde under Batu had killed a lot of Russians during their conquests in the 1200s, but that these were mainly war-related deaths and paled in comparison to the Tsar's blood lust. After Ivan sacked the Tatar garrison at Kazan in 1552, he had the mosques destroyed and the fortresses leveled. Not one to stop at inanimate destruction, he had the men eviscerated and beheaded, the women raped and transported into slavery, and the small children butchered because there was nobody left to care for them.

Matrona was unmoved. "Well, I still think the Tatars

deserved what they got."

Petr shook his head. "It says a lot about Muscovite rule that Christians must hide among the non-believing Inorodtsy, be they Muslim Bulgars, Tatars, or animists like the Voguls, Komis, and Ostyaks. These are the only places we are safe from our secular and spiritual leader, Tsar Ivan the Fourth."

Matrona was not about to be deterred by an unsolicited history lesson. "I've spent too many nights in hovels, tents, and lean-tos. According to you, the Tsar had agents in Nizhni Novgorod as well. Yet you and Anna spent the night among our people and left me in a Tatar shack."

Sneering, she pulled her robes up under her chin. "I imagine a Bolger shack on the Volga is not very different than a Tatar shack — filled with drafts, foul odors, and snot-nosed children!"

Petr was too tired and cold to argue. "Very well. As soon as I have secured the provisions and trade goods that we need, I will find accommodations for you."

"What about you?" Matrona asked. "Won't you stay with me? I don't want to be left alone?"

"I'll ask Anna to stay with you. I will be up much of the night preparing for our departure at first light. I don't want to stay in Kazan one more day than is absolutely necessary."

Matrona had mixed feelings about sharing her lodgings with the slave girl but sensed that she had pushed her brother as far as he was willing to go. Besides, she was uneasy about being alone in a stranger's house, and Anna would at least be familiar, if not necessarily welcome.

CHAPTER 17

Matrona smiled in satisfaction as she snuggled deep into the feather bed — a rare luxury even in Moscow or Novgorod. It had been a marvelous evening from the time they had arrived at the Moskvitin estate. Petr's contact, Boris Moskvitin, and his wife, Feuronia, accompanied by a dozen servants, met them on horseback at the main entrance to the Moskvitin estate — an elegant gesture in light of the harsh weather.

Once inside the Moskvitin's home, Matrona had been amazed at the opulence and finery displayed there. She had been surprised that this degree of sophistication existed this far from the center of the Empire. Even the dress of their host and hostess had been a delight. Master Moskvitin had been attired in the finest manner of Muscovite noble society. His apparel had consisted of multiple layers of clothing, which had befitted both the climate and the customs of the times that favored Greek fashion.

Moskvitin's headgear had also been layered, consisting of a small underlying silk skullcap, "tafya," with gold thread and bordered with pearls and precious stones. Worn over this had been a wide cap of black fox within which had been placed a "tiara," or long bonnet. The whole affair had stood upright for a Pope-like effect. Around his neck, Moskvitin had worn a jewel-encrusted three-inch wide collar.

Moskvitin's undergarments would have consisted of a shirt covered with a knee-length light silk garment called a "zipun," which buttoned down the front. The zipun, in turn, would be covered by a "kaftan" of gold cloth that hung to the knees. Around Moskvitin's waist had been a Persian girdle with attached cutting and eating utensils. The kaftan had been covered with a "feryaz," a loose silk garment trimmed with fur and gold lace. The outer garment, called an "okhaben," was made of fine cloth with long sleeves. It had a cape that was inlaid with pearls and attached with a jeweled broach. Since the many layers of clothing consisted largely of silk or other fine material, the total ensemble would have been surprisingly light.

Madam Moskvitin had worn a red silk skullcap with a white frontlet called an "ubrus." Over this had been worn a hood-like cap of gold cloth with fur trim. Around her neck, she had worn a jewel-encrusted collar that matched bracelets on both of her wrists. Her outer garment had been a loose floor-length scarlet gown with long sleeves. This gown, called an "opashen," was buttoned down the front with silver buttons and was set off by a broad cape edged with ermine. Under the outer garments, she had worn a long undergarment of silk called a "letnik."

The elegance of Madame Moskvitin had been diminished somewhat by her gaudy makeup. As was the custom in Moscow, she had painted her face in garish red and white colors. Matrona had found the effect hideous but had been careful to do nothing that would evidence her opinion. Her tact had been well rewarded. Madame Moskvitin had lavished attention on her as if she were her own lost daughter. She had declared that she could not have such an important guest take dinner without the benefit of proper attire.

Madame Moskvitin had given Matrona a beautiful blue gown with large gold buttons for the evening meal. She had stated that Matrona should consider it a gift. Madame Moskvitin had had it as a girl, and it no longer fit. Madame had applauded as Matrona had descended the stairwell, a picture of grace and beauty and the embodiment of refined nobility. Master Moskvitin's praise had been more subdued, but his furtive glances throughout the evening had demonstrated an acute appreciation of the ample cleavage revealed in the cut of the gown — and the carriage of its occupant.

Dinner had been taken with the noble women of the household. The Moskvitins had assumed that Anna was Matrona's servant and quickly ushered her upstairs to the servant's quarters. Matrona supposed she should feel a little guilty, but she was thoroughly enjoying her return to normalcy. Sooner or later, Anna would have to go back to her proper place, and Matrona was not going to let the fact that it was sooner, rather than later spoil her own evening.

Dinner had included two of Matrona's favorite dishes: "ikra," the roe of sturgeon that was being exported to the Italians, who called it "caviaro," and "pirogs," fritters filled with various fillings including minced meats, fish, and onions. There also had been, of course, much wine and vodka.

The ample food and alcohol consumed by Matrona had their way with her. After a few moments of warm reflection on the evening's pleasantries, she was fast asleep.

CHAPTER 18

Petr stared into the darkness. Some small evil was tugging at the edges of his consciousness, denying him sleep. He rolled the events of the day over and over again in his head, searching the edges and shadows for a telltale clue as to what was wrong.

Father Ivanov had been unsuccessful in getting directions to Chingi-Tura. Terrified of the Tsar, the local monks were uncooperative. With this exception, the day had otherwise gone smoothly enough. Late in the afternoon, the nasty wind that had been slashing at them for several days had finally abated. Boris Moskvitin had been delighted by their arrival, his enthusiasm only slightly dampened by Petr's insistence that he spend the evening in preparation for the journey up the Kama rather than partake of the hospitality of Moskvitin's home and hearth. Moskvitin obviously relished entertaining, and his disappointment with Petr's demurrer had been largely ameliorated by Petr's request that Moskvitin provide accommodations for Matrona and Anna.

Dressed in Muscovite finery suitable for a trip to the Kremlin, Moskvitin had appeared a bit of a dandy. But he had been gracious enough to assist Petr in securing the supplies needed for the long trip to Chingi-Tura. Most of the provisions had been taken from Safronov stores that remained intact despite the expansion of the Oprichnina in Kazan. Those supplies that had not been in these stores had been procured by Moskvitin and logged against Alexei's business accounts. Moskvitin had even dipped into his own private armory to

provide a dozen harquebuses and crossbows — an insufficient number to deter an army, or even a well-armed band of
Cossacks, but enough to dissuade any party of Inorodtsy that
might be encountered in the upper Kama or Urals.

Unfortunately, Moskvitin had limited supplies of gunpowder for the harquebuses. However, he had said that Alexander
Grigorov, one of his hunting companions, had more than
enough in store to supply Petr's needs. Moskvitin had invited
Petr to accompany him to procure the gunpowder. Petr had
expressed reluctance to reveal his presence and intentions to
anyone other than his father's agent. Moskvitin had insisted
that Petr come along, arguing that it would be difficult to
explain to Grigorov why he needed so much gunpowder for
his own use. Besides, Grigorov was a long-time business ally of
both Moskvitin and Petr's father. Moskvitin had been sure that
Grigorov could be trusted and pointed out that the Grigorov
estate was less than an hour's travel from the Moskvitin holdings. Petr had reluctantly agreed to accompany Moskvitin.

Upon their arrival, Grigorov had appeared delighted to meet
the youngest son of his "long-time friend Alexsei Safronov."
With much hugging and backslapping, he had insisted that
Petr and Boris join him in a vodka toast to friends and family and a tour of his estate. Not wishing to appear mysterious
or ungrateful, Petr had agreed to the tour. This had consumed
two hours that could have been better spent in preparation for
the journey ahead. The Grigorov estate had been unremark-
able except for the stables and carriage house, which appeared
impressive even by Novgorod or Moscow standards.

On reflection, this part of the tour had seemed more rushed
than their examination of the house, grounds, and other outbuildings. Most boyars were extremely proud of their equine
assets. Petr found it odd that the jewel of Grigorov's holdings
had received scant attention.

Petr rubbed his eyes, propped his head up with his coat,
smoothed out his sleeping robes, and tried to concentrate.

There was something troubling about the carriage house. Everything in Grigorov's demeanor had changed there. He seemed guarded — ill at ease. Once they had cleared the carriage house and stables, he had returned to being the gracious and boisterous host that had welcomed them upon their arrival.

Petr retraced their steps in his mind. They had walked quickly through the stables, pausing only to briefly admire a stallion that had caught Petr's eye. They had entered the carriage house through a workroom. There had been only one worker there, and he had quickly departed upon their entrance. Grigorov had dismissed him with a subtle wave of his hand. *Why had he left so abruptly?* Petr wondered. *We didn't pause for a conference or do anything that would have been compromised by the presence of staff.*

The stable hand had been working on something when they came in. *What was he up to?* Petr wracked his brain, but an impenetrable cloud of fatigue obscured any answer that may have been hidden there. He sighed deeply, pulled his sleeping robes up under his chin, and drifted off to sleep.

CHAPTER 19

Moskvitin lingered downstairs after the women had gone to bed. He considered sneaking into the bed chamber of the Safronov girl — Lord knows she seemed to enjoy the eyeballing he had given her. His ankles were sore from his wife's vicious kicks under the table. It was worth it, though. She was a delicious little Novgorodian morsel — a bit haughty but nonetheless delectable. Come to think of it, so was her servant. *Now, where the hell was she sleeping?* he wondered. *Well, I can't go rummaging through the house looking for diversions in the dark — no matter how delectable.*

In the end, greed won out over lust. Safronov was too good a business connection to lose over a woman. Moskvitin settled for a bit more vodka and one of his own servant girls who had come down to stoke a different fire. His sexual appetite was quickly sated on top of the clay stove. Spent, he dismissed the maiden and threw a sleeping mat on the pech', choosing the warmth of the stove to the cold reception that he was sure awaited him upstairs.

Before climbing onto the pech', Moskvitin went to the wood box in the corner of the room to fetch a few logs for the fire. Through the shuttered window above the box, he heard horses outside. *Probably a group of young boyars returning from some debauchery or other,* he thought. He smiled to himself, envying their lust and stamina. Ah, to be young again and quench his appetites in the night with no regard to time or propriety.

As he moved to the stove, Moskvitin heard several thumps on the outside of the house. *What the hell?* he thought. *I don't want them pissing all over the grounds, especially with guests in the house.* Angry now, he shuffled quickly to the main entrance.

"Partying is one thing; despoiling your neighbor's property is something else," he huffed to himself as he withdrew the bar that secured the door.

Stepping out into the yard, Moskvitin was immediately assaulted by thick, acrid smoke that caused his eyes to water uncontrollably. Coughing violently, he attempted to slide down the side of the building to escape the fumes. Instead he encountered a column of flames climbing the side of his home. He quickly moved away from the building with the intention of fetching the servants in the stables to fight the fire and seek additional help.

As he cleared the billowing smoke, Moskvitin detected several forms in the yard. He rubbed his eyes with his hands to clear the tears that obscured his vision. As he did so, he heard several guffaws from the darkness. As his vision gradually cleared, he made out several horsemen, all dressed in black. One of the horses looked familiar. He rubbed his eyes again, trying to clear them for a better look. As he looked up, one of the riders moved forward and raised his arm.

Moskvitin sensed movement — the hint of a shadow.

"Whaa—" The word died in his throat as the bolt from the crossbow passed between his eyes and out through the back of his head.

◊

It seemed like she had been asleep for only an hour or two when Matrona was awakened by a tug on her sleeve. Her eyelids were very heavy and resisted her weak efforts to raise them.

"Matrona, wake up!" It was Anna.

"Quickly, Matrona, you must get up. We have to get out of here now!"

Matrona was in no mood to be bothered at such an hour.

"Go away, foolish girl," she mumbled in annoyance. "Let me sleep. Didn't you hear Madame Moskvitin? Go back to the servant's quarters — you can't stay here!"

Switching her candle to her left hand, Anna grabbed Matrona's nightgown at the shoulders with her right hand and raised her into an upright position. "Get up now if you wish to live!"

The anger and fear in Anna's voice finally got Matrona's attention.

Matrona struggled to open her eyes. As soon as she raised her eyelids, her eyes smarted and slammed shut in a flood of tears. She rubbed frantically at them with her fists and tried to lie back down. Anna jerked her to her feet.

As soon as she was on her feet, Matrona began choking. She suddenly realized that the room was filled with smoke. With a rush of adrenaline, she was instantly alert to the peril that confronted her. Screaming in terror, she pulled away from Anna and ran for the door. Her mind clouded by fear and her vision obscured by smoke and darkness, she did not see the bench in her path. Matrona hit the bench in full flight, her momentum sending her cartwheeling into the doorframe. The last thing she remembered was a flash of light accompanied by a searing jolt of pain — then darkness.

Anna heard the thud when Matrona struck the doorframe, but Matrona had knocked the candle out of her hand, extinguishing the flame. With little light and the heavy smoke, Anna could not see Matrona. She called to her several times, but there was no answer. Anna dropped to the floor and crawled on her hands and knees, stopping frequently to sweep a hand out in front of her to locate Matrona. Anna was relieved to find that the smoke was much lighter near the floor, and she could breathe more easily. As she neared the doorway, the glow of the fire outside shining underneath it provided sufficient illumination for her to spot Matrona.

Crawling quickly to Matrona, Anna found her unconscious

but breathing. Anna stuck her head through the door open-ing and was horrified to see that the flames downstairs were eating into the vestibule and licking at the stairway. In a mat-ter of minutes, she would be cut off from their only escape route. She quickly grabbed Matrona by her gown and began to drag her through the door. Matrona's foot caught on the doorframe, and her gown tore away from Anna's grasp.

Frantically, Anna tried to get a better grip on the gown, only to have it tear away again. In order to improve her lever-age, Anna stood up with her back to the stairs. As soon as she was upright, the smoke assaulted her eyes, throat, and lungs. Gasping in agony, she reached down and grabbed two hand-fuls of Matrona's hair. She twisted the hair around her hands to gain a better purchase.

Anna squatted and, with a loud grunt, thrust herself back-ward, pulling Matrona free from the doorway. Blinded by the smoke and wheezing in pain, Anna carefully stepped back-ward, feeling for the top step with her toe. Locating it, she placed both feet on it and leaned forward to get a new grip on Matrona's hair. The bite of the smoke and the lack of oxy-gen were eroding her equilibrium. She almost fell down as she reached for Matrona. When she thrust backward, Matrona, now free from the doorframe, came more easily than Anna had anticipated. With a startled cry, she went over backward down the stairs. Matrona's weight falling across her legs pre-vented Anna from rolling down the stairs, but the back of her head struck the hard oak steps, and her world began to tumble through flashing lights and descending darkness.

CHAPTER 20

Petr tried to catch the reins of the big black stallion. It remained just out of reach. Frustrated, he tried a different tack. He took a carrot out of his pocket and stuck it out to the horse with his right hand, being careful not to extend his arm all the way. He didn't want to reveal the full extent of his reach to this clever creature. It was a bright day and very hot. Sweat ran into Petr's eyes, and he could barely make out the horse, but he could hear it pawing at the ground with its front hooves. It was interested — just a little more patience, and the horse would be his. He had never possessed such a horse. He pictured himself riding through a meadow of pink-purple flowers with Anna clutching his waist and breathing softly on the back of his neck.

The horse clopped forward. Petr willed his arm to quit quivering and relax. He felt the hot breath of the steed as it reached for the carrot. At the first hesitant tug, Petr released the carrot and grabbed the reins. The horse attempted to pull away, and for a moment, Petr had him, but the reins were rotten and slowly tore apart as the stallion pulled away from Petr's grasp.

The stallion ran over a little hill, and Petr dejectedly followed him. He tried to formulate another plan, but all thought eluded him in the glare of the sun and the bitterness of his disappointment. As he reached the top of the hill, he observed the horse entering a carriage house only half a verst or so away.

Now I have you! he thought. *All I have to do is close the doors, and you are mine.*

The walk to the carriage house seemed endless. First there was a pond that he skirted, and then a swamp to be waded — neither had been observable from the top of the hill. He was exhausted from the heat of the day and the suction of the swamp upon each step. He was drained of energy with each footfall.

Petr looked around, but nothing was recognizable. He could not determine the way forward and did not recognize the way he had come. Panic gripped him, and he began to hyperventilate. He was lost.

Frantically looking about, Petr saw movement off to his right. A slender woman of dark complexion stood at the edge of the swamp. She was waving to get his attention. She was beautiful and somehow familiar. She gestured for him to follow.

As he moved out of the swamp, Petr's feet seemed lighter, and his apprehension dissolved as the day brightened. The woman moved with an effortless grace that was mesmerizing. Try as he might, Petr could not cut the distance between them. At length, she came to a small hill and disappeared over the horizon. Petr hurried to the crest, but she was gone. But before him, in the distance, was a carriage house.

When, at last, Petr arrived at the carriage house, he circled it once. He was satisfied that there were no doors other than the one he had seen the horse enter. He entered the building and latched the door behind him. With the door closed, the interior was almost pitch black. In the gloom, his hearing grew keener, and he heard the rustling of mice in the hay. His own breathing was greatly magnified and seemed intrusive in the darkness. As hard as he listened, Petr could not hear the horse.

Somewhere in the darkness, Petr heard a scraping noise. He moved deeper into the building toward the noise. There was a small light in the distance. As Petr approached, he could make out a man carving or whittling on a piece of wood. The man worked with his head down and did not seem to notice Petr. Humming softly, he kept at his work as Petr approached.

Petr could not make out the object that the man was carving. He bent down to take a closer look, but the man placed a hand over it, obscuring Petr's vision. He wanted to see what it was — a small statue of the stallion, perhaps? Petr touched the man on the shoulder. The man looked up and smiled. It was a smile of deceit and betrayal — a Judas smile — it was Grigorov. Slowly his hand withdrew from the object. The smile on the object mirrored that of Grigorov, except it was not a human head — it was a dog's head.

Petr sat bolt upright in bed.

"My God. Grigorov is an Oprichniki," he shouted. "To horse and to arms."

The dozen men who, along with Father Ivanov, comprised the inner council of the refugees arose slowly from their sleeping mats on the monastery floor. Their planning session had lasted far into the night, and they were groggy from lack of sleep. Muttering in confusion, they fumbled wearily for their weapons.

"Quickly, men!" Petr shouted. "We have no time to spare. Anna, Matrona, and the Moskvitins are in grave danger!"

The men stumbled into each other as they exited the monastery door. Lacking the presence of mind to wait for directions and without knowing where they were going, at least half the men ran down the street in the opposite directions.

"Stop!" Petr yelled in exasperation. "Get your horses and follow me. It is at least four versts to the Moskvitin estate. It is too far to run on foot."

By this time, Father Ivanov had joined them.

"This way, men," he directed. "The stables are over here."

Ever the warrior, Andrei Stepanov was already in the saddle and ready to ride. Petr grabbed his reins and looked into Andrei's fierce Tatar eyes.

Petr spoke quietly so the others could not hear. "Be patient, my friend. We may need your fighting spirit this night. I don't want you riding into a trap alone. I may be able to get them headed in the right direction — barely — but I am no soldier — they know that. If fighting is required, they will need you to lead them into battle."

Andrei did not reply. He shifted impatiently in his saddle but did not leave. Like a coiled spring, he awaited his release to visit violence and vengeance on the hated Oprichniki. That opportunity had to wait a good five minutes longer as the tired men struggled in the darkness to saddle and mount their horses.

At last, they were in the saddle and on their way with Andrei and Petr in the lead and Ivanov at the back of the pack to restrain and encourage any stragglers. They pushed their mounts as much as they dared on the icy streets. The horses moved in muted thunder through the empty byways, their nostril blowing out small clouds of ice fog that obscured their riders. The men were silent — more surreal than menacing — gaunt men on a dark mission.

As they neared the Moskvitin estate, Petr saw a red glow in the sky in the direction of the residence. The warm glow sent chills down his back. It was either a bonfire or a house fire, and unless he had greatly misjudged Moskvitin, it was too late at night for the former. Ignoring the icy conditions, he lashed his mount into a full gallop. Behind him, a horse lost its footing and went down. The night was instantly filled with the shrieks of horses and the cries of men as two other horses tumbled over the fallen mount. Four of the riders fell out of the company to attend to the fallen riders. Petr and the rest pressed onward.

When the six remaining riders reached the entrance to the Moskvitin estate, they found the gate wide open and the night watchman lying face down in a pool of blood. He was impaled to the frozen ground by two crossbow bolts. As a weapon of war, the crossbow had been largely replaced by the harquebus. But due to its silent and deadly nature, the cross-bow remained the weapon of choice for ambush and murder.

The riders did not pause but made the sign of the cross as they galloped past the slain servant toward the conflagration that was the Moskvitin mansion. As they cleared the trees lining the lane into the estate, Petr saw a small band of riders with torches at the front of the house. At the center of the group was the nightmare stallion under its murderous master — Grigorov!

Sighting the approaching riders, Grigorov signaled to his band, and they rode off toward the back of the Moskvitin estate. Petr's anger impelled him to pursue the fleeing Oprichniki, but his concern for Anna and Matrona overrode his hot impulse for vengeance. One side of the house and the roof were totally engulfed in fire. A hundred feet from the house, Petr's mount slid to a halt. It refused to go any closer to the raging inferno that sucked the night air into a roaring vortex of noise and heat.

Petr dismounted and ran toward the house. *Where were his sister and Anna?* he wondered. *Where were the Moskvitins?* Then he spotted the body of Boris Moskvitin, and the sinking feeling in his stomach was so intense that it nearly brought him to his knees.

"My God," he shouted, "did they kill everyone before they torched the house?"

Andrei did not pause to answer but kicked open the door and bolted into the house. Petr was right behind him. Acrid smoke immediately assaulted their eyes, nearly blinding them. Petr fought to get his bearings. The fire on the outside wall had eaten through the shuttered windows and was lapping up the inside of the family room. The air from the open door fed the flames, and they shot toward the ceiling. The smoke cleared momentarily, and Petr caught sight of the stairway. Dangling over the side was an arm — the shapely arm of a young woman.

"There!" Petr croaked, his throat ravaged by the smoke and heat. "On the stairwell!"

Andrei sprang up the stairs with Petr on his heels. Matrona and Anna were just below the top landing — both unconscious. Andrei threw Matrona over his shoulder as if she weighed nothing at all and descended past Petr. Faint from smoke inhalation, Petr struggled to lift Anna. Twice he tried to get his shoulder under her, and twice he failed. He could feel his consciousness slipping away.

"No!" he screamed as the last of his adrenaline kicked in. He grabbed Anna by her hair and pushed himself down the stairs; he half crawled and half fell to the floor below. He retained his death grip on Anna's hair and thrust himself forward toward the door. Halfway there, he fell to his knees as his strength gave out, and he succumbed to the smoke. Growling like an animal and sobbing like a child, he strained to move forward. Petr's breath came in ever more shallow gasps. He felt himself slipping away — began to give in — drifting now — almost peaceful. And then there were hands — strong hands pulling him toward the light, even as it faded and slowly went out.

CHAPTER 21

In the darkness, there was only pain — it seared his lungs and tore at his throat. He tried to open his eyes. At first, his eyelids would not move, as if they had been sewn shut. He panicked in the darkness and strained to open his eyelids. Gradually they began to pull apart. As his swollen lids scraped over the dry surface of his eyeballs, he moaned loudly, and his hands instinctively shot toward his tortured eyes. Someone caught his wrists and pinned them to his sides.

"Be still, Petr — you're going to be alright."

It was Father Ivanov. Petr felt cool water flowing gently over his eyes, and the smarting slowly receded. Suddenly alert, Petr remembered the prostrate bodies of Anna and Matrona. He attempted to ask about their condition, trying to force the words through his scorched throat. But he could only muster a hoarse croak.

Ivanov smiled. "You sound like a wounded raven, my son. Perhaps you should let me do the talking for a while." Kneeling, he raised Petr's head and wet his lips with a small amount of water from a wooden ladle.

Petr sat up. "Anna!" he croaked. He tried to say his sister's name but only raised a rasping wheeze.

"Patience, Petr," the priest counseled. "You must go slowly, or you risk permanently ruining your voice. Anna and Matrona have both been revived. They could not have lain there long before our arrival. Praise God, they will both be fine due to the quick action of you and Andrei. However, I'm afraid that their power of speech is no better than yours."

Petr looked up at Ivanov and nodded his understanding. As he did so, he saw the reflection of flames flickering in the priest's eyes. With great effort, he threw off the robes that were sheltering him from the cold and thrust himself to his feet. Turning, his mouth gaped in horror and revulsion. What remained of the Moskvitin home was backlit by the blazing outbuildings that had caught fire from the house. The charred remains of the Moskvitins and their staff lay like grotesque steaming insects in the wreckage of the home.

Petr fell to his knees and pummeled the ground in rage. Spying his horse tied to a nearby carriage, he lurched to his feet and stumbled toward it — and his sword. Ivanov reached him first. He grabbed Petr by one shoulder and spun him around. Petr's face was a mask of hate. His eyes glowed red through layers of soot and ash.

"Kill!" he croaked. "Burn! Burn all!" Ivanov pulled Petr to him until their noses were only inches apart. The glare of the fire added to the blaze in the priest's eyes.

"Mark this well, my son. Some men's lives are measured in destruction and lust — lust for power, lust for revenge. The result is the same. Their legacy is ruined lives and scorched souls. If you reply in kind, this, too, will be your legacy. As these fires burn your heart, let them also cleanse your soul. Let this end here. Put it behind you. The path ahead is full of hardships. Revenge will be too great a burden to bear on this journey — for you and all the poor souls who rely on you to lead them to a safe haven."

His adrenaline spent, Petr fell to the ground — barely clinging to consciousness. Ivanov carried him to the carriage and gently placed him on a mound of fur robes. He poured a little more water through Petr's parched lips.

"Rest now, my son. You will be reunited with Anna and your sister soon enough."

Exhausted, Petr drifted into a restless sleep. In his dreams, he pursued dark riders through shadows and flames.

PART THREE

COSSACKS AND CALAMITY

CHAPTER 22

Kama River - Spring 1570

Anna awoke to the rattle of sleet against the side of the tent. Savoring the warmth and softness of her sleeping robes, she hunkered in and tried not to think about the raw day that awaited her outside. They were late in breaking camp, and she intended to take full advantage of the extra rest. Ivanov feared that any delay by the Novgorodians would give Grigorov an opportunity to alert his fellow Oprichniki in the Vyatka River. This would allow the Oprichniki to head off the refugees where the Vyatka joined the Kama. Consequently, Petr and the priest had been pushing them hard ever since they fled Kazan.

The refugees had passed the junction of the Vyatka and Kama two days ago, and there was little sign of any humans, including Oprichniki, if they could be considered human. Nevertheless, Petr and Andrei had posted sentries several versts from the camp in every direction except toward the river, which, due to the spring warming, had developed too many leads in its ice cap to allow for safe travel by any pursuers.

Anna had the tent all to herself. Petr had insisted that she and Matrona share a tent while their smoke-ravaged lungs recuperated from the fire in the Moskvitin house. As soon as she was well enough to complain, Matrona had demanded that Anna be moved to a tent with other servants. Petr had been angry, and rather than move Anna to another tent, he had moved Matrona in with a noble family. This family's eldest daughter had decided to take her chances with the Oprichniki and remain in Kazan rather than face the perils and hardship of the wilderness. Matrona's presence would help them fill the void left by the absence of their daughter.

Matrona relented, but it was clear that she was not happy with Petr's decision. In fact, it was quite clear to Anna that Matrona would never be happy as long as Anna was within a hundred versts of Petr. Matrona never acknowledged Anna's efforts to save her from the fire in Kazan. In fact, she had asserted that Anna had unnecessarily confused and frightened her. According to Matrona, the delay caused by Anna's panic resulted in both of them being trapped and overcome by smoke on the stairs. She also loudly pointed out that it was Andrei, and not her brother, who had come to her rescue.

For her part, Anna tried to keep her heart and mind free of any malice for Petr's sister. She understood that Matrona had led a sheltered and privileged life and was emotionally ill-equipped to handle the loss of her fiancé and the hardships of the trail. She supposed that Matrona needed the full attention and caring of her brother and felt that this would be denied her as long as Anna was on the scene.

In regard to Petr, however, Anna's heart and mind were far from free. There are forces of nature that are too strong to be bound by custom and tradition. One by one, the bonds of convention had been stripped away by hardship and misery. As they traveled deeper into the wilderness, the complex rules of *Domostroi* were but a faded memory, one locked within the walls of citadels that had long since disappeared from the western horizon. What was left was pure, honest, and strong — so strong that even the memory of her assault by the Oprichniki in Novgorod had been subdued and set aside. It would never be forgotten, but it could no longer cage the loving spirit that lay within her.

Forged in fire and fury, the bonds that connected Anna

and Petr were not to be denied. They were powerless to resist the current that swept them to a common destiny. She could no longer shun Petr — for his sake or hers. As winter gradually changed to spring, Anna's heart began to turn to Petr. Like a flower in the warm spring sunlight, she felt herself slowly opening to him.

Petr came to her the past evening, bringing boughs to freshen her bed and instilling in her head thoughts of receiving him there. She had tried to thank him, but while her lungs were healed, her voice was still wounded. The pain from the effort brought tears to her eyes. He reached out and gently traced the tear tracks down her face. Then, cupping her face in his hands, he looked into her eyes. They fell into each other's arms.

She was certain that they would have shared the tent, and the bed, had it not been for the arrival of the priest. He hailed the occupants of the tent before entering. Anna was sure that the blush on her cheeks and Petr's stammered greeting told the tale of their indiscretion. After all, Ivanov was widowed and could undoubtedly recognize the telltale signs of passion. Anna was certain that the blush on her cheeks glowed brightly in the gloom of the tent's interior.

Anna wondered if Ivanov had followed Petr. Petr's attraction to her was certainly all too apparent to anyone who was in frequent contact with him. Perhaps the priest intended to frustrate this union, a union that was at once unsanctified and contrary to the mores of Russian society.

Ivanov and Petr became engaged in a discussion of the travel plans and provisioning of the refugees. The discussion continued well into the evening. The later it got, the more miserable Anna became. It seemed that her dream of a relationship with Petr would come to no more than that, a dream.

I am just a foolish girl, she thought. *There is a gulf between our worlds that can never be breached. How brazen and stupid it was to try.*

She busied herself, rearranging her bed and straightening

up her meager possessions, to hide the tears that seeped from her eyes despite her best efforts to hold them back.

All the "what if?" and "if I but only" moments of her time on the trail flooded her thoughts:

What if I had not rejected his attention in Nizhni Novgorod?

If only I had been more sympathetic and paid more attention to Matrona.

What if I had sought the counsel of his friend Andrei?

If only I had been more direct — less difficult.

What if I had not divulged that I was a slave?

Anna knew that what was done was done and that no amount of wishing and hoping could undo her past actions, her station in life, or the hopelessness of her desires.

At length, Petr rose and took his leave from Ivanov. As he departed, their eyes met, and in his gaze, she saw desperation and despair that matched her own. Then he was gone into the night.

The priest's voice was quiet and soothing. "Your heart is heavy, my child. And your spirit that has bolstered so many of our people on this journey is now weak. Your face is etched in pain and despair. You must give these over to our Lord. Only his love and guidance can make you whole again."

Anna sank to the ground, and great sobs wracked her body. "Father, what I want is sinful and unholy, yet I cannot stop the yearning — even though I know I should!"

"No, child — what you desire is human. With all the madness and violence in this world, I doubt the Lord will look unkindly at a loving heart."

She looked up beseechingly at him. "But this love is unsanctified, and marriage between masters and slaves is against the Russian order."

He smiled and reached out to her, pulling her to her feet. "If you have looked around at all, which I know is difficult when one is young and in love, as once so was I — believe it or not — you would notice that all signs of Old Rus have long since disappeared over the horizon. The Tsar may claim these lands, but Russian order and Russian society have not yet taken root here. These are pagan lands, and I'm sure our Lord will look with favor on any Christian union that occurs here."

She shook her head. "But if Petr were to marry me, it would ruin his reputation in Novgorod!"

"Ah, at last, you mention his name," he said teasingly. "I was beginning to wonder who we were dealing with here."

"You know full well, as I suspect everyone else in the group does," she continued. "Even so, I cannot bring myself to call him by his first name. I am still a slave, and the Safronov name has great stature in Novgorod, as well as here, where the Safronovs are well known among the trading enterprises. To marry a slave would bring the entire family into disrepute."

"Novgorod the Great is no more," the priest countered. "Those that remain will be under the dominion of Muscovy. The Safronov name will only get you tortured and killed. And as far as this region is concerned . . ." He paused for a second to reflect and then continued.

"I've been gentle with Petr about this, but the Novgorodian traders, like the Muscovites that are replacing them, are little more than river pirates. From this land of the Urdmurts and Komis, through the lands of the Voguls and Ostyaks, they have stolen and plundered the natural wealth of the native peoples. The fur trade is ruined by overharvesting due to the greed of our Russian companies. No, the Novgorodians have no great stature here — only fear and hatred."

"There is still the matter of Matrona," she said dejectedly. "If I were to marry Petr, it would devastate her."

Ivanov shook his head. "No, you have been nothing but kind to her. Matrona must deal with her own demons. She has chosen a selfish path and must find the way back on her own — hopefully with God's help, if she will ask for it."

The priest kneeled, and she followed suit. "Now, let us pray on these matters."

They prayed silently, side by side, for several minutes. Then he rose and made the sign of the cross over her.

"Be at peace, my child. You are young and in love. Any happiness in these troubled times is an elixir for the soul. I will speak to Petr on this at the first opportunity."

Then he was gone into the night.

In the darkness of the tent, Anna wept tears of joy, and for the first time since she had floated on summer waters with her father in the land of the midnight sun, she was truly happy.

CHAPTER 23

The day was raw. The wind from the northwest brought a mixture of snow and rain that stung their faces and turned the snow pack into a granular mush. Men and horses alike struggled to make forward progress in the icy quagmire. Throughout the long winter trek, the refugees had prayed for a break in winter's icy grip. Now they longed for the once-firm footing that had been turned to slush by the warmer temperatures. Soon the snow would turn to mud, and those in sleighs would be on foot.

The Kama, though still icebound, was beginning to stir. Every day, more leads were opening in the ice, and the river was mumbling like an old man coming awake. It was no longer safe to travel on the river ice, and the refugees were forced to struggle along its banks. The traverse on shore was more difficult due to the uneven terrain and the lack of a well-defined trail. Often the path they followed appeared little more than a game trail, more suited to a hoofed animal than a large band of refugees.

Anna anxiously scanned the trail upriver. Petr and Father Ivanov had been gone for two days. The pair traveled ahead to scout out the trail and look for a location to make camp for an extended period of time should spring breakup make traveling totally impossible. Andrei, who was nursing a bad case of ague, was left in charge of the main body of refugees.

At first, Anna was not concerned. Lately, Petr seemed a new man. No longer the urbane artist from Novgorod the Great, he took to the wilderness as if he were born to it. In the early days of the journey, he had exuded an edgy bravado that Anna knew masked a tremulous spirit. Since they left Kazan, however, Petr had led the group forward with a quiet confidence that buoyed their spirits in the face of an unpleasant present and an uncertain future.

The events of the preceding day had become a cause for apprehension for the safety of the two scouts. Early in the day, the outriders had spotted several men observing the party from a distance. When they had ridden toward them, the strangers had melted into the thick brush, where the horses were unable to follow. The wet weather was unsuitable for the harquebus, and Andrei deemed it unwise to follow their trail into the brush for fear of an ambush.

Several more times today, figures had been seen in the forest, and it was clear that the refugees were under observation. Concerned about the intentions of the strangers, Anna had asked Andrei for his opinion of who they were. He suspected that they were Komis but did not know for certain. He, too, was suspicious of their intent.

Up until this point, Anna had been anxious about the conversation that she felt would certainly take place between Petr and Father Ivanov concerning her relationship with Petr. This concern had been replaced by her fear for the physical safety of Petr and Father Ivanov as they traveled lightly armed through potentially hostile territory.

Late in the afternoon, the weather worsened with increased wind and driving sleet. Andrei called an end to the day's trek, and the party made camp in a clearing on the lee side of a small ridge. It offered some protection from the wind without placing them dangerously near the forest, where it would be impossible to detect any impending danger.

After securing her tent, Anna climbed to a position just below the top of the ridge and maintained a vigil for the missing scouts. In the lowering gloom just before dark, she discerned a dark shape slowly making its way down the trail. Her heart sank as she saw that it was a single horse.

"Oh God!" she cried out. "Let it be Petr!"

She ran down the hill, calling to Andrei and a dozen or so men who were tending to a community fire. "A rider!" she shouted, waving and pointing. "A rider!"

"Where?" Andrei reached for his bow.

She pointed up the trail.

As the men rushed off to meet the rider, Anna stood immobilized, too fearful to follow or even look.

What will I do if it is not Petr? she thought. *How could I go on without him?*

Until now, she had not fully realized how central he had become to her existence. Over the many days on the trail, she had gradually come to realize that she loved him. Now it was instantly clear that her whole world revolved around him. He had become as essential as sunlight and air. Through the perils and hardships of her journey, he had been her strength. Now, in his absence, he was her weakness, and Anna, the survivor, had little experience with weakness.

Forcing herself to move, she walked slowly down the trail with her head down, not daring to look up.

Then she heard Andrei call out. "Be careful with him. He is in bad shape!"

Then she heard, "Petr ... Petr ... Can you hear me?"

Anna's head instantly snapped up. Before her was Petr's stallion, standing unsteadily on wobbly legs. Astride the stallion were two figures covered in ice and virtually frozen to his back. Sitting upright was Father Ivanov, who was holding on to Petr, slumped forward and barely conscious.

"We went through the ice," croaked the priest. "Crossing a feeder stream; it was safe yesterday. Should have known — my fault. Praise God that we are still alive."

He pried his left arm off of Petr's waist. His arm was stiff, as if frozen to Petr's cloak. "My horse drowned, thrashing at the ice. I was tangled in the reins. Petr pulled me out, but it exhausted him."

The men supported Petr as he was lowered to the ground.

Anna wanted to rush to him — throw her body onto him and pour her warmth and love into his frozen body. But she could not move. Decades of tradition and years of training held her back — kept her away — in her place.

Andrei quickly took charge. He ordered several men to pry large rocks out of the riverbank and place them in the fire. As the priest was led away to his tent, Andrei directed that Petr be placed in a tent where his frozen clothes could be removed and he could be placed under robes and furs to warm him. The tent was small to conserve the warmth.

In the flurry of activity, no one noticed the forlorn figure weeping quietly in the driving sleet and gathering gloom.

It was long after the heated stones had been tucked into Petr's bedding and the last man had returned to his tent or post that Anna made her way back to her own tent.

As she lay in her sleeping robes, she called out to God. "Father, forgive my selfishness for wishing that Petr instead of Father Ivanov would survive — and for taking so much of Petr from his sister. Let thy will be done, Lord. Show me the way, for I am weak and confused. But, oh God, I do love him so. Take me if it is your will, oh Lord, but please spare him."

CHAPTER 24

The current was slow but steady. Visibility was poor, as there was no moon. A dense fog hung over the water. The craft was narrow and unstable but easily cut through the water. He should be making good headway, but he kept bumping into things in the dark — soft things and heavy. He was glad that they were not hard, as the craft did not seem sturdy. It appeared to have been made from the skin of a birch tree, if such a thing were possible.

He pulled on his paddles with all his might, but the river was fighting him. There were more of the objects now, and he had trouble getting his paddle into the water. It felt like he was moving through a pumpkin patch — or cabbages, perhaps. He was very hungry. A cabbage would make a fine meal.

He boated one paddle and rested the other across both gunnels for stability. Keeping his weight centered, he carefully reached into the water and felt for one of the objects. The water was surprisingly warm; body temperature, or slightly warmer. Several objects bumped into his hand, but he was unable to grasp them. The current was swifter than he thought.

Something bumped the bow, and he swept his hand back and forth in the water, feeling for it. He felt a coarse and stringy object brush his hand. With one motion, he grasped the tendrils and heaved the thing into the boat. He couldn't see what it was at first — didn't want to — tried to look away. It bumped into his foot — then bumped again as if demanding attention. He felt his heart pulsing — heard it pounding like some giant drum in the canyon of his chest.

His eyes became very heavy — they strained at the sockets as his lids stretched and threatened to tear away. His neck bulged as the muscles struggled against the overwhelming weight of his eyes. They pulled his head down — his face forward.

The object rolled toward him — then back. It came to rest between his feet — inches from his face. He wanted to scream — tried to scream. But revulsion sucked the wind from his lungs, and terror squeezed his chest like a vice.

Between his feet was a rotted and bloated head. Worms crawled from the nostrils, and it stunk of decay. With the rolling of the craft, the eyes bulged hideously from the sockets, and the tongue lolled onto the deck. Even in its advance stage of decomposition, it was familiar — all too familiar — and that was the horror. It was Dimitri.

His head snapped up. The fog was heavy — and cold. He frantically groped for the head. It eluded his grasp, and he clawed at the deck in desperation. Finally he found it — his fingers puncturing the putrefying flesh. In revulsion, he hurled it out of the boat into the mist. He expected a splash — heard none, only a dull thud in the darkness. His skin crawled, and the hair stood up on the back of his neck and arms. He tried to paddle frantically away from this dreadfulness, but the craft barely moved. He was immersed in mud — or gore. He dared not look, but his eyelids would not close.

It became brighter. He began to rejoice that the fog was dissipating. But the lifting fog soon revealed his recent horror magnified. A sea of severed heads stretched to the horizon. As the heads undulated in the waves, their luminescent eyes bored into his soul — a thousand eyes projecting but one accusation.

His mind reeled with madness, and he began to sway from side to side. Fearing that he would upset his craft, he lay down on his back and clutched the gunnels. From the darkness, he heard a mellow, high-pitched sound like distant bugles.

Woo-ho

Woo-woo

Woo-ho

Suddenly, the sun breached the eastern horizon, and a golden shaft of light bathed two giant swans as they flew toward the rising sun. They passed so close that he could have touched them — wanted to — began to raise his hand — felt the soft caress of the wind from their flight feathers . . .

Petr opened his eyes — felt fingers lightly stroking his hair. He looked up.

It was Anna. "You had a bad dream, Master."

The images of the mist returned — chilling his soul. A frigid blast of air knifed through the tent flap. He trembled uncontrollably.

"I'm so cold. So awfully cold," he moaned.

She quickly removed her clothes, slipped beneath the robes, and pulled him to her. His conscience rebelled at first, but she was his love and so warm — so soft. They were alone in the darkness, and the world was far away. And he was cold and lonely and so very hungry for what she offered.

CHAPTER 25

When Petr awoke, Anna was gone. The rain and sleet that had chilled them to the bone yesterday had departed during the night. A shaft of sunlight thrust through an opening at the flap. It turned the murk of the tent's interior into a fine golden glow. Water droplets from the tent poles pattered onto the skin of the tent, lulling him toward sleep. The entire band of refugees was exhausted — Petr included, especially after yesterday's ordeal. The spring storms that alternated between snow, sleet, and freezing rain had taken their toll on everyone.

Outside the tent, Petr could hear the cheery *dee-dee-dee* of a nearby chickadee. He was warm and sated. Smiling, he turned onto his side and pulled the sleeping robe up to his neck.

Suddenly there was a great commotion in the camp. Petr could hear women screaming and the shouts and curses of angry men. He quickly pulled on his clothing and boots and exited the tent. People were running everywhere. The band of Novgorodian refugees had swelled to over two hundred at Kazan. It appeared that they were all on the run.

The blast from a harquebus brought a sudden halt to the milling of the crowd. Peter could see mounted men with pikes and harquebuses at the south end of the camp. Those with pikes were prodding the inhabitants of the tents into the open and herding them toward the center of the encampment. Not satisfied with the speed of this endeavor, one of the riders touched the match of his harquebus to the touchhole, sending another blast into the sky. It had the desired effect, and the refugees quickly streamed out ahead of the riders.

Petr headed for the tent of Anna and Matrona. There were no riders with pikes in his immediate vicinity, and he did not fear the harquebus. This precursor to the musket was inaccurate and difficult to fire. It had a slow match that was soaked in potassium nitrate and dried so that it smoldered when lit. The match ember had to be applied to the touchhole to ignite the piece. In damp weather, neither the match nor the powder were reliable. When a number of harquebuses were assembled on a fair day, the resultant volley could be devastating to massed troops. Fired singly, however, they served mostly to frighten civilians and troops unfamiliar with firearms.

Petr called to Anna and Matrona, who quickly emerged from their tent. When he saw Anna, his heart missed a beat in a flood of emotions that swept over him. He could see the fear in her eyes and wanted to gather her in his arms. His arms, however, were quickly occupied by his sobbing and terrified sister.

"Oh, Petr, what is it? Have the Oprichniki caught us?"

Petr stepped back and held his sister at arm's length. "You must get control of yourself, Matrona. The riders do not have any of the attire or paraphernalia of the Oprichniki. In any event, we will need our wits about us to confront this new danger."

Matrona choked back her sobs and collected herself. "Well, who are they then? They are certainly not very friendly!"

Petr studied the riders for a moment. Most had chain mail body armor, called "kol'cuga," over their winter wear. A few had short-sleeved chain mail shirts with square metal plates called "iushman;" others had another type of armor called "zertsalo" that consisted of a round metal plate over the chest with smaller plates over the arms and neck.

Petr said, "They could be Komi-Permyaks or Udmurts, perhaps even Cheremis. I have heard that there is a great deal of unrest among them due to the influx of Russians into this region. But from the look of them, I would guess that they are

Cossacks. Let us hope that they are 'gorodovyee kazaki' and that there is an ataman present to control them."

The Cossacks were adventurers, pillagers, and wild men of the frontier who constituted a constant annoyance to Ivan, the Christian Tsar, and the Muslim Suleiman the Magnificent. Originally mostly Tatar, the Cossacks were now a blend of Tatar and Slav. Some, the "gorodovyee kazaki," or town Cossacks, were fairly civilized and offered token allegiance to the Tsar. The free Cossacks, however, continued to constitute a threat to trade and settlements on both sides of the Urals.

As Petr, Matrona, and Anna joined the refugees assembled in the center of the encampment, Petr had an opportunity to observe the riders. About fifty in number, they were heavily armed with swords, pikes, and harquebuses. Most were swarthy and unkempt. They maintained a steady stream of curses and crude comments directed toward the women in the camp.

There were a few riders that hung back from the main group. They were silent and did not take part in herding the refugees. They appeared to be Western Russian: Muscovite, or even Novgorodian, perhaps.

Petr looked for Andrei but could not locate him. The situation was getting ugly, and Petr could use Andrei's sword and his presence. Unfortunately, Andrei and Father Ivanov had gone ahead to locate a campsite and would not return until midday.

The refugees outnumbered the riders, but a third were women and children, and most of the men were lightly armed, unskilled in martial arts, and exhausted.

When the refugees were fully assembled, a large Cossack with a grizzled full beard and a ferocious countenance rode forward to address the group. "You are trespassing on Stroganov land! By whose authority are you here?"

All eyes of the refugees turned to Petr. He felt a great weight settle on his shoulders. Petr took a deep breath to still his racing heart and stepped forward out of the crowd.

Petr was familiar with the Stroganovs. They were a wealthy and influential family. The Stroganovs were originally from Novgorod, but their political alliances had always been Muscovite. In 1445 and 1446, the family, under the guidance of Kouzma and Louka Stroganov, had helped ransom Tsar Vasily II from Tatar captivity. That deed had cemented the family's political influence in Moscow, and succeeding Tsars had granted them major trade and development rights on both sides of the Urals.

For the past two decades, the patriarch of the family had been Anika Stroganov. He was a patron of the arts and known for developing salt mines that made him rich and for building churches that further bolstered his political standing. Alexsei Safronov had maintained an active trading relationship with Anika. He had told Petr and Nikolai that the old man was in ill health. The family enterprises were now run by Grigorii Stroganov, Anika's eldest son. Petr hoped this knowledge would serve him now.

"I am Petr Safronov from Lord Novgorod the Great," he announced in a firm voice that he hoped sounded more confident than he felt. "My family has been friends and trading partners with the Stroganovs for many decades."

The burly Cossack guffawed and looked around as if sharing a joke. He then leaned menacingly forward in his saddle. "Then you should know, Petr Safronov, that the Stroganovs have enrolled his family in the Oprichnina — and you, and your wretched companions, do not look like Oprichniki to me."

"Well, you do not look much like an Oprichniki either, so I would guess that black attire and dog's heads are not needed to travel on the Kama," Petr replied forcefully.

"Besides," he lied, "I have read the Tsar's 1558 Charter to Grigorii, and he granted only trading and development rights. He did not grant the exclusive right to occupy the land. You would be wise to let us pass."

Petr heard of the charter from his father but had not read

it. He was banking on his assumption that none of the riders were literate and, even if they were, had not been afforded the opportunity to read the charter.

His antagonist was silent for a moment. *I have misjudged this one*, Petr thought. *He is both intelligent and cunning, and I may have overplayed my hand.*

The rider straightened his back, rose up in the saddle, and thumped his chest with a clenched fist. "I am Ivan Krasnoff. I am a Cossack! I wear what I choose, ride where I want, and come and go as I please. You, the Tsar, and the Oprichnina are so much dung to me," he roared.

He pointed at Petr. "I will decide what to do with you." Krasnoff studied Petr for a few long minutes before continuing.

"You probably assume that I have not read the Stroganov Charter, and you would be right. But you are not out of the woods yet, young Safronov. I will shortly determine the truthfulness of what you have told me." Krasnoff paused and looked over the band of refugees. "Where are you going with this motley band?"

Petr looked him hard in the eyes. "We are merely passing through on our way to Siberia. We have no intention of staying within Stroganov Charter Lands."

The Cossack raised his eyebrows, and then laughed uproariously. "You are taking this rabble 'beyond the stone'?" He used the Cossack term for crossing the Urals, perhaps referring to the large vertical rocks that lay along the Chusovaya River. "We should be merciful and kill you now!"

With that, he wheeled his horse to the north and trotted out of the encampment. The Western Russians followed him.

Watching them depart, Petr hoped that Andrei was his usually alert self and would manage to avoid being captured.

CHAPTER 26

After Krasnoff's departure, both refugees and Cossacks quieted down for a time. The Cossacks even permitted a few men to leave the group to relieve themselves in the nearby forest. No women asked for such an accommodation. Petr was not surprised, given the lecherous looks that the Cossacks directed toward every female over the age of ten.

Gradually, the sun climbed higher in the sky, and the refugees sought dry spots to seat themselves in the sea of mud that had once been a frozen trail. Many were forced to stand as the Cossacks would not allow them to spread out. Consequently, the refugees remained in a tightly packed throng along the trail.

As the day warmed well above freezing, clouds of small black flies emerged from the nearby swamp. They soon began to plague refugees, Cossacks, and horses alike. Petr was surprised that this horde of biting insects could arise from what had been, only hours before, an icy muskeg.

As the sun passed its zenith, the relatively peaceful coexistence between refugees and Cossacks began to deteriorate. The Cossacks began to curse the insects and their miserable surroundings. A short, stumpy Cossack began to gallop his horse up and down the trail, spattering everyone nearby with foul-smelling mud.

One of the Novgorodian men who was covered with mud from the Cossack's sport shouted out to him. "Why don't you relax for a while? Your leader should return soon, I should think."

The stumpy Cossack rode up to the man so that the nose of his horse was right up to the refugee's face. "No, you shouldn't think," he sneered. "Perhaps you don't understand the situation here. I do what I want — and you shut up if you value your life!"

Several of the other Cossacks moved in next to the short one. The refugees nearby began to shrink back from the confrontation. Encouraged by his newfound audience, the Cossack continued:

"I don't know where Krasnoff went, and I don't know when he will be back. What I do know is that I am damn tired of guarding this wretched mass of exiles. It would not trouble me to put you all to the sword. In fact, I would rather enjoy it. I haven't had any real entertainment since we burned a Vogel village last fall."

The Cossack turned to his companions. "What do you think, men? Shall we skewer a few of these Novgorodians just for fun?"

The crowd of refugees shrank even further back from the Cossacks. The speechmaker, buoyed by the attention he was receiving from his comrades, rode forward and began to jab at the crowd with his pike. As the individual refugees jumped away from the menacing blade, they sent their companions sprawling in the mud. This drew a hearty laugh from the Cossacks.

When he tired of this game, the sporting Cossack began to ride up and down the trail, eyeing the women. When he found one to his liking, he would stop and look her up and down with a long, lecherous stare. Then, pursing his lips and rolling his eyes, he would poke at her shoulders with the blunt end of the pike until she pirouetted for further examination by him and his colleagues.

"Look at this wench! Not as sturdy or as comfortable as a Cossack woman, mind you, but she could supply some sport on the trail, eh?"

Petr realized that he should get Anna and his sister out of sight as quickly as possible. He caught Matrona's eye and motioned with his head for her to move back into the crowd.

He looked for Anna. She was several feet away and frozen with the fear. The carnal assault that she had experienced in Novgorod was beginning to play out in front of her eyes once again. Petr slowly slipped up next to her and gently tugged at her sleeve. Startled, she whirled around to face him. With a gasp of relief, she buried herself in his arms.

He was overwhelmed by despair, by pity — by love. He wanted to cry — to shout — to take her inside him and run from this place.

The Cossack's pike slid between them — the sharp blade cutting their clothing. The squat Cossack sat with a smirk on his face, the pike in his hands, and danger in his eyes. "You don't think you can cut into our sport, now do you? We don't want to keep her — just borrow her for a time. There'll be something left for you — maybe."

He began to laugh, but it stuck in his throat as Petr suddenly stepped aside and jerked down on the pike. The Cossack went head-first into the mud. He looked up just in time to catch Petr's boot square in his face. All the sport left his body in a great shudder.

Petr stood shaking as the adrenaline coursed through his body. He was torn between flight and fight. But where could he flee? He couldn't abandon Anna, and there were too many of the Cossacks to fight.

A burly Cossack with a hooked nose rode up to Petr and pointed his harquebus at Petr's chest. "Well, you have fire in your belly, Novgorodian. I'll grant you that. But you'll soon have more fire than you can handle."

Petr wanted to duck — dodge the projectile before it found him — but knew he could not. If death did not find him, it would make its mark in the crowd beyond. The world slowed down. He watched the match as the glowing ember arched toward the touchhole. He closed his eyes — waited for the discharge — heard the blast — felt its hot breath on his face. But there was no pain, only silence — then a soft gasp, and a quiet thud.

Petr opened his eyes. Anna lay before him, a steaming red stain expanding on her breast. Her eyes searched for his — found them. Her face softened as if the pain had suddenly lifted. With a primal cry, Petr knelt beside her. With a trembling hand, she gently touched his face.

"Petr," she whispered — for the first and last time.

Petr collapsed onto the ground. Gently placing Anna's head in his lap, he rocked back and forth — staring at her — stroking her hair — gently at first, then harder — trying to will her back to life. Finally he stopped. Tears streaming down his face, he looked beseechingly into the sky — his arms were raised in futile supplication.

"Why?" he whispered.

He pounded the ground, smashing his knuckles into a bloody pulp. "Why?"

"Why God?" he thundered. "Why her? Why the innocent?"

Then Petr spotted the Cossack who had fired the fatal round. His eyes narrowed, and his face reddened in fury. The Cossack, seeing Petr's demeanor, hastily began to reload his harquebus. He reached into an ammunition pouch on his hip, but his panic overwhelmed his coordination, and he dropped the first ball he removed — then a second.

Petr jumped to his feet — his Tatar blade glistening in the afternoon sun. Other Cossacks moved in with their pikes at the ready, but Peter was so focused on Anna's murderer that he saw nothing else. He was poised to spring when the wrist of his blade hand was seized in a vice-like grip.

"Easy, my friend. Do not be so eager to throw away the gift that Anna just gave you."

It was Andrei. He encircled Petr's chest with his other arm and slowly dragged him back into the silent crowd. Petr's bloodlust began to recede into a gulf of grief and despair. Suddenly, he remembered Matrona. He frantically scanned the crowd to see if she was there. To his horror, he spotted her weeping at the side of Anna.

Unfortunately, the squat Cossack whom Petr had deposited in the mud had revived and had also spotted Matrona. He stood glowering above her — licking his bleeding lips. "So — all is not lost. We have a replacement for our sport — better than the first one, from what I can see." He poked at her clothes with his pike, chortling at his own cleverness.

Andrei released Petr and sprang forward to grasp the pike of a nearby Cossack. In one swift motion, he tossed the Cossack onto the ground as if he were no more than a pitchfork full of hay. Dodging vicious pike thrusts by two other Cossacks, he ran to confront the Cossack menacing Matrona.

"I'm taking this one, Tatar!" the Cossack snarled.

"You will have to kill me first, Cossack," Andrei replied in a firm and level voice.

An unfamiliar voice said, "That won't be necessary. There will be no more bloodletting this day."

The Cossacks moved aside to let this new speaker through. The Cossack who was squared off with Andrei was in no mood to give up his "sport," however. "Who dares to tell me what to do?" he snarled.

The speaker emerged from between the Cossacks. He was mounted on a beautiful Arabian stallion and clothed in a rich outer cloak, or "odnoryadka," of fine camel hair and fur. His cape was open to reveal an inner collar encrusted with pearls and other jewels. His boots, like his saddle, were of rich Persian leather called "saffian." His saddle was adorned with cloth of gold. The fine garments and stately bearing clearly marked him as a "boyarskiy," perhaps even an aristocrat.

He rose up in his saddle to speak. "I dare tell you what to do. You have been paid quite handsomely to do just exactly what I tell you. I gave strict orders that except for bandits or raiding parties, you were not to attack travelers in this region."

He turned to Krasnoff, who had just ridden up beside him. "He is one of yours, Krasnoff. I believe you have a Cossack tradition to handle situations such as this?"

"Well, I don't think we will find any sand, but we can improvise," Krasnoff replied.

The Cossack punishment for insubordination was to tie a bag of sand to the condemned man, place him in a sack, and throw him into the river.

Krasnoff pointed at the squat Cossack who had attempted to assault Matrona. "This one has always been a problem. It is time for the problem to go away."

Krasnoff waved his hand, and several Cossacks set upon the offending Cossack and trussed his arms and legs with leather straps.

The aristocrat rose in his saddle to address the crowd. "I am Yuri Kachalov, agent of the Stroganov family and administrator for this region." He looked down at Anna's remains and shook his head in obvious disgust. "Who shot this woman?"

The nearby Cossacks quickly moved away from Anna's killer, who stood defiantly glaring at Kachalov.

Kachalov was undaunted by the man's insolence. "Well, since your companions have been so kind in identifying you, perhaps they will also prepare you for the same treatment that your friend over there will receive."

He pointed to the Cossack who had been trussed and was now lying face down in the mud. The man struggled to keep from drowning in the ooze.

Krasnoff and several of his aides moved to bind the Cossack who shot Anna. As they approached him, the man spat fully in Krasnoff's face. Krasnoff calmly wiped the spittle from his face with his sleeve. He paused for a few moments, smiled — and then hit the Cossack with the back of his hand, sending him sprawling onto the ground.

The man struggled up on one knee, wiping the blood

from beneath his broken nose. "You call yourself a Cossack, Krasnoff. You are nothing but a dog groveling at the feet of any master who will throw you a few coins."

Krasnoff kicked the Cossack in the head so forcefully that he was thrown onto his back. Standing over the man, he pulled his head up by the hair. "A smart Cossack obeys his ataman. Since you are not very bright and have chosen to disobey, you will receive the Cossack punishment for insubordination."

Krasnoff bound the man's wrists and ankles and then motioned to one of his subordinates. "Bring me a sack."

When the sack, a large bag used to carry dry goods, was handed to Krasnoff, he pulled the open end over the head and shoulders of the stunned man. Two of Krasnoff's aides then grabbed the open end of the sack as Krasnoff lifted the man by his heels and dropped him into the sack like a fish in a creel. The open end was then lashed closed with a leather thong. In short order, the other bound Cossack was similarly bagged.

The Cossacks then carried their insubordinate companions to the edge of the river and set them down on the bank. Krasnoff leaned over the sacks to speak.

"We generally throw in a sack of sand to speed the punishment. But since you are such stalwart Cossacks, I'm sure you won't mind the extra swim."

Before the condemned men could be tossed into the river, Father Ivanov appeared out of the crowd and approached Kachalov. "Permit me to attend to the spiritual needs of these men before they are put to death."

It was more of a demand than a request, but Kachalov, recognizing the religious zeal in Ivanov's eyes and not willing to expend time or energy to confront it, readily acquiesced. "Very well — come away from those wretches so that the priest can attend to them — not that I think it will do any good."

Krasnoff guffawed loudly. "They are not Christians — or Muslims either, for that matter. So why are you wasting our time, priest?"

Ivanov was unperturbed by Krasnoff's outburst. "Their lack of religion explains their behavior — and yours, no doubt," he said calmly to Krasnoff as he brushed by him. "At least I can attend to their original sin, and perhaps, if they are truly repentant of their foul deeds, they will yet attain a state of grace. I will pray that it is so."

Petr had been silently watching the activities as they unfolded. He was in such a state of shock and grief that he was unable to participate in any act of retribution. He turned and walked into the crowd. He had little interest in watching yet another horrible death and even less in the salvation of the condemned Cossacks.

Father Ivanov noted Petr's departure and then kneeled to perform extreme unction over the ill-fated Cossacks. The murderous Cossack lay silently on the ground and said nothing as the priest performed the death ritual. The other Cossack, whose primary sins were insubordination and lust, sustained a low-wailing lamentation in a tongue that was unfamiliar to the priest. When Ivanov was finished, he made the sign of the cross over each man, rose, and returned to the crowd of refugees.

The Kama had begun to break up, but the spring floods from its headwaters in the central Urals had not yet arrived. Consequently, an ice shelf extended a dozen meters into the river. Beyond the ice shelf were open leads of water filled with slush and small ice blocks.

Four Cossacks grabbed each of their sacked comrades and proceeded gingerly out onto the ice shelf. If this shelf of undetermined thickness were to break, they would all perish.

This seemed of little consequence to Krasnoff, who hollered at his men to hurry up. "You men act more like Nogais than Cossacks. That ice will hold right up to two 'sazhen' at least."

When the men were about fourteen feet from the river's edge, they heaved the sacked men toward the open water.

Much to the amusement of the Cossacks on the shore, both sacks stopped several feet short of the nearest lead in the river ice. One of the lightest members of the river party cautiously edged toward the condemned men. He had gone only a meter or two when the ice shelf groaned and cracked under his weight. Panic-stricken, he spun around to run back, only to fall unceremoniously on his rump. Frantically, he clawed at the ice in a swimming motion that gained more derision than distance.

Gales of laughter erupted from the Cossacks on shore.

"Silence!" thundered Ivanov. "Have you no reverence for life — no regard for your fellow man! Indeed, perhaps you are animals and not men," bellowed the priest.

"We're as holy as your Tsar, priest — I understand he enjoys a little sport such as this himself!" bellowed a beefy Cossack. This comment brought another roar of laughter from his companions.

Kachalov, who had tired of this nonsense, rode up to the beefy Cossack and handed him a pike. "Perhaps you are as nimble on your feet as you are with your tongue. Go on out there and push those men into the water — and be quick about it."

The man blanched and began to tremble.

"Get on with it, man," Kachalov ordered. "We haven't got all day."

Greatly relieved that they were off the hook, the other Cossacks on the ice shelf patted their companion on the back and mumbled their encouragement as he trudged forlornly through them. Using the sharp end of the pike for support, the Cossack shuffled across the ice toward the condemned men. Twice, he fell only to bolt to his feet in terror. The Cossacks on shore bit their lips to keep from laughing. They did not want to join in their comrade's deadly, dangerous, and gruesomely comical detail.

When he neared the condemned men, the beefy Cossack eased onto his belly, and extending his arms as far as he could, he poked at them with the blunt end of the pike. Unfortunately, he could not gain enough purchase from this position to force the sacked men into the water. The man lay upon the ice, paralyzed with fear.

"For God's sake, man — get it over with!" shouted Kachalov.

The Cossack prodded the condemned men with the blunt end of the pike several more times to no avail. Then in desperation, he rotated the pike and pushed it into the sack containing Anna's killer. Even with the noise dampened by the cloth, the shriek of the man could be clearly heard by all on shore. A great red stain appeared on the side of the bag.

"That is enough!" shouted Ivanov.

He strode out onto the ice. The Cossacks in the execution detail quickly parted in the face of his withering glare. He stepped over the Cossack, who was sprawled in fear on the ice, grabbed the first sack, and dropped it over the edge of the ice into an open lead. There was an audible sucking sound, and the sack quickly disappeared under the ice. He then threw the second sack into the water. It circled lazily in the slush for several moments before it, too, was sucked under the ice.

Ivanov turned, grabbed the sprawled Cossack by his clothing, and dragged him over to his awe-stricken comrades. He then strode to shore and melted into the crowd.

CHAPTER 27

Petr lay on his bed of fir boughs, staring at the ceiling of the tent. Outside, Cossacks hooted and cursed as they gambled and argued at their guard posts near the edge of the encampment. The air was heavy with a hundred nervous conversations as the refugees sorted out the events of the day and speculated about what would happen tomorrow. Smoke from the cooking fires curled in through the tent flap, adding to the gloom of dusk and despondency. Rivulets of tears from the acrid smoke joined the stream of despair that was wrenched from his body and soul.

Petr was aware of none of this. His mind was ensnared in an endless web of remembrance and remorse. He was unprepared for grief. Before today, before Anna, he had lost no one. He had been close to no one, not even his family. His father had permitted more interaction within the family than was customary, but the members of the family were merely familiar, not really close.

The horror of the sack of Novgorod and their perilous flight through the Russian wilderness had changed all that. A number of people now meant a great deal to him: his sister, whom he had largely ignored until that fateful night when the Oprichniki descended on them; stalwart Andrei; the indefatigable Father Ivanov; and most of all, Anna — Anna from whom he had drawn courage for his flagging spirit and love for his empty heart.

She was gone now, gone to Rus', the Holy Russian Land. She had been interred in an icy ravine and covered with logs instead of earth because the ground was frozen, as frozen as the hearts of the men that inhabited this wretched land. Holy indeed! The Tsar was holy — the Church ordained it — the murdering, debauching, pillaging, torturing, holy Tsar.

And what of Anna; was her soul now in hell because she had lain with Petr? Because the same churchly hand that had anointed the foul Ivan had not passed over her before she died? And was her own remorse not enough to save her soul? Did she have remorse? Petr did not — only pain, and grief — and guilt. If only he had sent her to his tent. If only she had stayed in his tent. If he had been less confrontational — more diplomatic — swifter — slower . . . If only he had been more courageous and faced death head-on with his eyes open. He could have stopped her — should have stopped her.

The tent flap parted, and Father Ivanov stepped into the tent.

"Forgive the intrusion, my son, but knowing your heart, I feel we must speak."

Petr sat up — swiped at the tears with his sleeve — and attempted to collect himself.

"I appreciate your concern, Father, but I'm afraid there is little to be said — nothing to be done." He felt sobs welling up in his throat and lay back down on the mat.

Father Ivanov sat down next to Petr — grasping his shoulder firmly but gently. "I did not come here to give you a sermon, Petr. I am here as a friend — to talk — nothing more."

Petr took a deep breath — when he let it out, it came ragged with pain and despair. "Words cannot bring Anna back, Father. And the time for action is long past. There are things I could have said — should have said. But I said nothing. The kind words that swept my mind never crossed my lips. The love so deeply felt never gained expression. I have been the good Russian — cold, detached, and cruel in my silence. She gave her soul so that I might take carnal nourishment from her body. She gave her life so that I could live. I gave nothing and took everything."

The priest took a deep breath — let it out, rose, and paced back and forth several times before replying. "Do not place this burden on your heart or your conscience, Petr Alekseevich. The burden of things unsaid is universal. With each passing of someone dear, the silent litany of words unspoken echoes in our hearts and minds. Our lips are sealed by our humanity. Sometimes it is apprehension. Sometimes it is ignorance or confusion. But without malice, there is no guilt — no sin — only sadness and regret."

Petr sat up; his brows arched in anger — his face etched in bitterness.

"Forgive me, Father, but I do not fear sin. Anna was a kind and gentle soul — an angel here on earth. Yet she was enslaved, ravaged, and killed while the foulest of men reign in butchery over our blood-soaked land. Where is the heavenly justice? Why has the Lord turned his face from the loving and turned a blind eye to the wicked?"

"I cannot presume to know the mind of God, my son," the priest replied calmly. "The question of why bad things happen to good people has troubled church scholars for centuries. I think it will be many centuries before it is answered. Perhaps only in death will the answer be revealed to us."

Peter snapped, "If we die in sin, we go to hell. The church is very certain of this!" Petr continued, "Anna lay down with me, so her soul is doomed. But the Tsar can torture and murder thousands, and his soul is secure since he is God's agent on earth. What kind of God has such an agent?"

Father Ivanov was silent for several minutes. Petr's anger gradually subsided, slowly leeched away by his tears. He lay back down, silent and broken.

When the priest continued, it was almost a whisper. "Listen closely, my friend, for what I am about to say could cost me my life — and yours. You must not confuse the contrivances of man with the word of God. It has been many centuries since Jesus spoke to man, and then mainly in parables.

Over time, these parables have been twisted in many ways to suit the vanities and schemes of clerics and kings. Do not let these men drive you from God. Open your heart, and God will speak through it — love is the language and the salvation. Grieve for your loss, Petr, but do not mourn the death of Anna — for she is with God. You know this in your heart — I know you do!"

"I want to believe you, Father — truly I do," Petr replied. "But it is difficult to reconcile a kind and just God with our so-called Holy Russian Empire."

Ivanov's eyes narrowed, and he bristled with outrage. "This blending of the ecclesiastical and secular authorities is but another contrivance to benefit the clergy's greed and the monarchy's thirst for power. Twenty years ago, the monasteries possessed a third of the arable land in Russia. When confronted by Ivan IV Vasilevich the Terrible, Metropolitan Makariy became Makariy the sheep. He made a pact with this devil Tsar so that the Church could retain most of its landholdings. The cost was the installation of this madman as the spiritual ruler of Russia."

Petr slowly shook his head in disbelief. "Saying things like that has resulted in many of the free thinkers in Novgorod being tortured and purged, Father. You are a well-known Church zealot. I do not understand."

Ivanov smiled slightly. "The mask of the fanatic is my contrivance, Petr. You see — I am also a man. I'm afraid that such machinations come easily to men. That is why it is so difficult to find God with our minds. We must search within our hearts through prayer and meditation."

"But you still hold Mass, preach the Gospel, and attend to the Holy Obligations, Father," Petr retorted.

"I am a zealot for Jesus Christ, Petr. I will gladly endure dogma and politics to carry his word to the people in darkness. While I oppose many of the Church's tenets and virtually all of its administration, I keep my own counsel. I do not wish to end up like Matvey Bashkin or Feodosiy Kosoy."

Bashkin, who arose from the petty boyars, had been a heretical freethinker from Moscow. He had refused to worship icons and rejected most of the Church's sacraments. He and his followers had rejected bondage and serfdom. After being tried by a Church council, he had been imprisoned and later burned at the stake in 1554.

Kosoy had been a runaway serf who, in the 1550s, preached against Church landholdings, the Church hierarchy, monasticism, and obedience to religious and secular authorities. He had opposed the social order with its feudal organization of Church and State. He had rejected the Trinity and taught that the Church's liturgy and rites, as well as icons, prayers, and fasts, were the product of human legends. His evangelical teachings had centered on the principle of "love thy neighbor." He had been imprisoned but escaped to Lithuania.

Having lived in Novgorod, where there were many more heretics than in Moscow, Petr had heard of the teachings of Bashkin and Kosoy. Despite his shock and grief, he was astounded by Ivanov's revelations. "Are you a freethinker like Bashkin and Kosoy, Father?"

"No, Petr, I support most of the Church's fundamental sacraments. Even if they are not all divinely inspired, most are valuable tools for teaching Christ's message. The majority of men need structure to focus their thoughts and discipline their actions."

"Well, we Russians certainly don't lack structure and discipline, Father," Petr replied. "Between the Tsar and Metropolitan, our activities and even our thoughts are well regulated."

"Yes," the priest agreed. "Thanks to our Tsar, the Empire and the Church are inextricably intertwined. But here on the Kama, we are at the edge of that empire."

An angry shout followed by much laughter came from one of the Cossack guard posts.

The priest stood up and peered out from the tent flap.

"Listen to those voices, Petr. They are heathen voices. These men pay no allegiance to the Tsar or Metropolitan. They are no more evil or holy for it. They have no need for church and state. Yet they need Christ's love and forgiveness to lift their souls from barbarism and depravity. That is why I am on this journey — to carry the Word to the Ostyaks and Voguls — the Komi and Nogais — the Samoyeds and Nenets, and the unknown peoples to the east."

Petr stood up and approached the priest.

"Father, you are a good shepherd and a good friend. But my heart is locked in despair. There is no room for love. There is no light in my soul. It is black with hatred. God may forgive the Cossacks for their deeds here today, but I doubt that I ever will."

Father Ivanov shook his head sadly. "You must begin by forgiving yourself, Petr. Time and circumstances will take care of the rest. Will you receive my blessing, my son?"

Petr kneeled before the priest. "Yes, Father, but I doubt that the Eucharist will ever again cross these lips. I am sorry if this disappoints or offends you."

"Then I will pray for both of us, Petr Alekseevich. I have faith that the divine spark within you has not been extinguished. You may have forgotten the Lord, but he will remember you."

The priest made the sign of the cross over Petr, turned, and stepped out into a cold drizzle and the gathering dusk.

Matrona drifted in and out of sleep. Her eyes were closed, but she had the sense that the sun was well up. She was only slightly more awake than asleep. The morning camp's sounds of wood-chopping and rattling utensils seemed muted and far away. It had been a long and mostly sleepless night with the wind howling through trees, as if nature itself was grieving yesterday's human toll.

She felt the warmth of the sun on her face and opened her eyes to see if Petr or Andrei were about. The tent flap had been pulled back, and the sun blazing through the opening temporarily blinded her. She quickly closed her eyes but noted that the guard that Kachalov had placed in front of her tent had been changed during the night. She was relieved to note from his attire that this guard, like his predecessor, was a Muscovite rather than a Cossack.

After the insubordinate Cossacks had been executed, Kachalov had placed Andrei under guard. Matrona had been cowering at Andrei's side, clearly terrified by the presence of the Cossacks. She had begged Kachalov to place her in detention with Andrei. In response, Kachalov had ordered all but the four Cossacks holding Andrei to leave.

Kachalov then dismounted and addressed Andrei. He had pledged upon his honor as a boyar that no harm would come to either Andrei or Matrona. He stated that it was his intention to talk to the priest and Petr to figure out what to do with the refugees. But in the meantime, he would be taking no chances, and Andrei would remain in detention until morning.

In Kachalov's view, Andrei, with his fierce Tatar glare and outward belligerence, clearly presented the greatest threat to the order of the camp. Kachalov had kept this view to himself and ordered the Cossacks to place Andrei under guard. Andrei said nothing and did not resist as he was led away.

After the detention group departed, Kachalov approached Matrona. She shrunk from him as a horse shies from a snake.

"Do not run from me, my lady," he said. "For I am the only source of civilization you will find in this wilderness."

Matrona took several more steps backward.

Kachalov smiled and lowered his voice. "Please come closer so that I can talk to you without yelling. It is quite unseemly for a gentleman to shout at a lady."

Matrona shook her head but stopped and retreated no further.

Kachalov continued in a soothing tone. "It is wise that you fear the Cossacks. With all my master's wealth and prestige at my disposal, I can barely control them. But I assure you that I will let no harm come to you. You are a beautiful and sensitive woman, a rare treasure in this godforsaken region. It will be my honor and privilege to protect you and those close to you."

Matrona raised her chin and glared at Kachalov. "Under my current circumstances, I have no choice. I must trust you. However, you certainly make yourself sound a lot nobler than your conduct warrants."

Kachalov smiled. "I hope that in time, you will be able to put this madness behind you and will look upon me more favorably."

At first, Matrona protested the placement of a guard at her tent. Kachalov pointed out that there was a vast difference between being guarded and being under guard. The leer of a passing Cossack was all the argument she needed, and she had retired without further protest.

Matrona wept bitterly as she lay in the tent with the wind wailing through the forest. She felt abandoned and alone. The horrors of the previous day ran through her mind again and again. Time after time, the Cossacks had probed her body with their animal eyes. Over and over, the harquebus filled her mind — the match slowly entering the touchhole, the awful discharge, and the ugly hole appearing in Anna's breast. She wanted to run — to hide. She wanted out of this awful tent, this forbidding wilderness.

Where was Petr? Where was her brother? He should be here for her. In her mind, the crowd parted, and the harquebus appeared yet again. But this time, Petr was there, his face reflecting all that he felt — the shock, the despair — the love. Matrona pounded on her mat — not in anguish, but in rage. Suddenly, she stopped and sat bolt upright.

My God — I'm jealous.

The revelation hit her like a hammer. She wasn't grieving Anna's death or her brother's loss. She wasn't even traumatized by the gruesome execution of the Cossacks. She was feeling sorry for her own displacement, her misery, and her lack of love. She was feeling sorry for herself.

With the discovery of Dimitri's death, Matrona attributed all of her miseries to the loss of her fiancé. It gave her a reason to withdraw inward and cease communication with those around her. She realized now that what everyone mistook for grief was only the petulant sulking of a spoiled child. Even in the horror of Anna's death, she had found more resentment than grief.

Matrona had bonded with Anna at first — two fugitives sharing the same troubles and turmoil. But then Matrona watched her brother fall in love with Anna. Whereas she had once had all of Petr's attention, she then had been forced to share. She had resented this terribly. Consequently, she had become detached from Anna, angry that her brother had been more interested in this slave than his own sister's welfare.

Matrona threw herself onto the mat sobbing, but this time in remorse and shame. After she cried herself out, she began to take stock of her actions and her future.

CHAPTER 28

Kama Salt-Works

Slipping down the edge of the large wooden tub until the water was just below her nostrils, Matrona luxuriated in the warm, soapy water. This was her second bath in as many days, yet it still felt like years since she had been warm and clean. She remained conflicted about Yuri Kachalov, but she definitely loved his tub. She took full advantage of it for the two days they were at the saltery. Kachalov — she couldn't bring herself to call him Yuri despite his insistence — had settled her in his house. He took up residence in the small guest house that had been constructed for the infrequent visits by the Tsar's emissaries from Moscow. The rest of the Novgorodians were in tents uphill and upwind of the saltworks and its heavy smoke.

The Cassocks had departed downriver, and Matrona had been relieved to see them go. Petr had had a look of hatred every time he saw one of them, and she had been afraid he would do something reckless.

Matrona had to admit that Kachalov was generous, even gallant. But she knew that their ultimate safety depended on their ability to move out of Stroganov lands. The Stroganovs maintained their power and influence at the whim of the Tsar. The Stroganovs had huge land holdings in the Kama region and had consolidated the political and commercial power in the Western Urals. She doubted that Kachalov would risk the Stroganovs' wealth and influence to protect and nurture a band of Novgorodian refugees.

Matrona was glad to leave the responsibility for the safety of the refugees to Petr and Father Ivanov. Neither shrank from this burden, but the misery of the trail and the loss of Anna had taken a heavy and obvious toll on Petr. Gone was the youthful artist of a few short months ago, replaced by a haggard warrior who managed their destiny by instinct and force of will.

Matrona knew that she had changed as well. The spoiled and petulant girl that had fled Novgorod had been shaped and toughened by the hardship and grief of the trail. After Anna's death, she had taken an inward journey and did not like what she found there. With the help of Father Ivanov, she had resolved to take responsibility for her actions and meet head-on whatever challenges or opportunities life presented.

At that time, her greatest opportunity and challenge was Yuri Kachalov. Matrona could tell that he was smitten with her despite his best efforts to hide behind his command persona. In her mind, it was still in doubt whether his interest in her was due to her character and appearance or if it was merely a manifestation of the shortage of refined women on the frontier. For her part, she found him physically attractive but was put off by his excessive display of authority. She sensed that if she ever got him off his horse to hold a decent conversation, he may well prove to be a pleasant companion. At present, this remained purely speculative and would probably remain so for their short stay in the region.

For the time being, his interest in her served the needs of the Novgorodians. While she doubted Kachalov would harm the refugees in her absence, she was quite confident that without her, he would have pushed them quickly through the settlement and on into the wilderness despite their wretched physical state.

In the short time they had been at the saltworks, the spirits of the refugees had lifted substantially. From the camp, the chatter of women and the laughter of children filled the air.

A number of Novgorodian men were laboring at the works in payment for the provisions that had been supplied from the Stroganov's stores.

Matrona learned from a conversation with one of the few women in the Stroganov settlement that a raid from an outlaw band of Tatars in the fall had resulted in the loss of many of the Russian workmen. The ready supply of labor supplied by the Novgorodians undoubtedly contributed to Kachalov's decision to allow a lengthy respite for the refugees. She realized that he was on the very sharp horns of a dilemma. The presence of the Novgorodians offered a practical solution to a labor issue. It also created a dangerous political situation that could bring down not only Kachalov but his Stroganov masters as well.

The water in the tub was beginning to cool, and Matrona climbed out to fetch a cauldron of hot water from the hearth. At home, she would have had servants to perform such tasks, but home no longer existed. She paused for a moment, remembering the comfortable room in Novgorod that she had left behind, with its lavish carpets, rugs, pillows, and robes.

Matrona quickly banished the image of her former life of luxury from her mind. Novgorod was gone, washed away in a sea of blood. She was determined to confront her new life as a frontier woman head-on. Toward that end, she resolved to become self-reliant. She would start by learning domestic skills from the women in the settlement willing to teach her, even if a measure of subservience was required to attain these abilities.

As she stepped back into the tub, Matrona noticed how spare her flesh had become on her arduous journey. She had always taken secret pride in her ample breasts, which were now substantially reduced. As she slipped into the water, she thought of Yuri Kachalov staring at her from his horse. She was startled to find her nipples hardening and quickly tried to force this vision from her mind. It was stubborn, however, and she was soon awash in a sweet tension that she could neither eliminate nor control. Every touch of her fingers or ripple in the water sent a wave of pleasure through her very core.

She had felt such stirrings before, of course, but never this strongly. As she took a deep breath, the sensation of pleasure left as abruptly as it arrived. Suddenly the small hairs on the back of her neck stood up, and she was seized by a cold chill. She instinctively threw her hands across her breasts. She sensed that someone was in the room with her, and her eyes darted frantically from corner to corner, seeking the intruder. But she neither saw nor heard anything. *It is the Lord punishing me for my weakness of the flesh*, she thought. In any event, the fear and embarrassment meant that the pleasures of the bath were at an end. Matrona quickly dressed and prepared herself to face the new day that would soon be breaking over the Urals.

CHAPTER 29

Frol adjusted his position in the dense thicket. His body movements were so slight as to be imperceptible to anyone or anything less attentive than a hungry owl on the hunt. Only his eyes were in constant motion as he searched for any movement toward the house below.

The house was isolated. The natives in this region were peaceful, and the Stroganovs had constructed the saltery first. Just like the Russians, profit came before all else. Winter had halted work on the stockade, which would eventually shelter most of the inhabitants, but not yet.

Frol had been studying the movements of its occupant for several days and was ready to make his move. His horse was tethered several yards behind him in the darkness. There was not enough cover to conceal them both in the daylight. It was now or never.

Frol had slipped away from the main band of Cossacks during their first night on the trail back to the Don River. The Don was the homeland of one of two major branches of the Cossacks. Frol's "voisko," or clan, had heeded the call of the great Ataman Nikita Mamin to fight on behalf of Tsar Ivan against the marauding bands of Tatars that were making frequent incursions along the Volga and into the heart of Russia.

Under the leadership of their local ataman Krasnoff, Frol's band of Cossacks moved north. Krasnoff quickly abandoned Mamin's call to raid Tatar lands. He had agents in touch with the Stroganovs and knew that these lords of commerce had suffered substantial losses in men and profits. They would pay him dearly for what Mamin and the Tsar would have them do for free. Besides, the Volga villages along their journey to the Stroganov holdings would yield much more booty than the Tatars, and they would put up less resistance. The Cossacks could raid these villages at will on their way to and from the Kama salt works. If they happened to run into a band of raiding Tatars, it would provide an opportunity to serve all the masters, real and pretend.

Frol's last name, Tatarinov, indicated that his family's origin was Tatar, but that caused him little concern. The Cossacks were a mixing pot of Russians, Greeks, Tatars, Poles, Georgians, and many other Asian and European ethnic groups.

The word "Kazak" in Tatar meant "Freeman." For many years, the principle of the Cossacks was "S Donu vydachi net.": There is no extradition from the Don. Escaped Russian serfs and other refugees from throughout Asia and Europe found a safe haven among the Cossacks.

Frol found it bitterly ironic that he had lost his brother in an altercation with a band of refugees who, by tradition, should have been directed to the Don, where they would be welcomed into Cossack society. To be sure, there was no denying Bogdan's lechery and stupidity. But Frol could not tolerate Krasnoff's subservience to Kachalov and his Stroganov masters. If Kachalov had not been present, the punishment for Bogdan's lechery would have been a thrashing at best. Now, the boyar would have to pay, and since Kachalov had no relatives at hand, the object of his desire would have to suffice.

The young Novgorodian woman was certainly ripe, and it was clear that Kachalov was there to do the plucking. He had cleverly separated her from her companions and settled her in his own house, which was isolated from the rest of the compound. This undoubtedly impressed her and gave Kachalov greater access to her company. It also provided Frol an opportunity to abduct her from under Kachalov's nose. If she had stayed with the refugees, she would have been under the watchful eye of that half-breed Tatar who was never far from her side. Now she was isolated from him, her brother, and Kachalov.

Frol slowly slipped out from his cover and moved quickly toward the house. A light snow was falling, and he was barely perceptible in the pre-dawn shadows. He reached the house without being detected and edged along the outside wall until he was adjacent to the door frame.

◊

Matrona stoked the fire in the fireplace and began to brush her hair. It would take a while to heat the house to a comfortable temperature, and she was glad for the fur robe that Kachalov had provided. She smiled as she caught herself counting her brush strokes. Beauty habits die slowly, even here in the wilderness. As Matrona brushed, she quietly hummed an old nursery tune her mother had sung for her when she was a child. She remembered how safe and comfortable she had felt in her mother's arms as she had drifted slowly off to sleep.

But her childhood was a fantasy world now, severed by time and distance from her present reality. Gradually, Matrona forced her mind into the present. As she did so, she became aware of a faint intermittent tapping at the door. Her spirits quickly brightened. Kachalov had been feeding a huge raven who had quickly taken to the new occupant, who was twice as generous with the bread and table scraps. In a few short days, Matrona had the bird eating out of her hand. Now, each day, she looked forward to the tapping of the bird on the outside of the door. She had yet to think up a good name for the smart and affable bird. Perhaps today would be the day.

As she lifted the door latch, the thought crossed her mind that it was awfully early. The bird usually showed up after Alexsei checked on her. But it was too late. The door was thrown violently inward, the edge striking her across the face, knocking her onto the floor. Stunned, she had no time to react as a heavy sack was pulled over her head. The sack muffled her screams. She fought for air, and her mind reeled. As she struggled against the darkness, she was keenly aware that her naked legs were sprawled out from her robe. *Yuri will not want me now*, she thought as darkness descended.

◊

Frol was mesmerized by the sight of the nearly naked woman on the floor. For a brief moment, lust and greed battled for his commitment. It had been a long time since he had been with a woman, yet he knew an unspoiled woman would bring a higher price on the slave market. She was a haughty brat, and he had no doubt she was unspoiled. It would be a delight to wipe that arrogance off her face. A shout from the distant camp interceded in his internal debate. Any carnal release would be of little consequence if he was caught and they cut off his balls.

Frol rolled Matrona up in a bear rug, tied off both ends with a stout cord, and threw her over his shoulder. Oblivious to her weight, he sprinted up the hill to his horse. He tied her securely across his horse and, leading his mount on foot, he slipped quietly out of the thicket. Before the first ray of sunlight hit the cabin, he was well into the nearby forest. He moved quickly, as he had thoroughly reconnoitered this area in planning his escape.

Several versts into the forest, Frol located a small stream that flowed from the east to form a fork, one branch flowing west and one south. Dismounting, he walked his horse eastward up the main steam. The streambed would hide any marks of his passage, and any pursuers would assume he headed toward the Don, taking the southern branch of the fork. Even if the would-be rescuers split their search party, the majority would go south, thereby improving his chances for escape. There were many streams with countless tributaries in this region. At each junction, he would halve the remaining pursuers until there was only one remaining. And Frol was a Cossack. He was not afraid of any one man.

CHAPTER 30

Andrei studied the stream carefully. The sun was up, but it was a gray day and very dim in the larch forest. He was on his hands and knees, looking for the smallest mark that might provide a clue as to the direction taken by Matrona's abductor. The trail through the forest indicated that there was only one person involved in the kidnapping.

Andrei had routinely checked on Matrona at dawn. Today, he found her door wide open and Matrona missing. In his haste to escape, Matrona's abductor made a major mistake by not closing the door behind him. If the door had been closed, Andrei might have concluded she had left for the day. By the time her absence would have been noticed and a search of the saltery and refugee camp completed, most of the day could have passed. It took Andrei only a few minutes to get his horse, alert Ivanov, the first person he encountered at camp, and return to the trail. He doubted he was more than an hour or two behind in his pursuit.

The abductor was undoubtedly one of the Cossacks. The native Komi were not bold enough to attempt a kidnapping from the Stroganov enclave. Some of the Cossacks were still smarting from Kachalov's punishment of their brethren. One in particular, Frol, the brother of one of the executed Cossacks, had been eyeballing Matrona before the band left for the Don. Perhaps he had circled back to gain retribution.

After several minutes, Andrei found what he was looking for. One of the horse's hooves had clipped the edge of the stream bank upon entering the water. The angle of the indentation pointed upstream to the east. He gathered three pieces of dead wood and made an arrow pointing upstream to guide the search party that would eventually follow. Then he entered the water and proceeded upstream.

Andrei felt the small hairs on the back of his neck stand up. He was no coward, but this was a dangerous undertaking. He must stay in the stream in order to discover where Matrona's abductor exited onto its bank. But if his quarry checked his back trail, Andrei would be a sitting duck. He could wait until the rescue party arrived and have the safety of outriders, but that would afford Matrona's abductor time to cover his trail.

Andrei had one advantage. Matrona would be a burden to her abductor, slowing him down and distracting his attention. Andrei would risk the solo pursuit; his brother would expect no less.

◊

Matrona slowly became aware of her surroundings. Her temples throbbed with pain, and her ribs ached from being slung head down over her abductor's horse. She could hear water splashing from the horse's hooves and knew they were traveling in a stream. She guessed it was fairly small as she couldn't hear any flowing water. Her surmise was confirmed when she was smacked by a branch that was hanging over the stream. Her face smarted from the blow, but she remained still. She wasn't sure what would happen if her captor knew she was conscious, and she had no desire to find out.

Matrona hurt everywhere, but her instincts told her she had not been raped. Her abductor had been in a hurry. Perhaps he was waiting for a more opportune time when he was safe. Or perhaps he just wanted her conscious so he could enjoy her pain.

Her despair was interrupted by the slap of another branch. This one momentarily hung up in the cords securing the bearskin rug. As the branch pulled free, it loosened the cords. The stream must have been narrowing because the branch impacts became more frequent, each one gradually loosening the bonds securing her.

Matrona became fixated on her bonds. If only she could breathe fresh air and feel the breeze on her cheeks. It would be a measure of freedom, perhaps enough to sustain her through the ordeal to come. But the frequency of branch strikes diminished and then quit altogether.

Matrona slipped into deep despair. She was unaware of the passage of time. She was one with the horse, her body mindlessly accepting every lurch and jolt of its journey upstream. It could have been mere minutes or many hours before the horse came to a halt. Matrona was only vaguely aware that they had stopped. She remained perfectly still as gnarled fingers tugged at the cords, pulling the bear skin apart and removing the sack from her head.

As her head was jerked upward by her hair, Matrona opened her eyes. She had seen him before, the crooked nose and the long scar running down his cheek — one of the Cossacks. With a lecherous smile, he slowly bared his crooked yellow teeth and licked his battered lips. Matrona screamed twice before a heavy fist plunged her once more into darkness.

Frol jerked Matrona off the horse onto his shoulders. He spotted a low fir tree with widely spreading branches. It would provide adequate concealment for his captive. He threw Matrona onto the ground near the tree.

"Fucking bitch! If anyone is following us, they sure as hell know where we are. Now I'll have to cover my back trail. I might just fuck you and slit your throat when I get back."

Before he left, Frol wedged a stick in her mouth and secured it with a cord around the back of her head that was tied to both ends of the crude gag. He checked the tethers around the rug that encapsulated Matrona. Satisfied that she could neither move nor cry out, he kicked her under the concealing branches. Even in the gloom of the recess under the tree,

Matrona's golden tresses glowed with a subdued brilliance.

Frol cursed this new inconvenience and fetched a dark cloth from his pack. He kept it handy to look like an Oprichniki if any of the Tsar's men were about. He slid under the branches and tied the cloth loosely around her head.

With his victim having been immobilized and concealed, Frol led his horse up the steep embankment on the north side of the stream. Once at the top, he headed west for almost two versts until he located a dense grove of conifers that ran close to the stream. Hurrying now, with the fear of his pursuers growing with every minute, Frol led his horse away from the stream and tethered it out of sight and earshot.

He returned to the stream bank and found a perfect hiding spot under some tree branches. The spreading boughs concealed his presence, but he had enough room to accommodate the full use of his bow. If there was a single pursuer, Frol would dispatch him with an arrow. If there were many, he would stay concealed and slip away. The girl would probably die before they found her. He would lose some wealth but still gain his revenge.

◊

Andrei moved as swiftly as the unstable footing of the stream bed would allow. He knew he must be gaining on Matrona and her captor. There were fresh signs of their passage all along the stream: here a broken branch, and there a hoof mark in the stream bed that had not yet washed away.

Andrei left his horse behind as it slowed him down and made too much noise. Speed and stealth were his only earthly allies now. If Allah permitted, he would overtake his quarry before he left the stream and, more importantly, before the Cossack could check his back trail.

As he entered a stretch where conifers were densely packed along the banks, a squirrel began to chatter angrily. Andrei stopped. Was he disturbing the squirrel? Or was there some-one else in the forest?

The twang of the bowstring and the pain arrived simul-taneously. The impact of the arrow in his back drove Andrei face-first into the stream. From the bank behind him, he could hear his assailant's victory whoop. The arrow had entered his back and lodged in one of his ribs. Andrei struggled to breathe. His right lung was pierced and was quickly filling with blood.

He knew he would die, but not yet. Marshaling his remain-ing strength, he pushed himself up and stumbled forward. He must have surprised his attacker because he reached the far bank before the second arrow found him. It struck him in the scapula and deflected downward, piercing his diaphragm and coming to rest just under the skin of his stomach.

Lying on the stream bank, Andrei fought through the pain and impending darkness. He knew he had only minutes to live at best. He had but one chance of revenge. Twitching in mock death throes, he edged his knife from his belt. Then he was still.

◊

Frol shook his head. *Those Tatars are gritty little fuckers*, he thought, *even the half-breeds*. He didn't like wasting two arrows when one should have done the trick. Hopefully neither was broken. He didn't intend to waste a third.

As he approached the body, Frol noticed that the arrows had gone deep. Hopefully, they went all the way through, and he could pull them out of his victim's chest or abdomen. He kicked the body twice, but there were no signs of life. Frol drew his knife. Just to be sure, he would slit his victim's throat.

Frol kicked the body onto its back and bent to sever the jugular. There was a sudden blur of movement. Startled, Frol jumped back. He felt lightheaded, and something wet was running down his chest. He ran his hand up his shirt to his throat. His eyes bulged, and he tried to scream but could only gurgle. He almost made the opposite bank before darkness overtook him.

Andrei felt warmth on his face. The storm must have broken. He looked for the break in the clouds that rimmed the far horizon of the flat grassland. *Strange*, he thought, *I don't recall reaching the steppe*. A figure was riding toward him. At first, his vision blurred, and he could not make out the rider. Then his eyes cleared, and he smiled. Why, it was Dimitri, and someone was riding with him. As they came closer, he saw that it was Samara. "Allah be praised!" he shouted as he ran to embrace them.

CHAPTER 31

Pamoi was silent as a shadow as he dispassionately viewed the scene below. He was impressed by the Tatar's resilience to his wounds and his cunning in slaying the Cossack assailant. As a Komi, he had no love for either people, but he respected courage wherever it resided.

Friends of the Komi were few and far between on the eastern flank of the Kama watershed. Raids on Komi villages by Tatars, Cossacks, and other native peoples were frequent. Within the past month, a Vogul raiding party had sacked a Komi village only twenty versts north of this spot. The Voguls shared the same Finno-Ugric language base as the Komi. However, the Voguls were hardly of a familial disposition in their relationships with the Komi. The two peoples had been warring for as long as anyone could remember.

Pamoi maintained a low profile as he observed the scene below. He was on a scouting expedition, searching for the "Vorkuta," the place with the bears. This was the time of year when the bears would begin to come out of hibernation. He was on foot for reasons of stealth and the tendency of horses to panic when bears were about.

The bear was the totem of his tribe but had become scarce in this region since the arrival of the Stroganovs and their many mines and saltworks. These industries required vast supplies of timber for construction and fuel, and in many areas, the forest was largely denuded.

Pamoi used the name "Pitiu" when dealing with the Muscovites. The Muscovites referred to the Komi as the "Permian" or

"Permyak." In the late fourteenth century, Father Stephan Khrap, a monk of the Rostov Cloister, had begun converting the Komi to the Russian Orthodox Religion. For his efforts, Father Stephen had been canonized as Saint Stephen of Perm.

Church legend credited Saint Stephan with vanquishing the pagan shaman Pamoi in a test of faith by fire. True or not, the legend had been insufficient to convert the majority of the Komi to Orthodoxy. After Saint Stephen's death, the Muscovites had resorted to violence and coercion to complete the Komi religious conversion. Eventually, the Komi had become subjects of the Grand Duchy of Moscow. Upon their religious conversion and political subjugation, the Komi had begun a slow descent into serfdom, mainly under the jurisdiction of the Stroganovs, who had the Tsar's charter to the entire region.

Many Komi, including Pitiu's parents and ancestors, refused to accept the legend of Saint Stephen's victory over the shaman or follow the new religion. His parents named him Pamoi after the ancient shaman. As Pamoi, Pitiu had become a clandestine leader of the Komi people who still clung to their pagan roots. The pagan Komi remained in the forests and, whenever possible, traded with Novgorodians rather than Muscovites.

Novgorodian traders had preceded the Muscovites into the Kama Basin and the Urals. As early as the ninth century, they were exploring and developing commercial ties in the region. While many were little more than river pirates, their impact on the spiritual and cultural life of the Komi had been slight. The Tsar's charters to the Stroganovs had excluded Novgorodian operations in much of the territory. Unknown to Pamoi, the destruction of Novgorod that winter had forever eliminated Novgorod's commercial influence in the land of the Komi.

But to Pamoi, the present was of much greater concern than the past. He had been in a position to observe the duel destruction of the Tatar and Cossack, but if the Russians stumbled upon the scene, they might arrive at a different interpretation. The Komi could not afford to have the Russians think that they had slain the combatants.

Kachalov, the master of the local saltery, had shown little disposition to press the Komi into serfdom. He relied instead on expatriate Russians, preferring to maintain the local Komi as a natural buffer to the depredations of the Tatars and the Voguls. Pamoi had met with Kachalov on several occasions and found him to be honest and dependable. In turn, the local Komi had remained peaceful and assisted the Russians with food and fuel in times of shortage and hardship. The Komi could not afford to have this relationship altered by acts of outsiders. Leaving his horse on the ridge above the stream, Pamoi descended to the scene of the struggle.

Pamoi dragged the body of the Cossack across the stream and placed it near the Tatar. On closer examination, he could see that the man was only part Tatar, probably part Russian as well. This was all the more reason to tidy up the scene. The Cossack's bow was nowhere near the bodies. Pamoi searched under the trees and located the bow and quiver. He noticed the Cossack's tracks heading up the ridge through the trees.

Pamoi crossed the river and dropped the bow and quiver near the two bodies. He was careful not to make any tracks of his own that would indicate the presence of a third person. Then he covered the Cossack's tracks, as well as his own, by sweeping them away with a fir bough. He then went to where the Cossack had tethered his horse. The Cossack's horse was a good one, and despite the circumstances, Pamoi was delighted to take it for his own mount.

Pamoi was afraid that the slain Cossack may be one of a band of Cossacks that could threaten his village. He followed the Cossack's trail upstream along the north side of the high ridge. After a short time, he came to a place where the Cossack's trail vanished as if he had ascended into the sky to ride out to his destiny.

If the Cossack had such magical powers, he would probably still be alive. More than likely, he covered his trail in order to hide something nearby. Had he looted the nearby saltery and stashed his booty? Of course, it could also be a trap. Pamoi dismounted, and using the horse for a shield, he very carefully surveyed the surrounding area. Below him was a small clearing that was surrounded on the north and east by a grove of thick fir trees. The stream ran across its south side. It would be a good location for an ambush.

As if in answer to Pamoi's suspicion, the branches of one of the trees began to shake.

◊

At first, Matrona fought the return to a painful consciousness. The whole right side of her body throbbed. She felt like she had been kicked and was thankful that the thick bear hide had afforded some measure of protection. She was trussed up so tightly she couldn't tell if anything was broken. Her jaw ached, but she could not tell if it was broken with the wooden gag restricting its range of motion.

Matrona's breathing was labored, and she knew her ribs were badly bruised, if not broken. Her intake of air was further restricted by the wooden gag. She opened her eyes to darkness. Fighting off a claustrophobic panic, she collected her thoughts and began to take stock of her situation.

She could hear the stream flowing a short distance off to her left. She listened for the sound of her abductor or his horse, but heard nothing that would indicate their presence. Then she heard the *chick-che-day-day* of a chickadee. *Cheerful little creature*, she thought. *Easy for you; you're not trussed up like a fowl ready for market.* Another chickadee answered the first, this one only a few feet over her head.

Matrona doubted the birds would be so active if the Cossack

were around. She gathered herself and tried to sit up. Her head struck some small branches that blocked her attempt at rising. She noted that the cloth over her face got momentarily snarled in the branches, loosening its trusses. She sat up more forcefully. This time, the cloth was thoroughly snagged in the small branches that had been broken by her thrust. She moved her head cautiously up and down and felt the cord attaching the cloth move. She did this several times until the cord was hung up on her ears and nose.

She decided that in her current situation, facial features were expendable. Matrona jerked her head back violently. Light and pain arrived simultaneously. The pain was so intense that, for a moment, she thought she must have ripped her ears off. She carefully examined the ground and overhead branches but found no sign of them. Unless they were in the makeshift hood, they remained attached in some bruised and gnarled state.

She could see daylight through the tightly packed branches overhead. Occasionally, sunlight would stream through here and there. The storm of the previous night was breaking up. She knew it was a mixed blessing. If she could free herself, it would be easier to find her way back to the saltery, presuming she could slip around the Cossack, wherever he was. On the other hand, it was mid-afternoon, and even in late winter, without cloud cover, it would be bitterly cold overnight.

Matrona was reluctant to leave the relative sanctuary of the tree cave. The branches blocked the afternoon breeze, and she was quite warm in her robe and bear rug. But she had nothing on her feet. To travel any distance, she would have to fashion some type of foot covering, and that would best be done in daylight.

It took several tries before Matrona successfully rolled through the protective branches. As she lay face up on the light covering of snow, the sun shone through a break in the clouds, raising her spirits. She noticed that in rolling out from under the tree, her bonds had loosened substantially. She began squirming and soon found that by compressing her shoulders and sitting up and down repeatedly, the cord confining her shoulders shifted toward her neck, soon becoming loose altogether.

Matrona had less luck with the coil around her arms. Despite much vigorous squirming, she had little to show for her efforts beyond a copious sweat. The ground was much too slick to provide any friction on her bonds. She remembered some of her father's freight haulers used a long lever to lift a wagon out of a rut. She needed something similar to raise the bonds around her arms up over her shoulders.

Looking around, she spied a dead branch at the base of a tree on the other side of the clearing. With considerable effort, she rolled over to the tree, sat up next to the branch, and threw herself against it until it broke off. She then sat up against the tree and lowered herself until the broken shaft of the branch engaged the bonds around her arms.

Half of her plan worked well. The cord did get hung up as planned, but despite a good deal of writhing, her bonds only dug into the bearskin rug. Now she was anchored firmly to the tree. She fought back tears of frustration and fear that threatened to consume her. At least she would be visible to any rescue party, even if she couldn't talk or move.

◊

Pamoi moved behind a small group of firs on the ridge. Tethering his horse, he crawled forward under the tree until he could observe the clearing from a concealed position. The branches began shaking again, and Pamoi tensed. He anticipated that one or more warriors would come out into the clearing. He expected that they would be Cossacks awaiting the return of the dead warrior.

He almost jumped up in surprise when the mass of brown

fur came rolling out from under the tree. His first thought was that he had found the Vorkuta and awakened a sleeping bear. But something was very odd about this bear. As the form twitched and rolled, he caught glimpses of something light-colored attached to the hide. Occasionally a bear would have a blonde streak down its back, but this patch was too long and too light for a normal bear.

When the form suddenly sat up, Pamoi almost laughed. It was a woman wrapped up in a bear hide. He wanted to see a bear so badly that, despite the long golden tresses now blowing in the wind, his mind had invented one. As the woman writhed on the ground, Pamoi saw that she was tied up and was attempting to free her bonds. He deduced that she must have been the Cossack's captive and that he had stashed her under the tree while he checked his back trail.

This new situation perplexed Pamoi. If she was from the saltery and he rescued her, it would serve his people well in the eyes of the Russians. But her would-be rescuer was clearly of Tatar blood. Did the Cossack steal her from a band of Tatars in the area? If so, there would be no reward for Pamoi or his village, only bloodshed and destruction.

As he was pondering this predicament, the woman rolled to a tree and apparently became stuck on one of its branches. She wiggled and squirmed for a while and then remained still. In all the while that he watched, she never called out. She had either given up on a rescue party or was gagged. For his part, Pamoi was thankful for the silence. He would be certain to hear any sizable rescue party well before they arrived.

Of course, the woman could also be bait. The thick grove of conifer trees could conceal half the Kahn's Tatars with a brigade of Cossacks to boot.

He thought of his own daughter. What if the Tatars or Cossacks took her? What if she were alone and defenseless in the impending cold and darkness? Would a Tatar save her? Would a Muscovite? But they were not here now. He was here.

He could feel destiny and doom descending. Whatever he did, he was at the crossroads now. For better or worse, his fate was sealed.

The shadows were lengthening, and the temperature was dropping quickly. A short distance away, a wolf howled. Pamoi knew that if he didn't rescue her, she was unlikely to survive the night. The smart thing was to ride away. It was the one option with the least risk.

◊

The howl of the wolf made Matrona's blood run cold. It could not be more than two versts away. She wondered how far her scent traveled in the evening air. Was there any bear scent left in the hide after it was tanned? If there was, would it be enough to frighten off any wolves in the area?

Matrona remained very still, hardly breathing lest the mist from her breath carry her presence to the voracious beasts prowling the forest and the edge of her sanity. She heard something behind her in the trees. Was it her imagination? Perhaps only some birds getting ready to roost for the night?

There it was again. Not quite a footfall, but clearly something moving, something larger than a bird. She could hear breathing now, not labored but slow and steady. She braced herself for the crash of teeth. Her eyes rolled back into her sockets as she fell into the universal shock of prey in the grip of inevitable death.

◊

Pamoi jerked the woman up from the branch that had snagged her bonds. He held her in front of him as a shield in case this was, indeed, an ambush. There was only silence. Not even the woman made a sound. She was dead weight, so much so that Pamoi thought for a moment that she must have died.

However, holding his ear next to her mouth, he determined that she was breathing. Still, it was better that she was silent. Pamoi wanted to get away from this place. Then he would have time to think and do the proper thing. Leaving her bonds intact, he slung her over his horse and rode into the darkening forest.

CHAPTER 32

Kachalov was leading his horse, as it was too dark to ride. He stumbled over a large rock hidden in the dark waters of the shallow stream. He extended his arm and caught himself before tumbling into the water. Only his right sleeve was wet, and he could feel it quickly freezing in the frigid night air.

For the past several days, Kachalov had been off inspecting another Stroganov saltery fifteen versts upriver. He arrived at midday to receive the news that Matrona had been abducted and that Ivanov and Petr were leading a search party to rescue her. He tarried only long enough to get a fresh mount and was now, hopefully, close to catching up with the would-be rescuers. With any luck and some divine intervention, they had already freed her and were camped out for the night.

Since he left the saltery, Kachalov had been berating himself for hiding his true feelings from Matrona. He had done his best to act aloof and disinterested. Why? Was it manly pride, or was he afraid of possible consequences from the Stroganovs? Either way, he was a fool.

After another hour of slow going, he smelled wood smoke. As he negotiated a sharp bend in the stream, he saw a small fire in a nearby clearing. Easing closer, he could make out the face of one of his lieutenants, Skrynnikov, in the light of the flickering flames. He hailed the man, identifying himself to avoid being shot by any nearby sentry.

As he entered the camp, he could see the form of two bodies lying under robes on the edge of the clearing.

"Casualties?" he asked Skrynnikov — fighting to control

the anxiety that gripped his guts and knotted his throat.

"Yes, it is that Cossack called 'Frol' and the half-breed Tatar who was with the Novgorodians. Apparently Frol took the girl and ambushed the Tatar who was chasing them."

"You mean Andrei," Kachalov replied sharply. "He was a good man, Tatar or otherwise!"

"Anyway, they killed each other," the man replied.

"What about the girl?"

"We don't know. There was no sign of her nearby. That fool priest and her brother are out looking for her in the dark. She could be anywhere, tied to a tree or entertaining a camp full of Cossacks for all we know."

Kachalov could feel a tide of anger rising, but he would deal with the man's insolence and insensitivity later. He had no time for lessons now. "Which way did they go?"

"One of the woodcutters said that this stream is the outlet from a small lake about six versts above here. They are riding up the south bank and will circle the lake to return on the north bank."

It sounded like a good plan to Kachalov. If there was a band of Cossacks, they could be camped out by now, confident that their sentries would alert them of any large body of rescuers. If there were only one or two Cossacks, they might be trying to cover a lot of ground at night. If so, in their haste, they would be sure to leave tracks.

The rescue party had a number of harquebuses with them. He selected one with a good slow match to ensure ignition when he was ready to fire. They had also wisely brought along several auxiliary mounts in case of a protracted chase. Kachalov selected one of these and, despite the protest of his men, proceeded up the north bank of the stream. The moon was nearly full and was rising to a clear sky. There would be plenty of light to see tracks. It would be a frigid night. If Matrona was tied up and abandoned, every minute was critical. The wolves and wolverines would be out. If she were not rescued soon, it would not matter to them whether they gnawed on warm or frozen flesh.

◊

Matrona pulled the bearskin tighter against her body. The small fire provided barely enough heat to keep her from freezing. But she wasn't about to complain. Although her body ached and her mouth was sore from the Cossack's gag, she was free from her bonds. Her rescuer was assuming a risk by having any fire at all.

Once she had regained her senses, the man, a local native calling himself Pitiu, had explained their situation in broken but understandable Russian. The Cossack was dead, killed by a Tatar assailant. Pitiu had followed the Cossack's trail to where Matrona had been concealed. He was fearful that any rescue party from the saltery would shoot him on sight before the situation could be explained. His plan was to take her to his village and then go to the saltery alone to alert them that she was safe. It sounded like a wise plan to Matrona.

The eastern sky was beginning to brighten, and Pitiu rose to stoke the fire. He was not a large man, barely as tall as her and almost as fair. As he busied himself adjusting the wood in the fire, Matrona noticed movement in the nearby birch grove. In the early morning gloom, she made out what appeared to be the figure of a man. She rubbed her eyes to be sure. As she did, the figure raised a long stick. Her mind was catapulted to that awful day on the river when Anna was killed.

"Harquebus," she screamed, throwing herself at Pitiu. Her impact with the Komi and the report of the musket occurred simultaneously. Pitiu cried out in pain. Looking up, she saw a man rushing toward them with his sword drawn. Naked now, having been separated from her robes, Matrona threw herself across Pitiu.

"Matrona, get up so that I can dispatch this swine!"

She was stunned. "My God, it's you, Yuri! Put down your sword. This man saved me."

Kachalov reeled backward in disbelief. "He didn't beat you?" he stammered. "He didn't violate you?"

"No, Yuri — the Cossack beat me, and nobody violated me."

Kachalov fell to his knees. "Thank God," he whispered.

"Yes, and thank this man while you're at it. Hopefully, with God's grace, he is still alive."

Pitiu groaned as they rolled him over. The musket ball had ruined his shoulder but had not hit a vital organ. He opened his eyes and looked at Matrona. "Thank you. You saved me." Then he fainted.

They heard movement in the trees. Two more figures were rushing forward.

"Yuri! Matrona! Are you safe?"

It was Petr and Father Ivanov.

Suddenly, Matrona realized she was stark naked. She quickly clutched her robes around her.

Petr was gasping for air from his exertion. "We heard the shot. Did you kill another craven Cossack?"

"No, I severely wounded a friend," Kachalov replied morosely. "This Komi rescued Matrona, and I shot him."

"The Cossack is dead — killed by some Tatar," Matrona explained.

"It wasn't 'some Tatar' that killed him," Petr explained. "It was Andrei."

"Andrei!" Matrona smiled. "I could have guessed." Matrona saw the stricken look on Petr's face. "Where is Andrei, Petr?" she whispered.

"The Cossack ambushed him, Matrona — shot two arrows into Andrei's back. Andrei managed to kill the Cossack before he succumbed to his wounds. He is with Dimitri now."

"My God!" she moaned, sinking to the ground. "This is a black day."

She began tracing meaningless lines in the snow with her

finger. "We are dropping away one by one, Petr," she murmured. "Dimitri. Anna. Andrei." She paused for a few moments.

"Andrei was such a good man. He was always looking out for me. You know . . . I never said thank you . . . Such a good man."

"There are many good men left in the world," Ivanov interjected.

He bent over Pitiu. "And this is one of them. We had best attend to him before he slips away as well."

CHAPTER 33

Matrona placed a cool compress over Pitiu's forehead. Father Ivanov had dug the musket ball out of his shoulder as soon as they reached the saltery. For several days, Pitiu had shown improvement, but then his wound had begun to putrefy. Two days ago, he had developed a raging fever and began to slip in and out of consciousness.

Matrona and Father shared nursing duties. Matrona welcomed the opportunity to submerge her grief for Andrei in something positive. Both Matrona and the priest were impressed by the character of Pitiu. He did not appear to hold a grudge against any of them. In his lucid moments, he repeatedly thanked Matrona for trying to save his life. The fact that it was her rescue that placed him in peril did not appear to matter to him.

Ivanov had remarked that Pitiu was more Christian in his actions than any bishop or metropolitan of the Church that he had encountered. Realizing that the end was near for Pitiu, Ivanov had baptized him, although it was doubtful that the Komi had recognized the significance of the rite.

Matrona knew that it was the Cossack who bore ultimate responsibility for Pitiu's injury, that, and the perilous nature of frontier life that required quick and violent action. But, in her heart, Matrona could not help feeling responsible for Pitiu's injury. Only the Komi's kind and even disposition prevented her from falling into a state of depression.

Despite the steady counsel of Father Ivanov, Kachalov fell into despair for his part in Pitiu's shooting. He was inconsolable and a shell of his former self. He neglected his duties and the company of others, except for Father Ivanov, who did his best to break Kachalov's despondency.

Several times a day, Kachalov would shuffle morosely from the guest cabin to the main residence where Pitiu was being treated. At first, on each visit, he would apologize to Pitiu for the shooting. Eventually he would enter quietly and sit in the corner of the room, seemingly oblivious to the world around him. Gone were the arrogance of position and the swagger of command, replaced by a deep and abiding melancholy.

For her part, Matrona only had enough strength of fortitude and will to deal with the stricken Komi. As the day turned to evening, Pitiu's breathing became more labored, and she feared he would not last the night. When she was replaced by Father Ivanov, she requested that she be awakened if his condition worsened.

Sometime after midnight, the priest awoke her with the news that the end was near. He had performed extreme unction, and now it was just a matter of time before Pitiu slipped away. As she approached his sick bed, Matrona could feel the presence of death. But it was a gentler presence than she had experienced on the trail. She sensed a pending release, inevitable and benign.

As she bent to kiss Pitiu's forehead, he opened his eyes, which were clear and focused. "Bring me my belongings, please," he requested in a voice that was surprisingly strong. "That little sack there in the corner. Empty it on my bed."

She did as requested. There was an assortment of bone implements and something wrapped in a leather pouch.

"In the pouch there," he said, pointing to the pouch. "I want you to have it." His body shuddered, and she could see him struggle to collect himself. "You will know what to do. In time, it will be important."

She reached for the pouch. Inside, she could feel something hard. As she slowly and reverently extracted the object, she sensed something shift, something beyond her understanding. She looked to Pitiu. He was gone.

"What is it, child?" the priest asked softly.

"It is a bear, Father, a bronze bear."

"It must be some sort of pagan talisman," he replied.

"It is not evil, Father," she said, looking up.

The priest smiled. "I don't think so either. It is somehow important. I have come to believe the Lord moves in unusual and unseen ways, sometimes even through pagan means." He gently closed Pitiu's eyes. "There is the God spark in pagans such as Pitiu. Those kind and gentle souls that live the spirit of the liturgy we so vocally espouse and so often ignore."

◊

Kachalov could not sleep — had not slept in many nights. The events of the last few days washed over him like a flood. If only he had shown more restraint. The Komi would not be on his deathbed, and Matrona would still respect him. That is if she ever did respect him. From the beginning, he could have been more civil, more attentive, less martial and arrogant.

He realized that his plan of rescue had been based more on being a "hero" in Matrona's eyes than finding a safe resolution to the situation. He had fired on the Komi more to impress the girl than eliminate any real danger to her. Reflecting back, he could see that the Komi had not been armed and had been in no position to defend himself. Kachalov had had the elements of surprise and superior armaments.

Kachalov was losing faith in the Lord. He prayed often and fervently for the recovery of Pitiu after the shooting. Despite his entreaties, the Komi was slipping inexorably toward the grave. For the last several hours, Kachalov had been unable to pray. He could sense that the end was near for Pitiu. He dreaded the long ride to the Komi village to deliver the cruel news to the man's family. What was to become of Pitiu's wife and children? He could bring them to the saltery, but they would be among foreign people who could not be counted on to treat them well.

His thoughts turned to Skrynnikov, and the anger filled him once again. On the return journey to the saltery, Skrynnikov had repeatedly asked why they bothered to tend to a godless pagan who had no more worth than any forest animal. Kachalov had warned him to cease his insensitive drivel, but the man had persisted in his heartless comments.

After several hours of restraint, Kachalov had thrown Skrynnikov from his horse and drawn his sword to mete out quick and bloody punishment. Father Ivanov had quickly intervened, explaining that if Kachalov wanted to slash every insensitive brute in the world, it would take many more lifetimes than he was allotted.

Kachalov was so deep in tortured thought that he did not hear the door to the guest cabin open and close or detect the slim figure that quickly stepped inside. Only when the supple young body slipped under the covers and embraced him was he aware of her presence.

"Matrona, you mustn't; we mustn't," he protested.

"Pitiu has passed," she replied softly. "He has forgiven you. Now it is time for you to forgive yourself."

Then, with her lips, breath, hands, and body, she began to heal him as women have always healed their men.

◊

The next day, Father Ivanov heard their confessions. The following Sunday, Matrona and Kachalov were married.

The prosperous nobility of town and city were well served by the social rites of courtship. Those enmeshed in the wilderness of nature or poverty understood that love postponed was likely love denied. The harsh realities of survival did not defer to unrequited love.

As Matrona and Yuri exchanged vows, a great weight was lifted from Petr's shoulders. His sister had become a woman.

Her future welfare was no longer dependent on his protection. Her marriage would sustain her. Yuri was a good man and would prosper.

Petr took a deep breath. He must now look to the remaining refugees. They were still adrift in an uncharted wilderness. Caught between the twin perils of Tatar and Oprichniki, only through the grace of God and the strength and wisdom of Father Ivanov would they have any chance of survival.

PART FOUR

STROGANOVS
AND THE URALS

CHAPTER 34

Stroganov Stronghold - Confluence of Kama and Chusovaya Rivers

The stockade was well located on a high ridge. It formed a half circle with both ends terminating at the rim of a high cliff that dropped precipitously to the river below. The approach to the fort was steep and open, the trees having been cleared and used in the construction of the palisade that skirted the top of the ridge. Five large harquebuses, the kind called "harquebus a croc," were evenly located along the top of the palisade. With their three-and-a-half-ounce shot and thunderous report, they were sure to frighten most potential foes, be they native or Tatar. With the palisade's natural barriers and heavy armaments, it would take a small army to breach the fort's defenses.

It took four long days of riding for Kachalov's retinue of soldiers and civilians to reach the fort. Kachalov and Matrona rode in the front, with Petr and Father Ivanov in the rear. As they approached the main gate, Petr adjusted his posture to affect a more alert and confident air than he felt. They were all saddle-worn and weary, more than ready for sustenance and sleep.

As they entered the fort, the cold stares of the Stroganov men did little to lift the spirits of the travelers. Petr sensed no camaraderie between Kachalov's group from the saltery and the troop of men in the fort. Kachalov's men were workers who also performed military functions. For the most part, the men here were soldiers, conscripts from prisons or mercenaries.

The fort did not enclose a saltery or mine. This was a regional command center intended to guard the Kama and Chusovaya river passages and provide aid to saltery and mine sites as needed. Inside were barracks and an armory. Outside the armory was a large stack of harquebuses and another of halberds.

The harquebuses, a predecessor to the musket, would be particularly effective here on the frontier. Good suits of plate armor could stop a harquebus ball at a distance, but plate armor was rare among native peoples and the Siberian Tatars. If any attacking force got through the harquebus barrage, they would have to deal with the halberds. The halberd was a combination battle axe and pike on a long handle. It was as visually intimidating as the harquebus was through noise.

Petr was certain that inside the fort's armory, there would be a variety of bows, crossbows, and swords. The Stroganovs' wealth was based on trade. A well-stocked arsenal was essential to protecting the trade infrastructure, which was dependent on the domination of native peoples, the resistance to Tatar and Cossack raids, and the free flow of raw materials to the West.

The armory and barracks were consistent with the outside fortifications, but the building that was centered to the rear of the fort was as unexpected as it was magnificent. Even in the noble and boyar quarters of Novgorod or Moscow, the great house before them would have been the envy of its neighbors. Whereas the barracks and fortifications were all made of wood, the great house was mostly stone. Three stories high, it towered over the barracks and stockade. The second story had three large windows with glass panes, rare for the time period, even in the large Russian cities to the west.

A cobblestone path formed an arc that led counterclockwise to the great oak doors on the east side of the mansion. This lane was tree-lined with large firs that had been left standing when the area had been clear-cut for the stockade.

South of the great house, a number of workers were planting a garden. On the west side, several rows of fruit trees glowed in the afternoon sun. There, a short path led to a well, and several women were hauling water back to the house. It was a tranquil scene of domestic order amidst the imposing frontier fortifications.

Kachalov directed most of their band to the barracks, while he, Matrona, Petr, and Father Ivanov proceeded on to the great house. As they approached the front entrance, a number of servants in drab gray or brown clothing came out of a side door. They were accompanied by an overseer in a bright blue waistcoat, cut in the French fashion. He directed the servants to collect the visitors' mounts and take them to the stables. The overseer then led Kachalov's party up the stone steps to the main entry.

Upon entry into the foyer of the house, they were temporarily blinded as they transitioned from bright sunlight to the gloom of the interior. As their eyes adjusted to the faint light, they became aware of a thin middle-aged man with a patrician bearing awaiting their attention and recognition.

Instinctively, Petr straightened his stance and squared his shoulders; Kachalov did likewise. To his right, he could hear Matrona gasp. Only Father Ivanov appeared unaffected by the man's presence.

"I am Yakov Stroganov," the man said quietly with no show of emotion. "I would welcome my guests from Lord Novgorod the Great, but I am given to understand that this entity no longer exists. You are either my guests or my prisoners. I have not yet decided; perhaps you are both."

A slight smile crossed his face as he surveyed the travel-worn visitors.

"For the time being, you are much too untidy to grace my foyer." He motioned to the house servant. "In any event, there is no call to be uncivilized, so Yevgeni here will show you to your quarters."

Stroganov bowed slightly to Matrona. "Despite the harsh realities of frontier life, we do manage to keep *Domostroi* here. The women's quarters are limited, but I trust you will find them adequate to your needs."

He nodded to Ivanov. "We also have quarters for visiting clergy, Father. Perhaps in the morning, you will favor us by conducting Mass in our small church. It has been a while since we have had the benefit of a priest." Ivanov nodded his assent.

Stroganov directed a house servant to lead the way. "Collect our visitors for dinner in two hours, Yevgeni. Momentous decisions should never be made on an empty stomach." He paused for a second.

"Yuri, if your young wife can spare you for a moment, I would like to have a word before you freshen up."

◊

The dining room was splendid for any part of Russia, let alone the frontier. They were seated at one end of a table large enough to accommodate three times their number. The fact that there were chairs for everyone was unusual. At that time in Russia, chairs were rare and usually reserved for the master of the house. Around the room, in sideboards and cupboards, were goblets, tureens, plates, and bowls of not only the usual copper, wood, and pewter but also of gold and silver.

Petr had seen paintings of the inside of French and English mansions, and this room was easily comparable to those elegant households. The floor was covered with rich Oriental carpets, and the table had linen napkins with plates and cutlery for each individual. In most elegant homes of the time, plates were large and intended for sharing. Generally, only spoons were supplied individually.

The dinner was served by two house servants. It would not be considered a feast in Moscow or Novgorod, but compared to the food on the trail and at the saltery, it was a veritable banquet to the travelers. There was fresh bread, roast venison, fresh trout, boiled potatoes, pickled beets and beans, and plenty of wine to accompany the meal. For dessert, there was cake and pudding, which were accompanied by tea and port.

Throughout dinner, the conversation was congenial, dealing mainly with the weather and the hardships of frontier living. They circumvented the topics of politics and religion to avoid casting a pall over the meal. For his part, Stroganov appeared to enjoy the company of visitors who could match his intellect and refinement.

After dinner, a large fire was prepared in the adjacent sitting room. Although reluctant to leave and apprehensive of their future, Matrona, as was the custom of the day, excused herself for the evening.

Stroganov poured another round of port for his guests and himself. He then turned to Petr.

"Well, young Safronov, you do not look like the talented new artist that I heard about in Moscow. I heard that your icons were taking the Novgorod School to a whole new level of sophistication. I must say, you look more the warrior and less the painter."

"I'm afraid that these times require more of the sword and less of the paintbrush," Petr replied softly.

"Yes, and that is my dilemma as well," Stroganov said, standing. "Our family's past is tied to Novgorod, but our present and future are firmly anchored to the Tsar." Yakov went on to recount the Stroganov family history.

Spiridon had been the first Stroganov to come to prominence in Novgorod, in the late fourteenth century. At that time, Novgorod was a member of the Hanseatic League. Spiridon's grandson, Luka Kuzmich, had become a historical figure in 1445. He had paid a huge ransom for Prince Vasilii the Dark, who had been blinded and kept hostage by the Tatars.

In the early 1500s, the Stroganovs had been extracting salt in the Vychegda River Basin and founded the city of

Solvchegodsk. In 1558, Tsar Ivan the Terrible had granted Grigorii Stroganov a charter to develop 3,415,000 dessiatin of land on both sides of the Kama River up to its junction with the Chusovaya River. In 1566, Yakov had petitioned the Tsar to include the Stroganov lands in the Oprichnina. For this demonstration of loyalty, Yakov had received his own charter in 1568. His grant included the Chusovaya from its headwaters in the Urals to its junction with the Kama. With these charters, the Stroganovs had become the largest landholders in Russia.

"Surely, with your influence and wealth, you have little to fear from the Tsar," Petr interjected. "It is apparent that he trusts your reliability and industry. Besides, you are so far away from Moscow that he has little to fear. I doubt he knows that refugees from Novgorod are here."

"True, the Tsar may have already forgotten Novgorod," Stroganov replied. "His attention span is often as short as his temper. However, we have many trade rivals who would be delighted to inform the Tsar that the Stroganovs are sheltering spies and dissidents."

"But the reality is that we are neither spies nor dissidents!" Petr responded hotly.

"That is one reality," Stroganov continued evenly. "The Tsar has his own realities. It is dangerous to be too close or too far from the Tsar. Unfortunately we are both commercially and politically close, but geographically distant."

"The refugees have much to offer you. Here on the frontier, there must be a shortage of skilled craftsmen, and we have many in our camp," Father Ivanov interjected.

Stroganov smiled. "Yes, there is an opportunity as well as a threat. We need workers and soldiers. With our charter, we have responsibilities to develop this land, civilize the population, collect tribute from the native tribes and Tatars, and protect the frontier. The Sibir Khan, Kuchum, is located just over the Urals. We have absolutely no idea how large an army he commands or how many Siberian tribes owe allegiance to the Khanate. I have control of the Chusovaya on paper only. I know almost as little about the river as I do the Khan."

"Properly armed, these people could be quite the force!" Kachalov added enthusiastically.

"I'm afraid your heart rules your head, young captain. The Tsar would never stand for an armed Novgorodian force on the frontier, or anywhere else." Stroganov paused for a while, staring pensively into the fire. "You are fortunate, Kachalov; your lovely young wife has already lost her identity by merging it with yours. The rest of the refugees must disappear as well."

Stroganov could feel the others stiffen. "Do not be alarmed. I do not have the Tsar's taste for torture and death. We can assimilate some of your people into our communities, particularly the families. But there are too many single men. I don't know what to do with them."

He paused and shook his head. "Unlike my young captain here, I must make a commercial and political decision — but not today."

CHAPTER 35

Petr was up at first light. Apparently, they were not closely held prisoners, as his chambers and the exits of the great house were unguarded. He walked to the escarpment as the sun rose over the Urals. The light from the low-angle sun was diffracted by the morning mist, turning the Chusovaya into a great silver ribbon with pastel highlights of pink and purple. It was the most beautiful river that Petr had ever seen. He was held spellbound by its grace and majesty. Here was a natural setting to rival the resplendent view of Lord Novgorod the Great with the Great Cathedral of St. Sophia. Petr felt his soul soar for the first time since the horrors of Ivan's attack. He sensed that this river and his destiny were somehow inter-twined.

Petr heard footsteps behind and turned to find Yakov Stroganov, who said, "So, I see you are quite taken by my river."

"It is beautiful, yes," Petr replied, annoyed by the intrusion and arrogance.

Stroganov sensed Petr's displeasure. A hint of a smile crossed his face.

"I know; it seems like heresy to claim ownership of God's sublime works. In truth, all I control of the Chusovaya is about twenty versts of its banks up and down the river from here. Most of what I know of the Chusovaya is that its name comes from the Komi word 'chusva' that means 'rapid stream'— that and the fact that my scouts have a bad habit of never return-ing from their expeditions to its headwaters."

"It certainly looks like a natural pathway into the Urals," Petr responded.

"For part of the year, it is. But it is ice-locked in the late autumn and winter and doesn't break up until mid-April. The ice flows are gone for the most part by early May. There are also giant rocks in the river called 'boyets,' 'battlers,' that are a hazard for boats."

Stroganov clapped his hands. "But enough of rocks and rivers; let us have breakfast, and then I will announce your futures."

◊

It was a fine spring day with plenty of sunlight and just enough of a breeze to keep the mosquitoes at bay. However, the small party of refugees took little notice of the weather. Their full attention was directed to Yakov Stroganov, whose steel-gray eyes revealed little of their fate, a fate that he held as securely as any charter issued by the Tsar.

Stroganov took a deep breath. "I feel a great wheel turning, a wheel that we can neither stop nor avoid. We cannot escape the Tsar's authority or his notice. We can absorb all families into our mining and saltery communities. Unfortunately, if I am to retain my status, they must lose theirs — they will become serfs. I can only protect them if we Stroganovs retain our charters. Otherwise, we are all doomed."

"What of the single men?" Father Ivanov inquired.

"The Tsar is sure to consider any group of single men a threat, especially those who had any status in Novgorod. People like you, young Safronov. We can conceal most of them for a short while, but eventually, they must leave. I'm afraid it is exile or death for them."

Stroganov paused and looked directly at Petr. "But I can help them if you first help me, Petr."

Petr was equally apprehensive and intrigued. "What is it you need from me?"

"I need you to perform some tasks for me — as a slave,

more of a servant, really."

"A slave?" Petr gasped.

"Yes, at least temporarily, long enough to deflect the interest of the Tsar's men. Come; let me show you to your slave quarters."

Stroganov led them to the back of the great house. They passed through an ordinary door into a large, dark room. He fumbled for a moment, searching for a window. When, at last he flung open the shutters, the group stood in silent surprise. There in the interior of the room was a large workbench, surrounded on all sides by planks of lime, oak, spruce, and pine. Multiple shelves were filled with paints, linen, and linseed oil varnish, as well as ample supplies of gold and silver plating and foil.

"It's an icon studio!" Petr gasped. "This is better than my personal studio in Novgorod. There are enough supplies here for several artists."

"It is hoped that this studio will contribute to the Stroganov legacy," Stroganov replied. "Long after our fortune in land and commerce is squandered by the least of our heirs, our legacy in art will endure."

Stroganov smiled broadly at Petr. "At least, that is what we hope. In the interim, young Safronov, the icons you create will redeem both of us. You from servitude and I from my brothers, who will not appreciate my aiding and abetting perceived enemies of the State. They will not take kindly to any action on my part that could put us in disfavor with the Tsar."

"When do I start?" Petr asked, somewhat stunned by his change in fortune.

"Now would be good," Stroganov replied. "Now that I have accounted for your immediate safety, I must confer with Father Ivanov regarding the fate of the remaining Novgorodians."

◊

The studio was well-designed, with many windows perfectly positioned to illuminate the workspace. Petr had thrown them all open to let in the ample spring sunshine. He had yet to decide on the subject matter for his icon, so he busied himself with the preparation of the foundation. The first icon would be the centerpiece for an iconostasis, or icon screen. Consequently, Petr wanted it to be large. He selected several oak planks and began to attach them by means of struts, "shponki." These were recessed into the rear of the foundation to prevent warping.

After the planks were joined, Petr hollowed out the section to be painted with an adz to form a recess called the "kovcheg." He then roughened the kovcheg with a grater to increase the adhesion of the base coats to come. In final preparation for painting, Petr laid down a layer of linen, the "pavoloka," and layers of white chalk pigment suspended in fish glue, the "levkas" that formed the primer.

The icon preparatory work took several hours, and it was past midday before Petr was ready to paint. Before he could begin painting, he would need to draw the composition, the "risunok," or incise it, "graf'ja" it, onto the icon base. Now all he needed was a subject.

Iconographers had been working in Novgorod since the thirteenth century. With the arrival of Theophanes the Greek in the late fourteenth century, Novgorod had become the center of iconography for several centuries to come. His works, such as the frescoes in the Church of Transfiguration in Novgorod, *The Dormition of the Virgin*, *The Virgin of the Don*, and *The Virgin Mary*, had laid the foundation for artistic expression in Novgorod.

By the fifteenth century, Novgorod had become the cultural and spiritual center of Russia. There, the Byzantine iconographic tradition had been transformed into a bold and colorful technique that manifested the profound religious experience of Russia's Northern peoples. What became known as the "Novgorod School" had introduced style and realism to the art of iconography.

Eventually, competing schools of iconography had risen in Suzdal, Pskov, and Moscow. The Moscow School was closely aligned with ecclesiastic authorities that undertook to sublimate artistic license to Orthodox standards and dogma. However, when Petr had entered the trade, Novgorodian artists had continued to bring bright and colorful realism to their religious themes. The subjects undertaken by Novgorodian iconographers often depicted the lives of Russian saints and divine intervention in historical events of significance.

Petr sifted the lives of Russian saints through his mind, seeking a topic relevant to the frontier setting in which he found himself. His contemplation was disturbed by a clattering thunder within the stockade. All was quiet for a moment, and then there was one final report. It was all too familiar: the unmistakable sound of a harquebus. Petr's blood ran cold.

As Petr moved toward the open door, he was intercepted by Stroganov. "I hope we haven't disturbed your work, Petr."

"Well, I was startled," Petr replied. "I trust we are not under attack?"

"Certainly not," Stroganov continued. "In fact, we are just re-instilling some command and control on our military unit. One of our Cossack volunteers attempted to desert before his contract was up. I could have hanged him, of course, but I thought the execution could provide the harquebusiers with some practice. Obviously, they need it because the one I had kept in reserve had to finish the poor soul off at close range."

Stroganov was still clearly agitated over the botched execution. "Dreadful business, just dreadful — at least Ivanov gave him extreme unction."

He shifted his attention to Petr. "I'm sorry. This must be very disconcerting."

"On the contrary," Petr replied quietly. "It is a revelation."

◊

The beam of sunlight from the window fell directly on the kovcheg of the nascent icon. It afforded an ethereal luminosity that Petr found particularly inspiring for the commencement of this most spiritual of artistic endeavors. As he looked out the window, he could see the great boreal forest receding uninterrupted into the distant hills. He felt liberated by the frontier, free from the influence of political intrigue and Orthodox dogma that stifled artistic expression in all regions under direct Muscovite subjugation.

Icons have been described as the artistic expression of a searching soul. The wilderness set Petr's soul free to seek divine inspiration from outside the cocoon of civilization. This icon would be a window into the soul of not only Petr, but all those thrown into exile by the caprice and cruelty of the Tsar.

Petr began to mix egg tempera colors. Tradition called for beginning with an olive green background followed by dense, dark paints. But this icon would be different. He would use multiple layers of translucent color to reflect the radiance of Lord Novgorod the Great, a spiritual beacon in a land bereft of grace and virtue.

CHAPTER 36

Stroganov Stronghold - June 1570

The small church faced the East in order to represent the world of light, the divine light of reconciliation and redemption. The sun sets in the west; therefore, in Orthodoxy, one spiritually enters from the world of darkness into a world of light. On this morning, there was a hum of excitement as the small crowd of refugees and Stroganov company men filed across the church porch and into the nave. As was the tradition, the small group of women stood on the left and the larger group of men on the right. The church's altar lacked the elaborate adornment of those in Moscow and Novgorod. However, this simplicity served to accentuate the divine drama of the large gold cross suspended above the sanctuary and heightened the mystery and sense of anticipation surrounding the large veiled icon on the right side of the iconostasis.

In the sanctuary behind the iconostasis, Father Ivanov prepared for Mass. He was attended by two altar boys selected from the refugees from Novgorod. Only males attending to the Mass were permitted in the sanctuary. The iconostasis represented the division between the divine and secular worlds. While marking the division, it also served to unite these two worlds through the insight of the icons; hence, it constituted both a division and reconciliation.

As soon as the church was full, Father Ivanov commenced the Mass. As customary, the congregation stood throughout the service, with the men bareheaded and the adult women covering their hair with scarves. The Orthodox Mass was mystical, passionate, and time-consuming. But these inhabitants of the frontier appreciated the opportunity to participate in the Divine Liturgy. They lost little of their spiritual fervor as Father Ivanov proceeded through the Entrance and Vesting Prayers; the Liturgy of Preparation, the "Proskomedia"; the Liturgy of Catechumens; the Transition Litanies; and finally, the Liturgy of the Faithful, reaching its zenith in Holy Communion.

As Father Ivanov brought the Mass to its conclusion in celebration and thanksgiving, he moved through the royal doors in the center of the iconostasis. These doors were restricted to ordained clergy and contained icons of the four evangelists and the Annunciation. The icons had been imported from Moscow and were dark in coloration and simplistic in design.

Father Ivanov walked to a veiled icon and grasped the corner of the cloth covering. "We have a special reason for thanksgiving today," the priest began.

He chose his words carefully, avoiding any mention of Novgorod or the Tsar. "Petr Safronov, through the generous support of our host and patron, Yakov Stroganov, has created an icon to mark the transition of this pagan wilderness into the light of Orthodox Christianity. I am as eager as any of you to see his work,"

He motioned to Petr, who remained in the middle of the male parishioners, and then asked, "Petr, would you care to unveil your work?"

"No, Father, I am but a vessel of the Holy Spirit. It is more appropriate that you reveal this humble window to the Divine."

"Very well," the priest replied, smiling. He motioned for Yakov Stroganov to come forward, and they quickly pulled the veil from the icon so that its entirety was revealed at once.

A collective gasp filled the church as the splendor of Petr's work was revealed. Church dogma decreed that icons were "written, not painted" so as to minimize the contribution of the secular world through the work of the artist. This icon, however, demonstrated both artistry and spiritual passion of the highest order.

The icon contained three panels, each with a distinctive theme. The theme of the central panel was the baptism of Rus by Princess Olga of Kyiv. She had been the first saint of the Russian Orthodox Church and was known to posterity as "the holy, right-believing Empress Olga of Kyiv."

Princess Olga had been of Varangian heritage and was reputed to have come from Pskov. In 903, she had married Prince Igor I, who had been the son of Rurik, the founder of Russia. After her husband had been murdered in 945, Olga had become regent for her son Svyatoslav until he came of age in 964. In 957, she had visited Emperor Constantine VII in Constantinople and had been baptized into Christianity by Patriarch Polyeuctus.

Upon her return to Kyiv, Princess Olga had been unsuccessful in converting her son to Christianity. However, she had created a political faction interested in seeing Rus Christianized. Through her persistence, she had later been instrumental in converting her grandson Prince Vladimir of Rus into Orthodoxy, and with him, the whole of Rus had entered the Christian fold.

In the center panel, Petr depicted Saint Olga, attended by angels. She was in the center of the fortified city of Kyiv, directing a throng of citizens onto the Heavenly Ladder leading to paradise. At the top of the ladder was a great luminous light depicting the Divine Presence. In the foreground, her grandson, Vladimir the Great, with the assistance of a male angel, was holding the city's battlements against a Muslim assault. In the background, Vladimir's wife, Princess Anna, tended to the wounded and dying defenders of the city and the faith. Anna had been a Byzantine princess, the daughter of Byzantine Empress Theophano and Byzantine Emperor Romanus II.

The right panel of the icon depicted Apostle Peter entering the wilderness. On a great river, Saint Peter stood at the

bow of a boat looking to the east where a female angel, surrounded by divine light, beckoned the voyagers into the Urals.
The members of Peter's crew were pulling in a net of golden
fish representing infidel souls. On the left of the panel and
slightly to the rear of the boat, there were two groups of men
clad in black on the far riverbank. One band was burning clerics at the stake, while the other group was menacing a young
woman attired in pure white.

The maiden was protected by two male angels in robes of
brilliant red, a color favored by Novgorod iconographers. In
the background, on the horizon, rose St. Sophia's Cathedral,
the jewel of Lord Novgorod the Great, surrounded by fire. An
icon portrait of St. Sophia was transported into the wilderness
on Saint Peter's boat.

The left icon panel portrayed a dying man in a forest
clearing attended by a blonde woman. The woman was kneeling next to him and supporting his head while giving him
water. Saint Stephen of Perm was administering extreme unction while three female angels looked on as a dove, representing the man's soul, flew toward a heavenly light in the sky. A
large bear looked upon the scene from the edge of the forest.
The bear stood upon the carcasses of two dogs, their heads
snarling even in death. In the background, beyond the forest, was the Stroganov Chusovaya fortress. There was a large,
luminous Russian cross in the center of the stockade.

None present had ever seen a work of such brilliance and
luminosity. The Novgorod School of iconography was noted
for its independence, but the icon before them transcended
all that had come before it. Petr had incorporated the vigorous composition of Novgorod as well as the graceful figures
and rounded forms of the Yaroslavl School. He had used gold
highlighting in the robes of the principal characters in the
Pskov tradition and employed a light blue, reflective of the
Tver School, to enhance the sense of ascendant salvation portrayed throughout the work.

Iconographers in the Novgorod School often employed pure, unmixed colors. Petr chose instead to use multiple layers of translucent colors to impart an ethereal spirituality to the work. While the Metropolitan in Moscow would undoubtedly find the work heretical, those present could only stand in wonder at this window to the Divine Spirit.

So mesmerized were the men near the icon that they lingered, murmuring quietly to each other long after the service was concluded. Father Ivanov saw Matrona and Kachalov on the far side of the church, waiting for the men to leave so that she could cross into the male section to get a closer look at the masterpiece. He went to the couple and escorted them across the nave to the front of the icon.

"Look closely, and you will find some features that are quite familiar," he instructed.

Observing the right panel, Matrona felt almost giddy as she noted that St. Peter looked a good deal like Father Ivanov. The angel beckoning the men into the wilderness was a captivating dark-skinned woman of an unknown race. As Matrona shifted her focus to the far bank of the river, she became lightheaded and felt her knees begin to buckle. Kachalov sensed her instability and put his arm around her waist for support. Matrona took a deep breath. The woman being menaced by the black-clad figures was Petr's Anna. The angels protecting her were Dimitri and Andrei.

Matrona shifted her attention to the center panel. At first, she found nothing familiar, but then she gave a little cry and squeezed Kachalov's hand. She pointed to the male angel attending Vladimir the Great; it was Kachalov. Vladimir bore a striking resemblance to Yakov and was posed in a manner that was unmistakably Stroganov.

As Matrona viewed the final panel on the left, tears came to her eyes, and she wept uncontrollably. The scene depicted therein was of the death of Pitiu, and she was the woman in attendance. Even the bear bore a striking resemblance to the small bronze totem that accompanied her at all times.

Father Ivanov came forward and embraced her. "Some would find heresy in these manifestations of humanity. These are the same people who would use scenes of warfare to depict the presence of the loving Christ. This icon surely constitutes an emotional and spiritual release for Petr and a great blessing for this church and her people. I feel the hand of God in it."

CHAPTER 37

Stroganov Stronghold - Early July 1570

It was a hot and muggy afternoon. Petr was putting the finishing coat of hot linseed oil varnish on the second of four traditional icons he was painting for the royal doors of the church iconostasis. The varnish was drying very slowly in the humid weather. Petr had decided to call it a day and begin again in the morning when Stroganov arrived.

Stroganov said, "A courier from my brother has arrived with some alarming news. The Tsar is sending an envoy to inspect our operations. He and his entourage should arrive in late September."

Petr wiped the sweat from his brow with a cloth before responding, using the moment to collect his thoughts and steady his emotions. "I assume the bad news is that most of the Novgorodians best disappear by autumn?"

Noting that Stroganov seemed equally disturbed by the news, Petr smiled. "Is there any good news from your brother?"

"Some information that may be useful was included, more of a challenge, really. But we will take that up later; we need to contact Captain Kachalov and Father Ivanov for a meeting this evening."

◊

The evening meal was cleared, and the men retreated to Stroganov's study. Neither Petr nor Kachalov had informed Matrona of the situation precipitated by the visit from the Tsar's emissary. They felt she would be unduly troubled unless they could come up with a palatable plan before informing her.

The study, though small, was sumptuously appointed with fine carpets and tapestries. The men sat around a small table in the middle of the room, which was well-lighted by silver candelabra. At a side table, a house servant tended a "sbitennik." This precursor to the samovar resembled a metal teakettle fitted with a heater pipe and legs. A cold front had moved in, bringing chilly weather, and the servant was preparing "sbiten," a hot drink of honey and a variety of spices and berries.

After the sbiten was served, Stroganov began the conversation. "It is obvious from your icon, Petr, that you have discerned my plan for dispersing your refugees."

Petr replied, "Well, I don't know when they became my charge, but since we can't go north, south, or west without running into the Tsar's watchdogs, east is the only direction left to us."

"What do we know of the peoples to the east?" Father Ivanov inquired. "I've heard that there are people there that eat their dead — serve them up to their favored guests."

Stroganov laughed. "Well, if that is true, those people are far to the north and east. Most of what we know about the area east of the Urals comes from Novgorodian traders two hundred years ago and their soldiers who battled the Ugrians there a hundred years ago. But again, that was far away. Few, if any, Russians have journeyed up the Chusovaya and explored its basin and the lands directly to our east."

Kachalov offered, "I don't expect that any group you run into going east will be delighted to see a party of Russians from whatever region. Actually, the Komi and Voguls on this side of the Urals may be the most hostile. They are angry that we have pretty much cleaned out all the fur-bearing animals. I'm afraid our friend Pitiu was an exception, and my recklessness there certainly won't help."

Father Ivanov touched Kachalov on the shoulder. "Your guilt has been more than enough penance for your mistake, Yuri. You must let it go. It is but a small drop in a very large bucket of troubles, a bucket that is sure to spill over in time."

"If we are to flee into the Urals, we will need more provisions and armaments than we brought from Novgorod," Petr observed.

Stroganov nodded his agreement. "I am prepared to supply whatever is needed."

Petr was visibly shocked. "That is quite generous — no, that is extremely generous of you, Master Stroganov."

"You may call me Yakov. The icons you painted more than met any servitude I was due. Besides, we no longer need to keep up pretenses." He smiled and then went on.

"Besides, my offer is based on more than generosity. I badly need information about the geographical and political obstacles we will confront as we move into the Urals and beyond. This is what we presently know ...."

Stroganov explained what was known about the area to the east of the Urals, which consisted largely of the Ob and Irtysh river basins and their tributaries, the Tura and Tobol Rivers. While there had been little penetration by the Russians into the Urals up the Chusovaya, more was known from trade routes into the Ob and Irtysh region from the north and south. The region was controlled by the Khanate of Sibir, whose ruler was Kuchum Khan. Kuchum was a direct lineal descendent of Genghis Khan.

The region had once been subject to the rule of the Golden Horde. But in the mid-fifteenth century, the Golden Horde had shattered into the Nogai and Great Hordes and the Astiak, Kazan, Crimean, and Sibir Khanates. The Khanate of Sibir had consisted of the ruling Siberian Tatars and the subjugated Ostyaks, Voguls, Nenets, and Selk'ups.

Kuchum's predecessors, the pagan brothers Khans Yediger and Bekbulat, had agreed in 1556 to pay an annual tribute in furs to Tsar Ivan IV. But after ousting his pagan predecessors in 1563, the Muslim Kuchum had been reluctant to honor that agreement. Reports were coming in that Kuchum was referring to himself as the Tsar of Sibir. Reportedly, he was almost blind and relied on his son, Mahmetkul, to lead his armies.

The capital of the Khanate was Sibir, also called Isker in Tatar. Sibir was located on the right bank of the Irtysh River, two days travel up the Irtysh from its confluence with the Tobol River. Before the sixteenth century, under the Uzbek Khan Ibak, the capital of the Khanate had been Chingi-Tura, which remained a trading gateway between Siberia and Europe.

"Any journey into this region will be as dangerous as it is daunting," Petr observed. "What do you expect of us, in addition to disappearing?"

Stroganov replied, "Well, as Captain Kachalov has noted, the foreign demand for furs has all but eliminated fur-bearing animals north and west of the Urals. A prime sable pelt, unripped, with bellies and feet, is worth more than the yearly income of a peasant family. A black fox is worth ten times that. We need to tap the fur resources to the east."

"But most of the Novgorodians are not trappers; I doubt any are." Father Ivanov interjected.

Stroganov said, "We don't expect you to send back furs; if you did, it would be excellent but not expected. What we need most is information. I have heard there are silver, lead, and sulfur deposits in the eastern Urals. The Tobol basin is said to present excellent grazing opportunities for cattle. This all needs to be verified. I will send couriers with you. We also need an 'ostrog' at the headwaters of the Chusovaya for the same reason."

The ostrog was a fortified trading post. Small ostrogs were called "ostrozeks." They protected trading routes and provided a base for commerce and intelligence.

"An ostrog will not be well received by the Voguls, Ostyaks, or the Tatars," Kachalov observed. "In fact, I would expect it to be vigorously and violently opposed."

Stroganov stated, "That is why I will send a substantial force of soldiers with you. And most of them will have a harquebus. The Khan's troops, particularly the subjugated natives that are forced to take up arms, are unfamiliar with firearms. A few volleys of fire and lead might even gain you a few converts, Father."

"I would rather employ spiritual persuasion!" the priest retorted.

"I'm sure you would, Father, but violence on the frontier is a fact of life, and death. By establishing footholds in the Urals, we will satisfy the Tsar and keep him off your trail."

Petr didn't think Father Ivanov was much placated by the interchange and thought it best to change the subject. "This all seems very adventurous, but when do we come back?"

"I believe the better question is 'if' and not 'when,'" Stroganov replied. "The Tsar has a long memory, and this region is filling up with Muscovites at a rapid rate. It may be several years before it is safe to come west of the Urals."

"Well, they won't last several years east of the Urals!" Kachalov remarked.

Stroganov said, "There may be a third option. Petr, as you will recall, I told you about some information I had from my brother that may be useful but challenging."

Stroganov went on to explain what his brother had found out. The Stroganovs were exploring sea access to the Ob Basin through the Russian North. They were cooperating in trading ventures with the English and Dutch. To this end, they had purchased Lithuanian, Livonian, and Swedish prisoners of war from the ever-warring Ivan IV.

The Stroganovs had talked to a prisoner from Brussels who was incarcerated at the Yaroslavl prison, with the intent of purchasing him. His name was Oliver Brunnel, and he had a good deal of maritime experience in the Russian North. He had been arrested as a suspected spy. Brunnel firmly believed that seafarers could reach China by sailing through the Arctic Ocean.

"That sounds like a long way," Petr observed. "And a long, hungry way to boot. We don't even know our way over the Urals, let alone a route across the entire continent."

"Well, the first part I can help you with," Stroganov replied. "And let us hope that the second part will not be necessary."

Stroganov motioned to one of the house servants, who left the room only to return momentarily with a short, swarthy man with a round, weather-beaten face, long black hair, and piercing black eyes.

Stroganov went to him and placed his hand on the man's shoulder. "This is Bedi. Bedi is Tatar on his father's side and Ostyak on his mother's side. Kuchum's men killed his whole family except for Bedi, who was fortunate enough to be hunting at the time. Before that, he had to give up much of his fur harvest for the tribute to Ivan. So, you see, he hates the Khan and the Tsar. You might say he is the perfect guide for a bunch of Novgorodian refugees.

"Before your refugee band heads for the Urals, you and Bedi need to scout the route up the Chusovaya as far as possible. You will especially need to pick a location for the ostrog. Winter will be here all too soon, and you will need its protection and shelter from the elements.

"Just Bedi and me?" Petr inquired somewhat apprehensively.

Stroganov answered, "No, Bedi can pick out a dozen or so of my soldiers. I would stick with Russians. The locals can go feral on you as soon as they leave our stronghold here."

Petr wished he had as much faith in the Russians, who he found to be scurrilous for the most part.

CHAPTER 38

Upper Chusovaya - Late July 1570

Not everyone who courts death wants to die. That was certainly the case with Petr Safronov, although he was just now beginning to realize it. He was concealed under the low-lying branches of a pine tree that was perched on the western bank of a sizable river that flowed into the Chusovaya River about two versts downstream from his location. He had been part of a scouting party that had journeyed two weeks upstream from the Stroganov stronghold at the confluence of the Chusovaya and Kama. Now he was alone.

The cold waters hissed as the swift current undercut the stream bank where the river curved sharply away to the south just before it flowed into the Chusovaya. The lower portion of the bank had been devoured by the voracious waters, and a good third of the tree's roots hung unsupported in the air. Eventually the entire tree would slide into the river to join the hundreds of other sweepers that strained the stream of floating debris. Petr hoped this wouldn't be soon. There was no other suitable cover to conceal his presence from a large group of Voguls just around the bend.

As they journeyed upriver, the landscape adjoining the river had gradually given way from the larch, fir, and pine of the boreal forest to a riverine landscape of marshes and meadows with intermittent pine forests.

Petr had been fortunate to spot the lead element of the Voguls before his presence was discovered. He had just enough time to dive under the sheltering boughs of the low-bushy pine. Unfortunately, he had no opportunity to wipe out his tracks in the mud on the trail side of the tree. The surrounding stunted trees and low-lying shrubs precluded any attempt at a fast and undetected escape. Crawling would just leave a wider track in the mud.

The Voguls had stopped in a small clearing to prepare a cooking fire. Petr counted 32 men. There were no women. The group was too big for a hunting party, which meant it was on a raiding mission. Due to the sharp bend in the river, the Voguls were a quarter of a verst directly opposite Petr, but on the same bank. He took some comfort in this, as it would take them several minutes to run around the loop, time he would need if he had to outrun them.

It was late July, and the strength of the sun had returned, but the morning chill was still in the air, and the stream still ran turbid and cold. Due to the presence of the Voguls, Petr was unable to remove the extra layer of clothing required for the morning. As the sun reached its zenith, he began to sweat profusely. The sweat ran down his forehead in rivulets, stinging his eyes and obscuring his vision. To add to his discomfort, mosquitoes descended in hordes to feast upon every inch of his exposed skin. He dared not move. Petr closed his eyes in a vain attempt to distance his mind from his physical discomfort. He tried to concentrate on the situation at hand.

From the start, this had been a foolhardy mission; error upon compounded error ensued. Stroganov should never have permitted the dozen Stroganov men to go on this scouting expedition unescorted by Father Ivanov or someone with more authority than Bedi and him. Not that they would have listened to the Ostyak-Tatar guide in any event. In the eyes of the Russians, Bedi was twice cursed.

Like most Westerners, the Stroganov men looked upon Tatars with fear and loathing. Further, they had no respect for the indigenous people of the Urals, be they Ostyak, Komi, or

Vogul. Like most of the European voyagers before them, they were, at best, adventurers, and if presented with the opportunity, they quickly sank to piracy and barbarity without a second thought.

The Stroganov men had deserted the scouting expedition to pillage a nearby Mansi village. The inhabitants of the village had been slaughtered, and their homes pillaged. The Russian raiders were undoubtedly on their way out of the Urals with the booty of furs seized from the hapless villagers. This whole episode had resulted in halting their scouting expedition before they had journeyed very far into the upper reaches of the Chusovaya. The goal at hand was to explore the upper reaches farther up the river, several days travel from the present location.

The goal of scouting the exodus route for 150 Novgorodian refugees into the Urals had now turned into a survival exercise. Here, the rivers were wild, the climate harsh, and the inhabitants fierce. In order to survive, one traveled in stealth or in force. Force had been eliminated as an option with the desertion of the Russians. Petr and Bedi had figured the odds of one of them making it back to the Stroganov stronghold on the Kama would be increased if they split up.

Bedi had gone further up the Chusovaya to ascertain any obstacles created by the spring freshet. He would also scout the presence of any hostile forces that would be present in the fall. He also needed to locate a site for an "ostrozhek," or small fort. The fort would provide shelter for the Novgorodian refugees and Stroganov soldiers from the fierce Siberian winter and any attacks by the Tartars, Mansi, and Komi-Permyak inhabitants of the region. The ever-present Vogul raiding parties were a major concern as well. Incursions of Cossacks or warriors of Kuchum Khan, the Tatar ruler of the Ob River basin to the east of the Urals, while less likely, could not be ruled out. The upper Chusovaya was certainly within the reach of the Khan's Siberian stronghold at Chingi Tura.

For his part, Petr would head back, retracing their route up from the Stroganov stronghold on the Kama. It would not be an easy journey. When the Russians had deserted, they took all of the food and most of the gunpowder. Petr glanced at the harquebus lying next to him. He had only enough gunpowder and ammunition for three or four shots. If the Voguls attacked, he doubted that he could load fast enough to get more than one or two shots off. That is, if he could get the thing to fire. It was ill-suited to the damp riverine environment, which made the gunpowder and matchlock mechanism unreliable. Even under ideal conditions, the harquebus was mainly useful in mass shooting due to its weight and inaccuracy. Petr knew that as an individual fighting implement, it was best used as a club.

Food was Petr's primary concern. Already, he was feeling lightheaded from lack of nourishment. The berries that he had found were plentiful and delicious but did not supply the sustenance he needed for an arduous journey. Due to its inaccuracy, the harquebus was useless for hunting. Bedi had given him a crash course in setting snares for squirrels and hares and locating and spearing pike. He had also provided several fishhooks made of bone for fishing for carp and perch. These endeavors would be time-consuming, especially for a novice, and time was of the essence if he were to return to the Kama in time to prepare for a September departure.

Petr forced himself to ignore his hunger pangs and focus on his immediate predicament. The Voguls presented a fierce appearance. They were stocky and shorter than Western Russians. Their dark, tanned faces and arms indicated they had been in the field for an extended period of time. They certainly looked hostile, as all were armed, many with bows or crossbows and a few with harquebuses. There were many large packs lying about, and Petr assumed they contained booty obtained by sacking local villages.

Given the presence of the Vogul raiding party, Petr wondered about the fate of the deserters. The Voguls were much fiercer than the Mansi and Komi-Permyaks. They had no love for Russians, or any other non-Vogul for that matter. Perhaps the contents of the sacks scattered among the Voguls had been taken from the Russian deserters.

Petr's reflection on the plight of the Russians was interrupted by a commotion downstream from the Voguls' position. The whooping, hollering, and laughter of the small band of Voguls preceded their appearance on the trail by a good five minutes.

As they emerged from a bend in the trail, Petr was able to observe the source of their gaiety. Stumbling along in the midst of the Voguls were three bloodied members of the Russian scouting part. Petr recognized Shastalov, the leader of the deserters, whose right arm hung limply at his side. Either it was broken, or his shoulder was dislocated. He cried out in pain as he was poked and prodded by his captors.

The other two captives had been clubbed in the head so severely that they were unrecognizable. Petr wondered if the remaining nine members of the scouting party had escaped or been killed. He had worried that the deserting Russians would spread the word about the Novgorodian plans when they reached an area of Muscovy influence. He supposed that there was less of a chance of that now. He felt guilty about thinking this and pushed it aside. He realized there was little time, and no reason, to ponder the fate of the missing Russians.

There was a trail along the riverbank. It had obviously been used by animals and humans alike for many years. If the Voguls came upstream, they would use this trail and pass within a few paces of Petr's hideout. Even in their celebratory mood, he doubted they would fail to spot him. The only chance of escape he could see was to slip over the bank, hold onto the overhanging roots, and hope that he wasn't spotted. The trail was so close to the river that even a harquebus could hit him at that short range.

For the moment, he had a respite from danger as the

Voguls started a campfire. Several squatted down to cook, and most of the rest sat or stretched out on the ground. Three men got up and spread out to search for dry wood to replenish the fire. Petr noted that one of the men, who was headed his way, disappeared behind a grove of willows. He watched closely to see where the man ended up. He was somewhat relieved when the man reappeared near the campfire, but it would have been good to know the length of time the willows would block the Vogul's view of his position.

Petr closed his eyes to gain some relief from the sweat that was running down his forehead. It was insufferably hot, and the little pine offered scant protection from the withering rays of the afternoon sun. He fought the urge to doze. Inattention could be deadly. Still, the heat and the sound of the water dulled his senses. He imagined floating in the river, the cool waters washing the heat away. His mind drifted back to Novgorod, the carefree time he had spent with his father and brother on the Volkhov River at the outlet of Lake Ilimen. It had been a golden time. The late summer sun had been hot, and the lake and river had been gentle and cool.

He was jolted from his reverie by the shouts and curses coming from downstream. The Voguls were kicking and prodding their Russian captives to their feet. One of the badly beaten men wouldn't, or couldn't, get up despite the additional beating he was taking. A lone Vogul who was standing to the side calmly walked into the bedlam and lifted the Russian's head by the hair. Suddenly, Petr saw the flash of a blade across his throat and the instant convulsions of the victim. He made no sound that could be heard from Petr's hideout.

Petr's mind reeled in revulsion. He remembered the slaughter of pigs in the fall at their country estates, the squealing and screaming of the hogs as their throats were slit. If the cut was deep enough to sever the windpipe, there was only gurgling and wild eyes. It had been a tapestry of horror that was now being played out in human form.

Several Voguls grabbed the hapless Russian and threw him into the river before his death throes had subsided. The similarities of this atrocity to the barbarity of the Cossacks on the Kama River stunned Petr. Images of Anna, the blood in the snow, and the insanity of retribution came flooding back. He wanted to scream; he felt it rising in his throat, but movement across the stream distracted him. A familiar form, tawny, angelic, and primal, was moving at the edge of the forest. And then she was gone. But he felt something deep inside him stir; it held him back. He had responsibilities to the refugees, but that was not it. He wanted to delve into the sacred and produce great art, but that was not it. He knew that something important and sublime awaited him, something that pulled him inexorably to the East. Petr pulled himself together. It was a time for action, not a time for panic.

The Voguls downstream gathered their packs and weapons and prepared to move out. To Petr's dismay, they were heading in his direction. The leading element was already entering the stand of willows. A small group held up the rear. They had the Russian prisoners in tow and were busy prodding and tormenting them into movement.

Petr felt like a hare with hunters nearby. He twitched in anticipation of flight, afraid to move and afraid to remain. Timing was critical. He had to act before the first group emerged from the willows, as they would certainly spot his movement. The Voguls in the rear could also spot him if he moved too soon, but they were further away and distracted.

Petr could wait no longer. He thrust himself forward and over the edge of the riverbank.

CHAPTER 39

Stroganov Stronghold - July 1570

Matrona felt warm and cozy in the women's quarters, especially after the warm bath with scented soap from France. She sat at a small desk with a soft robe over her lap. It was a nice break from the small cabin that she shared with Yuri back at the saltery. Not that she would trade the freedom of their frontier home for the ordered luxury of the *Domostroi* household of the Stroganovs. She thoroughly enjoyed the carnal pleasures of married life and resented the barriers that upper-crust Russian society erected to thwart conjugal bliss.

She was sitting at a small desk with a bear-hide robe over her lap. It was the same robe in which she had been trussed up like a goose by her Cossack abductor. She kept it at the Stroganov complex because Yuri found it too painful a reminder of the demise of Pitiu to keep at home. Matrona, to the contrary, found it liberating. It reminded her of the resilience she had attained on the long, hard trail from Novgorod. She tried to convey some of her feelings in a journal she had begun after the funeral ceremony for Pitiu.

July 25, 1570

It has been a day of contradictions. At midday, it was hot, but this evening, it has been quite cold. I have my big bear on my lap to comfort me. My little bear has been put away to rest. I sense that much will be expected of him in the future, although I have no clear idea as to his ultimate fate, or ours for that matter.

Yuri has been very affectionate yet remote. It is clear that there is something important about to occur. Something that Yuri knows but is not at liberty to share with me. His concealment is not such a big thing. It is in the Novgorodian interest that plans are secret. Muscovy informants are everywhere. There may be secrets here at the Stroganov stronghold, but once we are home in our own bed, I will know everything. It is such a joy pulling information from him.

Petr is on an expedition up the Chusovaya. I suspect that this is a scouting expedition, and the men from Novgorod will be leaving soon after he returns. Boats loaded with supplies and weapons have been arriving for several weeks. There is no indication they are going downstream, and the supplies have not been stowed in the stockade's storehouses. Instead they have been placed on wooden platforms near the river and covered with tents or tarps.

I know that Petr will go with the men, whenever and wherever it may be. They look to him for leadership, he and Father Ivanov. But they will look mainly to Petr. Father Ivanov frightens them, not merely because he is clergy, but also his intensity.

I will miss Petr immensely, but I will survive. A few short months ago, I could not have endured his departure. But things are different now. I am no longer a spoiled maiden of the city. I am a frontier woman now and glad of it. I have taken what the frontier has thrown at me and used it to forge an inner strength that I otherwise could not have imagined.

In some ways, I am even stronger than Yuri. He still leans on his military status. I have had all status stripped from me and came through the better for it. I no longer yearn for Novgorod. If I had stayed, I would be little more than a pet playing parlor games. Here I am a full partner in forging a new existence in the wilderness. Perhaps we can create a better life than that we left and that which we found.

I am fortunate. I have found a measure of contentment here. I am afraid that Petr's destiny will be far more difficult.

I see the faraway look in his eyes. It is as if he is looking across the ages. He is driven by forces that he senses but does not fully understand. One can see this in his icon. The dark-skinned angel draws him to her, to the East — to his fate.

I must sleep now. So, it is off to my dreams — dreams of rivers and icons and Petr's angel. Perhaps Yuri will come to me. That would be so fine, so very fine.

CHAPTER 40

Upper Chusovaya - Late July 1570

The water was much colder than he had expected. Petr's chest muscles and testicles contracted violently, forcing the air out of his lungs and jolting his heart. He struggled to refill his lungs with air. The riverbank was sliding by at an alarming pace. He reached for a tree root sticking out of the bank, but he was numb — clumsy. He missed badly and lunged at another root that came up quickly in the swift current. This time, he managed to get his right hand wrapped around the root and hung on.

The force of the current twisted Petr around and added to the stress on the root, which was dry-rotted near the top of the bank. With a loud crack, it gave way, and he was once again hurtling downriver. The current pulled him under, and he kicked hard for the surface. He was heavy, and his efforts had little effect. His lungs screamed for air, but the surface eluded him. Suddenly, he realized that he still clutched the harquebus in his left hand. He dropped it, and with two strong kicks, he broke the surface and gulped a big breath of air.

Petr's relief at not drowning was short-lived. There was a shout from the Voguls on the riverbank, and a crossbow bolt cleaved the water inches from his head. The grim reality of his situation became very stark. The range of the Voguls' bows and crossbows easily covered the near bank out to the middle of the river. He didn't fear the harquebuses. He knew the Voguls would be lucky to hit the river, let alone a little head moving swiftly downstream.

Petr dove beneath the water and struck for the far shore. He gave mental thanks to God for the turbidity of the river and his father's swimming lessons. When his lungs gave out, he kicked to the surface. He was quickly bracketed by arrows and bolts, but the steep angle of their descent told him that he was near the limit of their range. He submerged once again, and when he resurfaced, the barrage of bolts and arrows was far short.

Heaving a sigh of relief, Petr floated for a few minutes, trying to regain some strength. He was numb from the cold water but knew it would be worse if he didn't have his wool sweater on. Even wet, it provided some warmth. He glanced at the far shore. He was a good distance downriver from the Vogul band and figured he had escaped unscathed. But he was dismayed to see a Vogul with a crossbow loping along the riverbank, tracking his movement downriver. Suddenly, the Vogul disappeared into a large stand of willows.

Petr suspected the Vogul was not gone for good but had a malicious plan for Petr's demise. But he had a more immediate situation that could prove dire. The river was sweeping him quickly toward the Chusovaya, and where it entered the larger river, it built up tall standing waves that were a definite drowning threat. He would be bounced around like a waterlogged piece of driftwood and ran the risk of being trapped in the waves until his strength failed and he drowned.

Petr's attention was so focused on the standing waves he failed to notice a large sweeper that was dead ahead. Flowing with the current, he did not feel like he was moving; rather, the partially submerged tree looked like it was coming at him, a giant broom that would sweep him under and into its submerged branches.

As he approached the sweeper, he could see the carcass of a moose calf caught in its branches. Not wishing a similar fate, he kicked and pulled with all his strength toward the middle of the river. The current was unbelievably strong, and despite his best efforts, he was inexorably swept into the waiting sweeper. As his feet impacted the branches, he could feel them clutch at his leggings like a monstrous living creature. Then he was under the water.

Petr kicked frantically. He had not taken a deep breath when he went under, and his lungs were burning from the lack of oxygen. His brain screamed that he was dying, the death throes of an ignominious end. He fought through it, continued to twist and kick.

Suddenly he was free. The same current that had put him in peril had now saved him. His weight, added to that of the moose calf, had been more than the branch could hold, and it had snapped, freeing them both. Petr sucked in air and caught a glimpse of the blue sky above, a natural icon and perhaps an omen. And then he was in the standing waves.

The waves jostled him about, and he knew he had to kick his way through to the Chusovaya, but his strength was failing him. His body was pulling his blood into his core to protect his vital organs, leaving his limbs deprived of blood and oxygen. He was numb — flailing. Suddenly, a pungent odor assaulted his nostrils. The stench was overpowering, but it acted like smelling salts and momentarily revived his senses.

Something bumped into the back of his head. He swiveled in the water and discovered the revolting carcass of the dead moose calf bobbing about like a hideous cork. The gasses of decomposition had filled the inside of the body, making it buoyant. Petr retched, grabbed a putrid leg, and hung on. He found that with the added buoyancy, he was able to float and conserve energy.

Petr clenched his teeth and tried not to breathe too deeply. He had no food in his stomach, and if he got the dry heaves, it would further sap his failing energy. He concentrated his attention on the near bank of the river. He saw that, ever so slowly, he and his rotting companion were making headway.

After what seemed like an interminable period of time, but was probably only minutes, they were at last at the junction of the two rivers. Petr said a quick prayer of gratitude for the strange salvation and kicked his way into the Chusovaya.

The Chusovaya current was no swifter than that of its tributary, but it seemed heavier, more forceful. Petr raised his head and craned his neck to get his bearings. He was in the middle of the river in the strongest current. Up ahead, the river made a sharp turn to the left, the main current gnawing against the right bank. And there, perched above the roiling waters, was Petr's Vogul nemesis. He had obviously cut across the countryside to put himself in an ideal position to skewer Petr as he drifted by, well within the range of the Vogul's crossbow.

The Vogul had already spotted Petr. He waved and beckoned derisively for Petr to come closer. He was obviously in a good mood, knowing that he would get at least two, and maybe three, shots at Petr at point-blank range. Petr let go of the moose carcass and tried swimming away from the cut bank, but his efforts were feeble — useless. As he drifted toward shore, he could see the Vogul's face. Swarthy from sun and wind, his face had a deep scar running from his right ear, across his mouth, and ending on the left side of his chin. He smiled broadly, but his eyes were serious, and his overall countenance was menacing.

Petr dove under the water to escape, but in his reduced state, he could not hold his breath very long. As he broke surface, he saw the crossbow aimed directly at him. Suddenly, there was a brown blur, and the crossbow, and the Vogul holding it, disappeared. Petr could not see what was happening. Suddenly, there were loud growls and blood-curdling screams, and then silence. Well downstream now, Petr looked back and saw a huge brown bear on the riverbank. The bear was looking directly at him. He felt no menace — just release and a sense of recognition.

The river picked up speed. Ahead, Petr saw a huge rock protruding from the water and reaching a height equal to the tree line on the riverbank. Petr maneuvered as best he could toward the outcropping. He knew that there would be an eddy created where the main current flowed around the rock. The trick was to get as close to the rock as possible and get drawn into the eddy without hitting the obstacle. He was almost successful. The rock came at him fast, too fast. His right shoulder impacted the rock, spinning him around and under the water. Petr stretched his arms to stop his rotation and kicked toward the surface. When he came up, he was in calm water in the middle of the eddy. Fortunately, the rock had been worn smooth by the current, and his shoulder was bruised, but there was no break or dislocation.

Petr rested in the calm water, moving just enough to keep himself afloat. Unfortunately, he would need to confront the river current again before he could reach shore. He did not believe he could make it in his enfeebled state. His mind was as numb as his body. He looked up at the blue mid-afternoon sky. *This is not such a bad place to die*, he thought. *Too bad, though; that sky would make a great backdrop for an icon, an icon I'll never get to create.*

As he lowered his head, Petr's peripheral vision caught some movement on shore. He swung his body in that direction and was astonished to see the woman of his dream-vision standing there looking at him. She was dressed in finely tanned animal hides decorated with small shells and feathers. Her raven black hair hung below her waist. Her movement was graceful, and it was clear that she was slender and supple. Her bronzed skin seemed burnished rather than weathered. Her face was finely featured with wide-set, luminous brown eyes and an angelic countenance.

Petr longed to meet this ethereal presence. Knew he never would and wept. She shook her head, scolding his negative thoughts. She turned around as if to leave. His mind screamed,

"Don't leave!" She turned around and beckoned to him.

Maybe if I aim up-current, I can get across before I succumb, he thought. *It's worth a try. Better to die trying than give up. If I give up, all that has happened, or will happen, is meaningless.*

He struck for the shore, kicking and clawing with all his last reserves of strength and energy. He tumbled under the current, clutching and scratching at the loose gravel on the riverbed. Realizing that it was much shallower than he anticipated, he gathered his legs under his body and thrust forward. His feet got little purchase in the loose grave, and he rose to the surface only to be pushed under again. Again, he thrust with both legs. This time, the bottom was firm, but the current caught him as if it were a living entity unwilling to release him. The world spun in a dizzying blur. He lost all sense of time and place.

As his senses returned, he felt ripples gently lapping at his back. He looked up. She was still there, a bronze glow in the diffused forest light. Her raven tresses were splayed in alluring abandon, and her presence called to unmet dreams and aching memories to be. She beckoned once and walked into the forest.

Petr staggered to his feet and stumbled after her. He pushed through the willows into a stand of fir trees. There was a clearing with something dark on the ground at its far edge. He looked for the woman, but she was gone, if she was ever really there. Petr's body shook with exhaustion. He tried to call out, but his vision blurred and faded before he could utter a sound.

◊

Petr awakened to the sounds of the boreal forest with the river splashing and gurgling in the background. A breeze sighed softly through the fir trees, and a fish jumped in the river. He wondered about the woman in his visions who had saved him yet again. He knew she would be gone. He heard what sounded like doves very close to him. Opening his eyes very slowly, he spied a brace of large black grouse less than a stone's throw away. He was very hungry; a grouse or two would be just what he needed.

The grouse were pecking around in the duff under the fir trees and seemed oblivious to his presence. He knew that grouse were not the smartest birds and would often freeze in plain sight, hoping you would walk by. But he wasn't walking and feared that any quick movement would send them into flight. Moving only his eyes, he spotted a fist-sized rock next to his right leg. He slowly reached for it with his right arm, managing to absorb, if not ignore, the pain in his bruised shoulder. He was pleased to find that he had a serviceable range of motion despite the pain.

Keeping his eyes on the grouse, Petr gradually worked on getting the rock out of the dirt and needles in which it was embedded. He only moved when the grouse were looking away. At last, he had it firmly in his right hand. He slowly flexed the muscles in his arms and legs. They were all stiff and sore. His feet were raw and sore as the river, at some point, had taken his boots. He knew he couldn't jump to his feet with any alacrity. The birds would be long gone before he staggered erect.

Petr gritted his teeth and, all in one motion, sat up and hurled the rock. He missed his intended target, but the rock bounced once and struck the companion bird with a glancing blow. Stunned and with a broken wing, the bird fluttered about in a frantic figure-eight. Petr lurched to his feet in pursuit of the wounded bird. Stiff and clumsy, he twice failed to catch the bird and finally resorted to flopping his body down on top of it. Not wanting a repeat performance of his physical ineptitude, he smothered the bird with his body until it quit struggling. He then wrung its neck just to be sure. He hated killing, even when necessary. In the custom of the Mansi and Komi, he thanked the bird's spirit.

With his meal secured, Petr began to take stock of his situation. He could tell by the slant of the sun and the dew on the grass in the middle of the clearing that it was still early morning. That was good. Even if the Voguls returned, they would probably not arrive for several hours. But it was foolhardy to stay here any longer than necessary. Nevertheless, the journey downriver would be difficult as he had no hat or shoes, and his harquebus was at the bottom of the river. He was happy to discover that his knife had remained in its sheath and the bone fishing hooks were still in his pocket.

Petr surveyed his surroundings to see what kind of resources nature might provide. He crossed the clearing to examine the dark object on the far side. He was delighted to find it was a dugout canoe. Judging from the small shrubs growing around it, it had been there awhile. But it was not rotted and was still functional. Unfortunately, there were no paddles to be found; the river would have to do all the work. He said a silent prayer to God and his tawny messenger for providing him with a means of salvation. He also acknowledged the original owner of the canoe. Hopefully, it had merely washed away in a spring flood, and the owner had not met with tragedy.

Petr knew that to make it back to the Kama, he would need something on his feet besides skin and blisters. There was a small stand of alder trees near the river. He hobbled over and found one that had a large area of smooth bark. He cut a slab of bark off with his knife, then placing his right foot on the slab, he traced its outline and cut it to fit. He repeated the process for his left foot and cut several more blanks to keep in reserve. Next, he collected moss and dug up tree roots. He used the moss as a cushion between his foot and the bark and then lashed the whole assemblage to his feet with the roots. Except for a couple of beetles squirming between his toes, it was a surprisingly comfortable arrangement.

The fear of returning Voguls was ever-present. He hurried to cut a number of fir boughs to use as a rudder. He then found a sturdy sapling and cut and trimmed a long pole to maneuver in shallow water and fend off boulders and other river obstacles. It was mid-morning before he was able to drag the canoe to the river and load it.

As Petr tossed the grouse into the canoe, he considered slicing off a piece of raw breast and consuming it on the spot. He decided he was hungry but not that ravenous. Settling into the canoe, he found that it was unstable but functional. It had plenty of freeboard to keep the river out in any rapids or standing waves he might encounter.

◊

It was mid-afternoon, and Petr was well downriver from his launch site. The little canoe proved very agile, and he had only used his pole once to fend off a large rock formation in the middle of the current. Hunger was his constant companion. He could think of little else. Ahead of his position in the middle of the river, a pair of ducks erupted noisily into flight near the right bank. Drawn by the commotion, he noticed a small wispy smoke column on the right bank. He did not see any people.

Using the fir boughs, Petr was able to maneuver close enough to the left bank to pole ashore. He climbed a small ridge near the tree line and observed the opposite bank long enough to ensure that there were no people in the immediate vicinity. The smoke drifted up from a small campfire that had burned out over the course of the day. He guessed that it was a cooking fire for breakfast. He wondered whether the individual or group had gone upriver or down. He hoped up because he had not seen anyone since escaping the Voguls, and whatever threat there had been then had passed.

Going ashore on the far bank would be risky, but Petr wanted that fire, risk or no risk. He doubted his makeshift footwear would hold up in a lengthy trek back upriver to the campfire site. He could not go directly across the river as the current would take him far downstream before he made the other side. Holding tight to the canoe, he waded upstream to give himself sufficient space to cross over and land near the campfire. At first, the current near shore was quite tame, but after a few minutes, it increased in velocity until he could hardly stand upright.

Leaning into the strong current, Petr feared slipping on the loose gravel of the riverbed and letting go of the canoe. It was now or never. He jumped into the canoe and pushed off with his pole as hard as he could. He had to squat because it was too wobbly to stand. He pushed twice more with his pole before the water was too deep to reach the bottom. The fir boughs were an inefficient rudder, and he feared he would not make the other bank anywhere near the fire site. But as he approached his objective, he saw two boulders just under the water. The one on the right was larger, and there was an eddy big enough to accommodate the canoe just below it. Sweeping frantically at the current with his fir boughs, he managed to place the canoe directly between the rocks. As he entered the channel between the rocks, he pushed off the smaller one with his pole and thrust the canoe into the eddy.

As Petr poled the canoe toward the riverbank, he was dismayed to see that smoke was no longer rising from the campfire. Once ashore, he sprinted to the fire site. He gently blew the light gray ash away and probed beneath the heavier ash below with a small stick. To his delight, a tiny wisp of smoke rose from a buried coal. He quickly gathered light kindling from the lower branches of a nearby pine. Placing a few dry twigs over the coal, he blew briskly until the twigs ignited. In no time, he had a small fire going. He added larger driftwood to make a bed of coals for cooking and set about preparing his meal.

He plucked the grouse over the river so that the feathers would float away and not leave a telltale sign of his recent presence. He then gutted the bird, setting aside the entrails for fish bait. Rather than wash the grouse in the muddy river, he walked over to a small clear stream that was close by. As he bent over to rinse off the grouse carcass, he was delighted to discover a large number of crayfish scurrying about the bottom of the creek. He collected a dozen and, wrapping them up in his shirt, headed back to the fire.

Later, with the clear blue sky and roasted grouse juice running down his chin, the world at last seemed beautiful and benign. He cooked the crayfish on hot rocks near the fire for a later meal. But now that he was fed and felt his strength returning, he became apprehensive of being discovered. Preparing to leave, he searched the nearby forest for tree fungus. He collected two large pieces and placed them in the fire until they were coals. He then nestled the fungus coals into moss using sedges to secure the packet. With any luck, he would still have embers to start a new fire come nightfall.

Using two pieces of driftwood, Petr dismantled the fire by throwing the larger pieces of burning wood into the river. He then smothered the remaining coals with mud from the riverbank until there was no smoke showing. He would be well downriver before any smoke worked its way to the surface.

As he pushed off from shore, Petr felt more confident than he had in days. He had food, the means of making fire, and a river craft sufficient to get him to the Kama. Even his bark shoes were working out well.

◊

It was mid-morning, and Matrona was writing in her journal. Thoughts of her brother's safety consumed her waking minutes. This is only a short scouting trip, she thought. What will it be like when he is gone for a long time, perhaps forever?

There was a light knock at the door. Thinking it was a servant, she ignored it. She really wasn't ready to meet the day and all of its realities. But the knocking resumed, louder and more insistent. Perturbed, she swung the door open and, to her surprise and delight, found her brother. It was a much thinner, browner, and mosquito-bitten version of Petr that stood beaming before her. She leaped into his embrace, thankful that she would have a few weeks more with him before he departed beyond the stone.

Later, after Petr left for a bath and hearty meal, Matrona reflected on Petr's encounter with the bear. It was clear to her that Pitiu's bear spirit was looking after them, a guardian between intersecting worlds.

CHAPTER 41

Chusovaya River Landing, Early September 1570

Petr sat alone on the high ground above the boat landing. It was going to be a clear day, auspicious for the beginning of such a long journey. A journey from which, he knew in his heart, he would never return. The mist rising from the river matched his own feelings, at once melancholy and uplifting. The river mist was transformed by the pastel rays of the birthing sun. The fleet of simple "strugi" floated like a celestial armada on this ethereal firmament. The falsetto wail of an arctic loon sent a chill through his soul.

As the mist lifted, he could see that the boats rode low in the water. They were filled with enough winter supplies for 250 men. The largess or cunning — only time would tell — of Yakov Stroganov had provided bountiful stores of rye flour, buckwheat, roasted oats, and salt. The provisions would be sufficient only if the boats made it through the upper Chusovaya.

He could hear the sounds of the fort coming alive: the clank of gathered arms and the muffled curses from within the refugee tents as men reluctantly entered their last day in civilization.

He heard a rustling, and Matrona was beside him, gently rubbing his back. He put his arm around her shoulders but did not look, fearing the flood of emotion that her eyes would surely engender.

"I do not fear the journey, but I dread our parting," he said softly. "As do I, Petr."

"Yuri is a good man; otherwise, I would remain."

"Yes, brother, I know. But your destiny is elsewhere. We both know this. I fought it for a while. I was a girl then. But that was long ago, in versts and hardship, if not in time."

"Perhaps you will be reunited with Mother and Father someday, Matrona."

"Yes, Yuri has pledged to help; time will tell."

She leaned over and gently kissed him on the head. "I will not watch you leave Petr; my heart could not bear it. Yuri and I will depart as soon as I return."

They sat in silence for a time, their heads hanging low in thought and remembrance. Then she gently tugged his sleeve.

"I must go now, Petr, before the little girl returns and begs you to stay. But know that wherever you go, my love and prayers reside with you, always."

She pressed a small object into his hand. "Pitiu gave me this. He said I would know what to do with it. I don't know why or how, but it is important to your journey."

Then, as suddenly as she came, she was gone.

Petr looked at the object in his hand. It was a small bronze bear.

EPILOGUE

Downwind is a dangerous place to be in bear country. Armed only with adrenalin and a can of rocks, Albert Johnson glanced nervously into the alder thickets lining the riverbank. A city boy from Seattle, he had been warned not to surprise any of the brown bears that inhabited the Kasilof basin. With its poor eyesight, the river noise masking his approach, and an unfavorable wind, any bear upstream of Johnson was sure to be surprised. This fact alone was sufficient to keep Johnson on the gravel bar as he slowly worked his way upstream against the light breeze blowing down from Tustamena Lake. The swarms of mosquitoes infesting the sloughs abutting the main stream were an added incentive.

Johnson practically jumped out of his boots when a large king salmon exploded from the churning river and landed with a loud thwack. He rattled his can of stones vigorously and peered anxiously into the underbrush. His fight-or-flight instinct was at an all-time high, and he wished that he was someplace else.

Johnson was a history major. He was fascinated with the period of Russian occupation of Alaska. As part of a research project, he had read a 1944 article by T. S. Farrelly entitled "A Lost Colony of Novgorod in Alaska." It reported the discovery of a Russian settlement on the Kasilov River by a federal survey crew in 1937. Some commentators dated the settlement to the late sixteenth century. This was at odds with the historical consensus that the first Russian settlement had been in Kodiak in 1784, two hundred years later than the purported

Kasilof site. And, more troubling, the Kasilof site had never been located again after the initial 1937 report.

Johnson was determined to find and explore this lost settlement. He took a summer job at a cannery in nearby Kenai so that he could spend his off hours exploring the lower Kasilof. Unfortunately, he failed to factor in mosquitoes and bears. Now, on the edge of the river, he was being slowly eaten by the former while dreading his potential consumption by the latter.

As he rounded a sharp bend in the river, Johnson spotted a promising ridge a hundred yards from the river. It had several stands of spruce and offered a good view upstream and downstream. More importantly, he could reach the ridge through an open grassy area that would not require thrashing through the thick underbrush.

It did not take long for Johnson's inexperience to manifest itself. About halfway up the ridge, he found himself in a stand of grass that stood well over his head. The grass was so thick that he could not have spotted a bear a paw's length away.

In a near panic, Johnson thrashed his way uphill until he eventually stumbled into a clearing. Wiping the sweat from his eyes with his handkerchief, he looked around. His panic soon turned to joy as he observed several depressions. Each contained the remnants of log dwellings. He had found the lost settlement; or its equivalent.

At first, Johnson dug aimlessly around the depressions with his trenching tool. Too excited for any methodology beyond rampant curiosity, he moved quickly from spot to spot. After the passage of several hours, he realized that daylight was fading and that he had best concentrate his search. He picked an area with the greatest number of exposed logs and carefully excavated around and under the pile.

After a half-hour of digging, Johnson's shovel hit something hard. Using his knife, he carefully worked the dirt away from the object. It was a carving of a small bear made of bronze. As the sun went behind a cloud, Johnson looked up with alarm. The sun was going down. He did not want to be walking in the near dark with bears about. Any more digging would have to wait.

Johnson took a GPS reading to mark his discovery's location. He quickly picked up the little bear and brushed off the remaining dirt. Suddenly, he sensed something in the tall grass. He looked up to see a large brown mass hurtling through the underbrush.

Good Lord. I didn't know they could move that fast!

As his consciousness faded into darkness, he could hear a conversation in the clearing — Russian.

GLOSSARY & GAZETTEER

Beyond the Stone. Russian medieval expression for traveling over the Ural Mountains into Siberia.

Boyars. The highest members of the Russian aristocratic class, second only to the ruling princes. Ivan the Terrible distrusted many of the boyars, particularly ones who had foreign commercial or family ties.

Chusovaya River. The Chusovaya originates on the eastern side of the Urals and flows through the mountains to the western side and into the Kama River, to which it is a major tributary.

Cossacks. The Cossacks were adventurers, pillagers, and wild men of the frontier who constituted a constant annoyance to civilized society. Originally mostly Tatar, the Cossacks became a blend of Tatar and Slav. Some, the "gorodovyee kazaki," or town Cossacks, were fairly civilized and offered token allegiance to the Tsar. The free Cossacks, however, continued to constitute a threat to trade and settlements on both sides of the Urals.

Domostroi or *Domostroy.* A manual for "domestic order" originally produced in sixteenth-century Russia to instruct and guide the boyar elite in every facet of domestic life. A patriarchal set of manuscripts, it set out extensive rules for the treatment and conduct of women. It was written at the behest of Ivan the Terrible (Ivan the IV) in the years before he became terrible.

Grozny. Ivan Grozny — "Ivan the Terrible," "Ivan the Formidable," or "Ivan the Fearsome;" an epithet for Tsar Ivan IV.

Ivan IV. Ivan IV Vasilyevich was the Grand Prince of Moscow from 1533 to 1547 and the first Tsar of Russia from 1547 to 1584.

Kama River. The longest left bank tributary to the Volga, entering just below the city of Kazan. In medieval times, it was the principal roadway into the Ural Mountains and Siberia.

Metropolitan. The Metropolitan was the head of the Russian Orthodox Church during the Middle Ages. Cyril the IV was Metropolitan of all of Russia from 1568-1572 during the times of terror of Tsar Ivan the Terrible (IV).

Novgorod. Also known as Novgorod the Great, Lord Novgorod the Great, or Novgorod Veliky, it is one of the oldest and most important cities in Russia. Novgorod was a principal medieval Russian commercial, cultural, and political center. Novgorod was forcibly annexed to the Duchy of Moscow by Ivan III in 1478 and sacked by Tsar Ivan the Terrible (Ivan IV) in 1570.

Oprichniki. Tsar Ivan the Terrible's bodyguards or henchmen, who secured and administered the Oprichnina on his behalf.

Oprichnina. A personal estate established by Ivan the IV from 1565 to 1572. It included land seized from the boyars, the feudal aristocracy that had largely governed local and regional affairs prior to the Tsar's consolidation of power. Commonly, "oprichnina" was the widow's share of a noble's estate that could not be taken by other heirs. It attests to Ivan's paranoia that he considered himself as vulnerable as a widow.

Tatars or Tartars. Turkic-speaking peoples who lived in West-Central Russia along the Volga River and its tributary, the

Kama, and into the Ural Mountains and western Siberia. The Tatars were fierce warriors and part of the Golden Horde that fought Ivan IV.

Verst. A former Russian unit of distance measurement equaling approximately 0.7 miles or 1.07 kilometers.

Volga River. One of the great rivers in Europe that provided a major pathway for commerce and invasion in medieval Russia. Flowing through Central Russia to the Caspian Sea, it is the longest river in Europe with the largest discharge and catchment basin. To emphasize its importance, it was often referred to as "Mother Volga."

Zemshchina. *Land held by boyars outside the Oprichnina.* In areas largely consisting of Oprichnina lands, Oprichniki seized the land and forced the boyar owners onto other zemshchina land more remote from the Oprichnina.

ACKNOWLEDGEMENTS

The heart of *The Muse in a Time of Madness* (Muse) lies in Alaska. Alaska is a refuge for those who are rootless or lost. Whether it is the muse of this tale or Robert Service's *The Spell of the Yukon*, which led me to Alaska as a young man, the appeal of the Great Land is irresistible to those with a wandering soul. The muse of this story persists to the present day. I have seen her in Minto and felt her presence whenever I have heard the summer call of an Arctic loon or was swathed in a shimmering aurora at -45° F.

Three faculty members of the University of Alaska set me on a path to conceive and write this novel. Fred Dean, my Department Head in Wildlife Management, encouraged me to expand my education beyond a scientific field of study. Professor Donald Kaufman convinced me that I had the creative ability to write fiction. Fr. William Loyens of the Anthropology Department instilled a desire to understand and appreciate the Indigenous peoples of Alaska and the world.

A work of historical fiction requires a great deal of research to ensure the background authenticity of the story. Much of the research for *Muse* was conducted in *The Alaska Collection* of the Z.J. Loussac Library in Anchorage. The staff there were ever-helpful and encouraging.

Prose alone cannot convey the landscape and tone of the time. Chohnny Sousa provided the artwork and mapping to bring the Medieval Russian era into perspective.

I must give a great deal of thanks to the Soul-Making Keats Literary Competition (SMK) team for increasing my creative fervor by acknowledging my prose and poetry entries over the last several years, especially the recognition for *Muse* in their novel-excerpt competition. The Epilogue for *Muse* received an

SMK short story award under the title "Talisman." "Talisman" was published as flash fiction in *On the Run Fiction*.

I am most thankful to my family, Theron, Jeremy, Emily, Kenny, Joyce, and Erica, who have supported my work with unflagging enthusiasm. My sister, Audrey, and friends Joanne Huff, Claudene Wharton, and Julie Espalin have helped me hone the narrative of this novel. Cathy and Ed Smith, Clif and Beth Usher, and Mary Rose Martin have given me immeasurable encouragement. I'm ever thankful to my friend Dean Kawi for bouncing me out of my publication doldrums. SMK judge Gail Kenna, an accomplished author and keen observer of the world, has greatly encouraged and inspired my work.

A special thanks to the late Lizeth Ramirez-Barroeta, whose exemplary life and courageous battle with cancer were an inspiration. Her appreciation of my poetry during her struggle was both humbling and invigorating when I had reached a low point in drive and creativity.

Last, and far from least, I must thank the entire Atmosphere Press team, especially Bryce for his incisive editing and Ronaldo for his cover design work.

ABOUT ATMOSPHERE PRESS

Founded in 2015, Atmosphere Press was built on the principles of Honesty, Transparency, Professionalism, Kindness, and Making Your Book Awesome. As an ethical and author-friendly hybrid press, we stay true to that founding mission today.

If you're a reader, enter our giveaway for a free book here:

SCAN TO ENTER
BOOK GIVEAWAY

If you're a writer, submit your manuscript for consideration here:

SCAN TO SUBMIT
MANUSCRIPT

And always feel free to visit Atmosphere Press and our authors online at atmospherepress.com. See you there soon!

ABOUT THE AUTHOR

FRANCIS FLAVIN is a poet and writer. Originally from rural upstate New York, he has lived extensively in Alaska, Colorado, Nevada, and the Philippines. His writing draws upon his experience as an educator, hockey player, fish and game field worker, public interest lawyer, governmental investigator, and adventurer on four continents. He has also been a successful advocate for civil and indigenous rights.

Francis's written work has been published nationally and internationally in *Poetry Quarterly, Beyond Words Literary Magazine, Inwood Indiana, Blueline, Pacific Review, Moonstone Arts Center, La Piccioletta Barca, Three Line Poetry, The Closed Eye Open, Tempered Runes* and *The Plentitudes*, among others. He was the Winner of the 2021 Poetry Quarterly Rebecca Lard Award and has received recognition for humor and flash fiction (two), short story (two), novel excerpt (three), creative nonfiction and personal essay categories in the Soul-Making Keats Literary Competition, the social impact category of the Chicagoland Poetry Contest, the Partisan Press Working People's Poetry Competition (winner) and the personal essay and rhymed poetry categories of the 2020 Writer's Digest awards.

Printed in the USA
CPSIA information can be obtained
at www.ICGtesting.com
JSHW081638240624
65196JS00005B/13/J